PIONEER DESIRE

THE O'ROURKE FAMILY MONTANA SAGA, BOOK TWO

RAMONA FLIGHTNER

GRIZZLY DAMSEL PUBLISHING

Mum,
Since I was a girl, you've
understood my love of reading,
always encouraging me to
read "just one more page."
Now, your love and faith in me
encourage me to create
the stories I love to write.
Thank you.

CHAPTER 1

Fort Benton, Montana Territory; July 1865

Ardan O'Rourke walked down the boardwalk in Fort Benton, Montana Territory, his smooth gait hitching at the sight of a beautiful woman sitting alone at a window seat inside the café. Although he never ate the inedible food on offer at Buford Hunt's establishment, today Ardan was tempted to skip the noontime family meal and meet this woman. He forced his gaze away from the café, glancing across the street at the sun shimmering off the Missouri River.

Most who arrived in the frontier town of Fort Benton ventured farther into the Territory to towns such as Helena or Virginia City, in search of gold or other riches. As his gaze returned to the attractive woman sitting next to Buford's café window, he wondered if she would stay in town or soon leave Fort Benton. Curiosity won out, and he approached the café.

Hesitating at the entrance to the café, Ardan once again questioned his desire to meet the mysterious newcomer. He grimaced as the owner of the café, Buford Hunt, approached him, beaming and bellowing his hello.

"Ardan," Buford said in his carrying voice. "How wonderful you've finally decided to sample the café's delicious fare." His hand clamped onto Ardan's, pulling him toward the newcomers inside the café. After greeting a few of the newly arrived, Buford led him to the beautiful woman with red-gold hair and a cautious gaze.

"Hello, ma'am," Ardan said in a deferential tone.

The small slip of a woman stared at Ardan as though he were an apparition, and he couldn't determine if she wished for him to disappear or to remain. He rubbed at the back of his neck and gave her an encouraging nod, hoping she would speak. He couldn't help from noticing the pretty flush on her cheeks or the warmth in her cognac-colored eyes. At least he hoped it was warmth and not dread he saw.

When she still didn't reply to his polite greeting, Ardan flushed as Buford Hunt watched him with a speculative gleam in his eyes. The last thing Ardan needed was for the gossiping café owner to wander over to his family's warehouse for a chat about how Ardan had appeared flummoxed by this unknown woman.

He took a step back and nodded at her again as Buford was called away by another patron. "I'm Ardan O'Rourke, and I hope you feel welcome in town," he said, while doffing his hat this time.

"One of the famous O'Rourkes," she said in a deep smoky voice, as she brushed at her gold-colored skirt, her voice filled with derision. "I should have recognized you," she said, looking him up and down.

He stood tall, any warmth he had felt for her leeching away at her implied criticism of his family and especially his father. After all, Ardan was the spitting image of Seamus O'Rourke. Tall, with broad shoulders, black hair, and piercing blue eyes. "Da is a good man." Like his father, his voice held a hint of the Ireland of his youth.

"If you deem him so, then you must be as deceitful as he is," she said with a roll of her eyes, as she turned to stare out the window and ignore him.

He leaned forward, gently gripping her arm, preventing her from brushing him off as though he were a gnat. "Remember, ma'am," he said in a low voice laced with warning. "You're the newcomer here. My family is respected and admired in this town. Don't make enemies where you don't have to." His gaze was filled with caution. "And don't go spreadin' your lies."

"A successful business doesn't make you respected, no matter what you believe."

He stiffened beside her before releasing her arm. "Our business is successful, aye. And you will find we are not delusional, nor deceitful. And we *are* respectable." He spoke in a clipped monotone, unwelcoming of her implied criticism of his family or their store. The *O'Rourke and Sons General Store* supplied needed goods to the year-round townsfolk, and the store also outfitted the thousands of transient men who traveled to the Territory in search of gold. As his father, Seamus, often said, the real riches came from tending to the dreamers. "Good day, ma'am."

Ardan walked past her and out of the café. He no longer wished to face Buford Hunt's questions or the inquisitive stares of other patrons if he were to eat there. Although he had thought a meal away from his family would soothe his restlessness, he reconciled with returning home for the midday meal. Kevin would be there, his closest brother and best friend. However, Kevin would be occupied with flirting with his new wife.

Ardan kicked at a piece of dried horse dung, battling impatience with himself. He would never begrudge Kevin his hard-won happiness. After all Kevin and Aileen had suffered in their struggle to finally marry, Ardan rejoiced in their triumph. However, as the eldest O'Rourke, Ardan had always shared his concerns, fears, and deepest thoughts with his brother Kevin. Now he felt out of sorts because Kevin had Aileen—although Ardan had no wish to intrude on their time together, especially not during their first month as newlyweds.

With a deepening respect for the third O'Rourke brother, Declan, Ardan turned for home. Declan had confessed last month that he had always felt alone among his large family. Ardan and Kevin were best friends. Eamon and Finn were so alike—in appearance, thought, and action—that they were referred to as the twins. Niall, Oran, and Bryan formed another close unit. Only Niamh and Declan had been the odd ones out. Now Ardan felt like one too.

He paused, staring at the cliffs standing like sentries over the Missouri River. Fort Benton was a burgeoning town on the banks of the large river and was the innermost port in the world, nearly 2,300 river miles from Saint Louis. Steamboats carried passengers and freight up the river in a two-month-long journey fraught with the constant peril of fire, Indian attack, or becoming stranded on a sandbar. Now that the river ran low, ships no longer made the journey all the way to Fort Benton and had to dock farther downriver, with stagecoaches and oxen carts ferrying passengers and freight to the town. No boats would arrive to town again until next summer.

Ardan recalled his recent journey up the river with his brother Kevin from Saint Louis. They had spent the winter in the large city, stockpiling supplies for their family store. Although he knew they would need new supplies to be delivered next summer from Saint Louis, his mother had informed his father that she didn't want her sons to be away for months at a time.

Thus, Ardan knew his father frantically worked on a list of all merchandise to be sent to them the following year by their employee and friend who worked in their warehouse there. Ardan shied away from thinking about his mother and her sudden reappearance in their lives after a nearly eighteen-year-long absence. Although he rejoiced at her return, he continued to fear her eventual abandonment again.

Instead he thought about the recent two-month trip up the Missouri River with his brother. He had thought he would spend the time telling tall tales with Kevin and getting to know some of the men traveling to the Territory in search of gold. However, Kevin's world had been upended. Although the long journey had been tedious, Kevin had met Aileen O'Keefe on the steamboat. Ardan had entertained her miserable aunt so Kevin and Aileen could have time alone and their affection and love had blossomed during the two month journey. Ardan knew he would always be thankful that Kevin found such happiness with such a wonderful woman. Ardan turned from studying the river, walking at a brisk pace toward home and a meal.

Ardan knew he'd missed the usual time for his family's midday meal during his interaction with the frustrating woman at the café and his time spent ruminating by the river. However, his mother always kept food ready, in case any of them arrived hungry and in search of something to eat.

His parents' house was large, with a kitchen built on the back of it. Da said, in case of fire, it would better protect the house. Ardan believed it was because Da realized, after the house was in construction, that they needed more space and added it on. Ardan walked past the chicken coop, the small vegetable garden, and approached the back stoop with the entrance to the kitchen.

After cleaning his boots on a rug outside, he doffed his hat, hung it on a peg inside the back door to the kitchen, and entered the comfortable room—his favorite space in the house. A large table, barely big enough for all the O'Rourkes to eat together, hugged one wall when not in use. Along the wall with the doorway stood the stove, set on a brick platform with bricks lining the back wall. On the other wall, across from the table, was the sink and counter space area, with shelves over part of it and a window in the middle. A hutch with plates stood in the corner.

"Hello, Mum," he murmured, as he nodded to his mother.

"Ardan," she exclaimed, her hands in soapy water as she washed dishes. "I hadn't thought you'd come home today. You've missed the family meal, but there's always food." She dried her hands and pulled out a bowl, ladled it full of stew, and set a few pieces of bread by him as he sat.

He stared at the bread a long moment and then glanced at his mother. "Brown bread," he whispered.

"Yes," she said with a satisfied smile, as she swiped back her auburn hair with streaks of gray. "It's taken me a while to find the proper mix of ingredients here, but I think it tastes quite good." She waited with an expectant expression for him to taste it.

He stared from her to the bread and back again. "What are we celebratin'?" he asked, his voice thick with the Irish accent of his youth. Unconsciously he leaned forward, smelling it. He closed his eyes as a groan of appreciation leaked out at the scent. As a boy in

5

Ireland, they only ever had bread for a celebration. A birthday, a holiday, or if the crop was a tremendous success.

"What's the matter, Ardan?" Mary O'Rourke asked, her delight fading as she watched her eldest son with concern and confusion.

"It reminds me of home," Ardan whispered, his eyes closed once more as he pictured the small stone cottage he had shared with his parents and five siblings near Limerick, Ireland, before they were evicted in 1847 during the potato famine. He saw the large room with the stone fireplace, a peat fire always burning, either to heat the room or to cook their simple meals. His mother, a bundle of purposeful energy as she cooked, knitted, and cared for them. His father, always with a ready smile and a tall tale to enliven their evenings before they went to bed. The sense of home that had been missing here until she had returned to them last month. He cleared his throat as he was perilously close to tears.

"Oh, my boy," Mary said, as she took a step closer to him.

He opened the startling cobalt-blue eyes he'd inherited from his father and watched as his mother reached a hand out, as though to grip his shoulder. To comfort him in some way. Rather than touch him, her hand dropped to her side, and she stared at him with a soul-deep yearning. Instead of confronting the multitude of emotions battering him, Ardan reached for the crock of butter with a shaky hand and spread a liberal amount over the bread. His eyes closed again at the first bite. "Thank you, Mum," he said in a near-reverent tone.

"I'm glad you like it," she said, as she turned away to face the stove, her shoulders back and her head held high, as though marshaling her emotions. "Your brothers can't remember a time when we had bread in Ireland."

He swallowed his bite of bread and took a swig of black tea. "Eamon and Finn would have been too young," he said. "Was Kevin not home for the midday meal?"

She looked over her shoulder with a tranquil expression, as though she had not experienced a great emotional maelstrom. "No, he returned to see Aileen for his midday break. As he should." She smiled with satisfaction at her second-oldest son's marriage. "'Tis a joy to know he's so happy."

"Aye," Ardan said. "I've never seen him so content. Although I've never known him to miss a meal." He flushed as his mother battled a wry expression. He cleared his throat and dropped his gaze, belatedly realizing another reason his brother was so eager for time alone with his wife. "I met a woman today who's taken an instant dislike to us," he said.

Mary poured herself a cup of tea and joined him at the table. "Oh, that seems unlikely." Her hazel eyes shone with bewilderment. "How do you know you don't like someone if you don't know them?"

Ardan shrugged. "I don't know, Mum, but I must say that I didn't like her much either. We won't be missing that lass's company at any family dinners."

~

Deirdre Finnegan sat at the table in the café near the window. She hated eating alone and wanted the distraction of looking outside. She also detested the appreciative looks cast her way by nearly all the men she had encountered and wanted to appear engaged so that none greeted her after Ardan O'Rourke's hasty departure. She feared her strategy wouldn't be successful, but it was worth a try. She had learned men loved a challenge, attempting to succeed where another had failed.

She smiled in her practiced, impersonal manner as the café owner approached her. After deflecting his impertinent prying questions, she ordered the daily special. She knew it would never compare with what she was accustomed to eating, but she hoped it would be edible, as this was the only café in town.

Her unfocused gaze stared outside as her mind raced with questions, and she fought panic. Why was she always so rash? Why hadn't she thought things through better? She gripped her hands together on her lap, as she took deep calming breaths. When would she stop looking over her shoulder in fear?

She jumped in her seat when the bowl of congealed food was set in front her. As the proprietor was about to walk away, she called out, "Excuse me, Mr. Hunt?" When he looked at her with a raised eyebrow, she asked, "What is this?" She nodded to the food in front of her.

"Some sort of hash. My cook wouldn't say."

She blanched as she looked at what she hoped was food in the chipped ceramic bowl, but it looked worse than the dried horse dung found in the street. "Do you mean to tell me that you paid someone to create this travesty?"

"You tell me, ma'am, where I'm supposed to find me a cook when all anyone can think about is gold. Gold!" he proclaimed, the hint of the South still in his voice. "Ain't no one willin' to spend time in town when they're fixin' to strike it rich in Helena or Virginia City."

She pushed away the bowl without taking a bite. She glanced around at the half-empty tables. "Do you have more customers when you have a better cook?"

"Of course, ma'am," he snapped. "I might be slow, but I ain't stupid."

She frowned at his response and shook her head. "I meant no offense." She pasted on her friendliest smile, although it remained impersonal. "Might I have a look at your kitchen?" she asked. When he balked, she said, "I know my way around a café kitchen, Mr. Hunt, and I believe we could aid each other." She waited, her gaze steady as she watched him consider her.

"Come," he said. He led her through the dining room area to the kitchen, separated by a swinging door on a hinge, like she'd seen at saloon entrances. She stopped short after stepping inside.

"This is worse than I could have imagined," she breathed. The kitchen was a disaster. Dirty pots and pans were everywhere; the sink overflowed with dirty dishes, and nothing was prepared for the evening meal. "Where is your cook now?"

Buford scratched at his head. In his early forties, his brown hair was thinning, and he combed it over his head to conceal a growing bald spot. "I'm uncertain. He has a tendency to disappear at the most inopportune moments."

She shook her head. "Perhaps you are wrong. This appears to be an auspicious time for me to inform you that I ran a successful café before arriving in Fort Benton. I will need a few days to clean this kitchen and to ensure I have the supplies I need, but soon you will have people clamoring to eat here."

"I can't close for a few days!"

"You'll have to, unless you want to poison your customers." She met his irate glare. "And I'll need every bit of that time, if you want me to take on the Herculean task of setting this disaster to rights." She waited as she saw him stare at the kitchen that looked like a tornado had struck.

"Fine," he said.

"One more thing, Mr. Hunt," she said. "I know you will have great success because of me. I refuse to be paid only a pittance for my work as though I am nothing more than hired help." She watched as he bristled. "I understand you own the space. However, I imagine its reputation is dubious at present. If you refuse me, I will find a way to open a competing café, and I promise I will steal away all your customers."

"What do you want?" he asked as he stared at her, as though she were an exotic creature and not a woman asserting herself.

"I want us to be equal partners, for you wouldn't have any income without me." She met his shocked gaze. "We split the profits."

"That's highway robbery," he gasped.

"Think about it, Mr. Hunt. Either 50 percent of a thriving business or 100 percent of next to nothing." She waved her arm around, indicating the catastrophic state of his kitchen.

"Fine, but, if you're a charlatan, I'll make up what you owe me by selling you to the Bordello."

She held out her hand and waited until he grasped hers, shaking it with a firm grip, ignoring his wounded male pride and his sputtering about places called the Bordello. She'd heard it all before and had learned it better to ignore men when their pride had been ruffled.

When Buford Hunt marched out the front door, she turned to stare at the mess she had to clean up. Releasing her grip from her skirts, she ran a shaking hand through her hair and let out a deep

9

breath. A smile burst forth as she realized she had just bluffed her way into a job in Fort Benton. She only prayed Mr. Hunt kept to his side of their bargain and paid her what she was due. For she had ten dollars to her name and had no idea how she would survive if this endeavor failed.

~

Ardan wandered into the warehouse on Main Street to find his brothers Kevin and Declan chatting, as they rearranged merchandise. However, there wasn't much to do as they waited for another small shipment of goods to arrive from Saint Louis. During times like this, when at least one sibling was not busy, Ardan wondered at his parents' reluctance to have a few of the brothers establish another store in Saint Louis. Or in Virginia City or Helena. Some other place outside of Fort Benton.

However, his father was adamant that the family remain together. Ardan knew Da would understand if Ardan had a desire to leave—to travel and to explore and to see some of the world. However, he'd never desired adventure. He closed his eyes, fighting the image of the woman he'd seen today. Of her allure before she spoke disdainfully of his family. Her hair that looked silky soft and shone like a red-gold fire in the sunlight. His fingers twitched as though itching to tease it out of the confining bun she wore. Her eyes, both expressive and full of secrets at the same time. Her subtle scent of lilacs in full bloom.

"Ardan, lad," his father called out to him, jerking him from his reverie. "Are you havin' a wakin' dream?" Seamus O'Rourke asked. Although in his early fifties, he maintained a youthful vitality, and his blue eyes always sparkled with joy these days. Ever since his first wife, Mary, had returned from the dead the previous month and had reconciled with Seamus, he had exhibited an unfettered delight with the world around him. However, today he seemed slightly less effusive.

"No, Da." Ardan approached him and followed him into his office. "Are you well?" he asked, as he sat in the chair across from his father's desk. He saw the ever-present inventory list for the store that Seamus would need to send downriver soon. "Do you need help determinin' what else we should order for next year?"

Seamus sighed as he tapped the list. "'Tisn't determinin' what we should order but how much. Will there be more men next year or as many or less?" Seamus raised his hands, as though to say he had no idea. "How are we to know, lad?"

"Order 20 percent more," Ardan said. "If we don't have enough supplies, we'll raise the prices." He shrugged. "You can only do so much." After a moment, where he watched his father scribble on the sheet of paper in front of him, Ardan broke the silence. "Are you certain you don't want me to return to Saint Louis?"

Seamus looked up, his pencil stilled, and his alert gaze wholly focused on his son. "I just got you back, Ardan. I don't want you or any of the lads separated from us again so soon." He sighed, setting aside his pencil. "'Twould be easier knowin' you, Kevin, or Declan were there, purchasin' the quality goods we have become known for." He rubbed at his temples, an action he always did when he was worried about something.

"I can return to Saint Louis," Ardan said. "I survived last winter there."

"Aye, but you had Kevin for company. This time, you'd be alone," Seamus said, as he sat back in his chair, making it creak. "We have a month to six weeks before the last ship will leave to head south. I'll talk this over with your mother." He quieted when he saw Ardan's expression. "What is it, lad?"

Ardan's gaze was haunted when he looked at his father. "She made brown bread."

Seamus stilled at his son's whispered words.

"Aye. For the first time in eighteen years, 'twas like home."

Seamus paused as he saw Ardan battling strong emotions. "She's not leavin', lad," he said in a voice as gentle as the one he had used to soothe the younger Ardan of his fears, when the wind had rattled their cottage so loudly that he feared the banshees were keening.

Bowing his head, Ardan clasped his hands together in front of him. "She's been back over a month. I should trust that she will remain. But

I find that hard. Especially after praying for her and wee Maggie over the last eighteen years."

"Time will prove her steadfastness," Seamus said. "She never wanted to be separated from us."

Although Ardan nodded, he couldn't banish the doubt that remained buried in his soul like a burr. "Today I met a woman who detests us," he said, unwilling to continue discussing his mother's return with his father. He knew his father only rejoiced at her reappearance in their life and was unwilling to understand Ardan's continued trepidation.

"Ah, Miss Deirdre Finnegan," Seamus said, as he closed his eyes and shook his head. "Or *Mrs.* Finnegan. I never quite determined which one." He chuckled. "A firebrand, that one. Irate that Kevin had married. Said I'd misled her."

"How?" Ardan asked.

"She saw the advertisement I placed in a paper back east for a mail order bride. Came all this way, thinkin' I was waitin' for her. Or one of you lads were." He chuckled. "Should have seen her, her face as flushed as her hair."

"I met her at the café. Buford wanted me to meet the new arrivals." He paused, his gaze confused as he met his father's. "Her attitude toward me changed the moment she knew who I was. As though the name O'Rourke were akin to the devil himself."

Seamus rose and paced the short distance to the window and back again. "There's nothin' I could have done to prevent her from travelin' all this way. I had no notion she planned on arrivin' on our doorstep until I received a letter from her, once she arrived at Cow Island, just before Kevin's marriage to Aileen." He rubbed at his head and frowned. "I wonder how she paid for her ticket?" He exchanged a long look with his son, as the price for a ticket to Fort Benton had risen to exorbitant prices with the gold rush. "Well, 'tisn't my concern. Unless Declan wants to marry her."

Ardan grimaced. "I'd find it unlikely any man would want to marry that woman."

∾

Deirdre stood with her hands on her hips as she stared at the kitchen. The inedible food had been placed in a bucket to be fed to a neighbor who had pigs; other scraps were saved for Mr. Hunt's chickens, and she had washed more pots than she had thought possible. She still wanted to scrub every surface in the kitchen and the floor, but that would be tomorrow's work.

After swiping at her head, she arched her back and groaned at her aching muscles. With a satisfied smile, she relished the burning pain, as it meant she had done an honest day's work. At the approaching footsteps, she turned toward the door leading to the café's seating area.

Mr. Hunt stood staring at the pile of pots and pans drying beside the sink. "Surely you can cook tomorrow," he said, a note of entreaty in his voice.

"No," Deirdre stated. "This entire kitchen needs to be cleaned before I will cook in it. If you help me, there is a slim chance I could prepare something for tomorrow's evening meal."

He sputtered and flushed and jutted out his slight paunch, as though in outrage. "That is not something I am accustomed to."

She lifted one shoulder, as though it were no concern of hers. "Well then, you will have to wait another day while I clean. You should have taken more care to prevent your kitchen from sliding into such disarray, Mr. Hunt." She reached for the lantern hanging from the hook in the center of the ceiling, intent on carrying it to the front door with her as she left for the day. It would be ready for her to light upon her arrival in the wee morning hours.

She brushed past Buford and exited to the street. Although it was past 8:00 p.m., the sun had yet to set. The soft evening light gave a romantic glow to the river and its cliffs, but she did not pause long to appreciate the natural beauty. Men's shouts and hollers roused her from her short reverie, and she hurried back to her hotel room, eager for a quick wash and a well-deserved rest.

~

Madam Nora stood in the shadows between the café and the laundry next door. Although most women in town seemed fearful of the men's attentions, Nora knew the men were more afraid of losing her high regard. For, if they did, they would be barred from her establishment, the Bordello. Thus, Nora felt no trepidation as she loitered in the shadows near the café. Tonight, Nora had paused to listen in on the first interesting conversation to be had in over a week, and she gave silent thanks she had felt a need to stretch her legs.

She watched as the woman she had determined was Buford's new cook, a Mrs. Finnegan, departed in the direction of the hotel. Moving out of the shadows, Nora looked inside to see Buford with hands on his hips, a look of consternation on his face. "Must be because she outwitted him." A sly smile spread. "Let's see if a woman can outwit him twice in one night," she murmured to herself.

"Buford," she called out, as he stepped onto the boardwalk, turned, and locked the front door of the café, failing to hide the cunning in her smile or in her voice. "I hear congratulations are in order at your new chef."

"That's still to be determined," he said sullenly. "She hasn't cooked a thing yet and insists the café must close another day so she can clean the kitchen. The insolence of the woman!"

"Oh, yes, how dreadful of her not to want to sicken half the town," Nora murmured, humor lighting her gaze. "I saw her scurry away from here a few moments ago. I presume to the hotel?"

Buford shrugged. "It's no concern of mine where she spends her evenings."

With a *tsk*ing sound and a sashay of her hips, Nora approached Buford. A satisfied gleam in her eyes, she noted how he watched her move, and she knew her subtle rose scent would waft around him. "You are a fool, Buford." When he bristled, she shook her head. "As a businesswoman, I would advise you to keep your employee content." She glanced to the darkened second story of the café, empty for over a year. "Why wouldn't you have her live upstairs?"

He sputtered and glared at her. "Why should I offer her those rooms? She's a single woman. She doesn't need so much space." His gaze turned calculating. "Perhaps I should. I could recoup the money I was tricked into paying her to be my cook."

Nora approached Buford, placing a hand on his arm to help soothe his ruffled male pride, as she spoke in a soft, yet forceful voice. "No, Buford, not at a price. For free. For working hard to reestablish your café as a center in town where folk actually want to gather to eat."

"Free?" he sputtered.

She nodded, her gaze serious and brooking no argument. "If she lives upstairs, she never has to worry about men bothering her as she goes to and from work. She will have the time to prepare all manner of delicious food for you to sell, something that has been sorely lacking since the Tompkins family departed. The free board might entice her to remain working with you, long after she discovers the onerous proposition of having you as a partner."

"Blasted woman," he muttered, and he sighed heavily, his gaze distant, as though he were considering all she had said. "Fine, I'll do it. Although I won't always countenance your meddling."

Nora smiled as she strolled away from him. "Better to accept my meddling rather than being barred from the Bordello." Her smile broadened when he shuddered at the thought. She walked in the direction of her business, satisfied Mrs. Finnegan would have a greater chance of success, now that she was to live above the café.

Deirdre stood in the hotel entryway, conversing with the hotel owner, Mr. Foster, as her mind raced with ways she could cut their conversation short. Although friendly, Mr. Foster was too overt in his attentions, and she wished she could escape his flattery, as it made her feel cheap and tawdry rather than pleased.

"Thank you so much for your kindness, Mr. Foster," Deirdre blurted out, "but I find myself feeling unwell. If you will excuse me?" She barely heard his exclamations of concern for her as she barreled upstairs. When he called after her to detain her once more, she paused with a sigh on the second-floor landing. "Yes, Mr. Foster?"

"You have a visitor, ma'am."

"Who would call at such a late hour?" she asked, half convinced Mr. Foster had invented someone to entice her downstairs again for more conversation.

"Get down here now, Mrs. Finnegan. I need a word with you," Buford hollered up the stairs.

"Mr. Hunt," Deirdre sighed with a groan, trudging down the stairs. "Hello, sir."

"Finally you show me the respect I deserve," he snapped, his face ruddy and his eyes glowing with dissatisfaction.

Frowning, Deirdre looked at him in confusion, as she walked down the stairs. "Is something amiss? Have you found another cook?"

He glowered at her and shook his head. "You know I haven't, you saucy woman." He shook his head as Mr. Foster hissed at him to lower his voice, so as not to bother other hotel guests. However, at the loud cheers and general raucous behavior coming from the adjoining saloon, Buford rolled his eyes, as he knew few would sleep well until the men inside decided to call it a night.

"I'm tired, Mr. Hunt," Mrs. Finnegan said. "I've had a long day, and I have an even longer day ahead of me tomorrow. If you had any sense, you'd let me rest, so I can put your kitchen to rights, and then I can open the café the day after tomorrow." Mrs. Finnegan faced him, now on the first floor of the hotel once again, while she leaned against the banister for support.

"Are you residing here, ma'am?" Buford asked, his voice lowered.

"Of course I am," she said with a roll of her eyes. "I'd never wander the hallways of such an establishment if I didn't."

"I have a house nearby," he said.

"How nice for you," she said with a huff, turning to climb the stairs again.

"No, you misunderstand," he said, reaching forward to grab her arm. "I have a house nearby that I live in. However, the café building also has rooms above on the second floor that remain empty. If you like, you may move in and consider those rooms the cook's quarters."

"I'm certain they are more expensive than my simple room here. I do not live an extravagant life." She stared at him impassively.

"No, you misunderstand," he repeated, flushing as he noted Mr. Foster watching their exchange with avid interest. "You may live in those rooms for free. It's where the previous owners and cook lived, and I purchased that property from them, after I already owned my house."

"Were the previous owners successful with the café?" she asked.

He ginned ruefully. "Yes. I hadn't realized what a wonderful team Harold and Irene made. He sweet-talked the customers, and she cooked simple, yet delicious food. The café was always busy, and I know they made a tidy profit. I thought it would be easy to take over from them." His fingers tapped at the banister. "Never thought it'd be so hard to find a decent, reliable cook."

She smiled at him. "Well, now you have. And I'd be delighted to live upstairs. It'll make it easier for me to arrive at work to get the bread going early in the morning." She saw his eyes light up at the prospect of homemade bread. "Now, Mr. Hunt, I believe I've earned a rest. I'll see you tomorrow."

She watched as Buford left and then turned to Mr. Foster. "Mr. Foster, as I'm certain you overheard"—her voice was filled with wry irony—"I will be vacating my rooms tomorrow. I thank you for your hospitality." She spun on her heel and ascended the stairs quickly to forestall any further conversation.

After entering her room, she quickly washed off the day's grime as best she could in a sponge bath and donned a clean nightgown. With a groan, she collapsed onto her bed. Now that the day's hectic activity was over, thoughts and impressions of this town nearly overwhelmed her.

When she had first arrived, asking for directions to the O'Rourke home, she had heard about the store and the warehouse, plus about Kevin's recent nuptials. Then, at the O'Rourke warehouse, when she found that Seamus O'Rourke had not anticipated her arrival, she had lashed out. She curled onto her side with her arms wrapped around herself. "Fool," she whispered. "Always allowing fear to fuel you."

However, in that moment, when she had learned of his son's marriage, she had thought all her hopes and dreams were dashed. It wasn't until she had fled and spoken with Mr. Hunt that she realized Mr. O'Rourke had more than one son. "Fool," she muttered again. She feared Seamus O'Rourke thought her a madwoman and would never want her for one of his available sons.

Although, if his only interested son were the overbearing, pompous one who had spoken with her at the café today, she'd rather remain a widow forever. Shivering as she remembered the deep blue of his eyes, she fought the yearning to be worthy of a man's concern and regard again. To feel cherished again.

With a disgusted grunt, she breathed in and out to force herself asleep and to still her mind of racing thoughts and free it from flights of fancy. She would be reasonable and self-reliant. Banishing foolish thoughts, she reminded herself the last thing she wanted in her next marriage was love.

CHAPTER 2

The following day, Ardan worked in the family store with his younger brothers, Eamon and Finn. They were affectionately called the twins because they looked so much alike, thought alike, finished each other's sentences, and were inseparable. Although Eamon was older, at twenty-two, he did not act any more mature than his twenty-year-old brother. The store was largely their domain, and Ardan knew they were experts at peddling their goods to the men arriving in Fort Benton, eager to travel to the gold mines farther afield in Montana Territory.

Ardan half listened to the twins prattle and extol the virtue of one mining implement over another, while Ardan worked alone to restock shelves. Although he could have had any one of his younger brothers do the task, he needed something to relieve him of his pent-up energy. If the bullwhacker Cormac Ahern arrived soon, Ardan determined he would travel with him to the next steamboat landing at Cow Island, some 120 miles away, to help load supplies onto wagons for their return to Fort Benton. Anything to ease his restlessness.

As he moved around their store, he considered his plan to return to Saint Louis. Last winter had been tolerable because he had had Kevin for company. Ardan was uncertain what he would do were he to travel alone. He had no desire to play endless games of poker, and he knew few people there for him to partake of much society.

Tilting his head to one side, he listened as Buford Hunt spoke with Eamon about having supplies delivered to his café later in the day. After Buford strolled out, Ardan wandered to the front area in a lull between patrons. "If you need someone to deliver supplies, I can do it," he said. "I've nothin' better to do today."

Finn stared at him in confusion. "I thought you always said the benefit of being the eldest brother was that you didn't have to do the menial tasks, like delivering supplies."

Ardan shrugged and grinned at his brother, who was the spitting image of his younger self. "No, the benefit is that I can decide what I do and don't want to do." He winked as Eamon laughed, and Finn rolled his eyes.

A few hours later, Ardan pulled the loaded cart along the dirt path behind the buildings on Front Street until he arrived at the rear entrance to the café. He walked up the few steps and knocked on the door. When no answer came, he pushed open the door and stepped inside. He paused, eyes widening as he beheld the sparkling space. "Wow," he breathed, as he turned in a slow circle.

"You're dirtying the floor with your shoes," said an irritated woman behind him.

He spun and smiled, as he met the equally irritated gaze of the woman from yesterday. "Hello again. Is it Miss or Mrs. Finnegan?"

She flushed, her lips pursed together, before she said, "Mrs. Finnegan."

"And where would Mr. Finnegan be?" His blue eyes twinkled with merriment, as he noted his presence made her even more irritable.

"In a mass grave in Mississippi."

He stilled, his smile frozen, as he met her defiant stare. "I beg your pardon, ma'am." He held up his hands, as though in supplication. "I never meant ..." He broke off his apology when he noted no soft-ening in her expression. He waved toward the rear door. "I have supplies."

She motioned for him to get them and opened the door to a small larder. "If you could bring them in and set the boxes on the table, I'll sort them out."

"I can help you, Mrs. Finnegan," Ardan said, as he watched her with unveiled curiosity.

"There's no need. I've organized kitchens before, and I have a system."

Understanding he had been summarily dismissed, Ardan returned outside to begin lugging in her cooking supplies. He set everything on the butcher block table in the middle of the large kitchen and then crammed his hands into his pockets. "May I do anything else to help you?"

She firmed her mouth and then nodded. "Yes. I know no one in town, and Mr. Hunt has made himself scarce today. The only time I've seen him, I gave him a list of supplies I needed. Other than that, I have no idea where he is."

"Ah, as to that, ma'am, I suspect he's savorin' his free day." His fingers tapped on the tabletop. "He's most likely at the Sunrise."

"Sunrise occurred hours ago, Mr. O'Rourke," she said, her brows furrowed with confusion at his blatant misunderstanding.

"No, ma'am," Ardan said, a chuckle as his eyes twinkled. "The Sunrise is the most popular saloon in Fort Benton. I heard Buford tell Eamon and Finn at the store that he would go there before heading … elsewhere." He flushed and shook his head. "I wouldn't seek him out again today."

"Eamon and Finn?"

"Two of my brothers. They run the family store. You should call me Ardan, as there are so many of us O'Rourkes that you'll never keep us straight." He winked at her, and his smile broadened as her shoulders straightened so much he thought she'd topple backward.

"Mr. O'Rourke, I'm certain I don't need—" Her protest was interrupted by a pounding on the front door. She turned to stare in that direction but did not go to answer it. She paled as the pounding intensified.

"Are you well, lass?" Ardan asked. When she shivered as though in fear, Ardan marched from the kitchen through the empty café and to the front door. He yanked it open and glared at the two men standing on the opposite side. "What?"

"We want us some food," said the taller of the two, a rifle slung over his shoulder, as he attempted to push Ardan aside.

Ardan stood his ground and crossed his arms over his chest. "Not today. A new cook arrived, and the café's closed 'til tomorrow. Find somewhere else to eat." He saw them exchange a glance and took a step forward. "Try anything, and I'll report you to the sheriff."

He watched them saunter off, muttering under their breaths about uppity Irishmen, waiting until they were a fair distance away before he shut and locked the door again. He ensured the notice informing patrons that the café was closed was readily visible before returning to the kitchen.

Pausing at the entrance to the kitchen, he frowned when he didn't see Mrs. Finnegan. However, he heard muttering in the larder and poked his head in. "Trouble?" he asked, as he saw her kick at a heavy ceramic jar.

"Did you ever eat here?" she demanded.

"Not since the Tompkinses left town and sold it to Buford, although I've considered it a few times."

She gave a huff of exasperation. "I'm surprised Mr. Hunt's cooks didn't poison the whole town. He could have started an epidemic with the rancid food I've found."

Ardan paled at the thought and shook his head. "Do what you must to prevent such a thing, Mrs. Finnegan." He ducked his head rather than meet her inquisitive stare. "What was supposed to be in that large jug?"

"I think it's a butter churn, but it's so foul smelling that it makes me ill."

Ardan picked it up and carried it outside, with her on his heels, ignoring her protests. "I've nothin' better to do today, and you need some help if you are to set this place to rights by mornin'." He nodded in the direction of the front door. "Those were hungry men lookin' for food. I imagine they'll be lined up tomorrow early, waitin' for a meal. I'd pray you can cook as well as Buford claims."

She fisted her hands on her hips and shook her head, although her eyes shone with intrigue and appreciation. Letting out a deep breath, she said, "Thank you … for your help, Mr. O'Rourke."

"*Ardan.* Seven more Mr. O'Rourkes are in this town, not counting Da. Nine male siblings total, if you count my two half brothers who Da has adopted as his own. Reserve your *Mr. O'Rourke*s for my da." He winked at her and set off with her butter churn. "I'll be back," he called over his shoulder.

~

Deirdre stared after Ardan as he carried the heavy churn, as though it weighed no more than a feather. She attempted, and failed, to ignore the way the muscles in his shoulders and back flexed as he moved. For a large man, he was too graceful for his own good. "For *my* own good," she mumbled to herself.

Rather than stand on her stoop and stare after him like a lovesick girl, she entered the kitchen and latched the door after her. She stared around the kitchen with satisfaction. Every surface sparkled, and she knew she could serve nourishing food with pride tomorrow.

Ignoring yet another knock at the front door, she put away the new supplies as she planned the simple meals she would prepare for tomorrow. Uncertain of how many men she would need food for, she thought it better to plan for too many than too little. A near constant knock had sounded out front, as though men were attempting to see if any food scraps were to be had. However, none had come to the back door except Ardan.

She flushed as she remembered how she had reacted when Ardan had been here at the initial pounding on the front door. Closing her eyes, she took a deep breath to still her racing heart. A knock never upset her, but the sound of a fist demanding entrance brought back her worst memories. Memories she wished she could forget.

Shaking her head to clear it of her reverie, she pulled out a cloth to swipe down the counters one more time. Unable to prevent it, her thoughts returned to Ardan. His effortless strength as he brought in crates of supplies or hefted the butter churn. The twinkle of amusement in his gaze and then the remorse when he realized he'd misspoken. Although she wanted to dislike him, she feared he would be a hard man to hate.

"You don't have to hate him," she muttered to herself. "Just avoid him." With that, she attempted to focus on her remaining tasks, although her gaze frequently flitted to the back door, awaiting his return.

Ardan walked away from the café's back door, uncertain how he would clean out the butter churn. He half considered going to the store and seeing if they had another one there, but this was a solid ceramic piece, and he thought it would be a shame to destroy it. "Maggie!" he called out, as he saw his youngest sister sitting on the back steps of his parents' house. She looked like a younger version of their mother, with her auburn hair and build, although her eyes were their da's startling cobalt blue. "Want to help me with a project?"

She rose and met him near the chicken coop, only a hint of trepidation in her gaze. "What do you have there, Ardan?" she asked. She bent forward to better look at the churn, and her nose wrinkled as she backed up a step. "Did something die inside it?"

Laughing, Ardan shook his head. "No, but 'tis a right mess. Mrs. Finnegan is putting the café to rights, and I delivered her new supplies today. She was working on this, an' I thought I'd help her."

Maggie gave him a searching look before motioning for him to wait. After entering the house, she exited with a bar of soap, a long wooden spoon, and two towels. By the back door, she grabbed a shovel. "Come. Let's go to the small stream, and see if we can wash this out."

"A shovel, Maggie?" Ardan asked, as he walked beside her.

"To bury that vile stuff inside. I fear it would kill the chickens!" She fought a smile as he laughed.

He slung an arm over her shoulder, carrying the churn against his side. Maggie was his youngest sister at nearly eighteen, and he had thought her lost to them. As lost as his mum. However, last month, he had discovered that not only had his mother survived his sister's birth after their arrival from Ireland to Montreal in 1847 but so had his wee baby sister.

He had spent nearly eighteen years, praying every night for his dead mum and sister, only to find them in town, planning to travel to Virginia City. Beaten and bruised, both his mother and his youngest sister had escaped living with a violent man who now looked for gold deep in the Territory. Ardan prayed their tormentor never returned, for Maggie was finally overcoming her fears and turning into the confident, spirited sister he had always imagined her to be.

Allowing Maggie to lead them away from town, he relaxed as he enjoyed his time with his youngest sister. The impatience he had felt earlier in the day had dissipated, and he relished having a purpose. Even if it meant dealing with a churn filled with rancid butter. The ability to aid Mrs. Finnegan also filled him with pleasure, although he ignored that thought and focused on the robin's-egg blue sky, the horsehair clouds, and the gentle breeze ruffling his hair. "I should have insisted you wear a hat," he said.

"I should have remembered," Maggie said with a giggle. "Come. Let's get this chore done, and then I'll find some shade." Like Kevin, Niamh, and their mother, Maggie had a tendency to burn much faster than the rest of the brothers, who looked like their da.

After following a small path through waist-high burnished-gold grass, they approached a small stream. Maggie handed Ardan the shovel and pointed for him to dig a hole away from the water. He watched as she nearly retched when she lifted the lid off the churn.

"Oh, this is disgusting," she gasped. She turned her head away, taking deep breaths of fresh air. "How could someone not know this was festerin' away?"

Ardan smiled at his sister, as she sounded more like his Irish siblings and their parents every day. He had begun to suspect she had a knack for picking up accents and mimicking those around her, and worried she had originally learned that skill to deflect notice of herself by the abusive men who had raised her. Pushing aside that concern, he motioned for her to hand the churn to him, and he took it from her, dumping it upside down.

His smile faded as he saw his sister watching him with a curious expression. "What?" he asked.

She shrugged. "You're smiling more," she murmured. "When I first came to the house, you were always serious and almost never smiled. Now you laugh and grin at least once a day."

He scowled at her, pausing in running water through the churn in his attempt to clean it. "I'm not an ogre, Maggie."

She shook her head and hitched up her skirts as she rushed into the creek. Gripping his arm, she shook her head. "That's not what I meant. It's like you're finally allowing yourself to enjoy life, Ardan. Since we came back." She paused and dropped her head. "I'm being foolish."

"No, lass, you aren't." He closed his eyes. "More joy has been in our house in the past few weeks than in the past eighteen years combined." He opened his eyes, revealing the longing, hope, and terror within. "'Tis wondrous and terrifyin' at the same time."

Maggie nodded. "I know. What happens when I lose you all again?" she whispered.

He took a step toward her, water sloshing at his feet and spraying her skirts. He gripped her shoulder with a free hand and gave her a gentle squeeze. "No, Maggie. You'll always have someone. There are too many of us for you to ever be alone again." He waited until the panic receded from her gaze and then nodded. "Come. Let's finish this work before you look like a ripe tomato." He smiled again as she giggled at his teasing.

Working with Maggie to clean the churn for the next forty-five minutes, they chatted about any topic that interested her. However, one topic she never discussed was their sister Niamh. Their eldest sister, married to the lazy Connor Ahern since her arrival to Fort Benton, had never reconciled with their mother, and had yet to fully welcome Maggie either.

"What's Mrs. Finnegan like?" Maggie asked, as she stood in the stream with her skirts tied around her knees, shaking the water around inside the churn.

"Prickly," Ardan said without thinking, which earned an intrigued stare from his sister. "Doesn't like to accept help, even when she needs it. A widow."

"Oh, the poor woman," Maggie said, as she swiped at her forehead and effectively doused herself with stream water. "I should just give up and jump in the stream right now for a bath." She laughed at her soaked clothes.

Ardan took the churn from her and took over scrubbing the inside again. He knew that it would soon be cleaned out and ready to use. "She thought Kevin would be waitin' here to marry her."

Maggie's eyes rounded in shock, as she gaped at her eldest brother. "You're not joking." At his quick shake of his head, she held her palms to her cheeks. "Oh, what did Da do?"

"Nothin'," Ardan said, as he started on the final rinse of the butter churn, half smiling at her calling their father "Da." She used to intentionally call him "Father," as though to keep herself separate from her other siblings. And to keep their father at arm's length. "Seems she acted like a madwoman, saying she'd been 'duped by a duplicitous fiend, and, if there were any justice in the world, she'd never have to hear the name O'Rourke again.'" He chuckled.

Maggie couldn't stop a fit of giggles. "And then you delivered her supplies today."

"Aye, 'twas a surprise to find her there as the new cook, but I took that opportunity to inform her nine other O'Rourke men besides me were in town, not counting Da, and she should call me by my first name. Thought she'd faint when I told her the total number of O'Rourke men here."

"Oh my," Maggie whispered. She accepted his hand as he helped her out of the creek. She pushed and pulled at her skirts until they hung around her ankles again. "We should have her to supper one evening."

"Absolutely not," Ardan said, any joy in their conversation evaporating. "I might enjoy sparrin' with the woman for a few moments,

27

but the last thing I'd want is for her to ruin one of our family meals."

He turned away, ignoring his sister, as he focused on ensuring the churn was dry enough to haul back to the café and to return to Mrs. Finnegan.

"Aileen doesn't ruin our meals," Maggie said quietly, as she watched him with the deep cobalt eyes of their father. "Mother and Da always welcome those who come during supper."

"That's not the point, Maggie. Aileen's part of the family now, an' Kevin loves her," Ardan said, running a hand though his ebony hair and making it stand on end. He patted at it and let out a huff of breath. "This Mrs. Finnegan? She's a cantankerous woman. And I fear she'd only come because she's lookin' for another husband. Not because she desires friendship."

Maggie shrugged and began the short walk back to their house. "Even if you claim you plan to go to your grave a bachelor, Declan wants to marry. Why shouldn't he have the opportunity to get to know her?"

"'Tisn't a *claim*, Maggie. I've never desired a wife. That sort of responsibility."

She paused and faced him, confusion in her gaze as she stared at him. "Why not? You were raised by a good, decent man who never failed to show you love. Why wouldn't you want to marry?"

He clenched his jaw tight until the muscles ticked. "You don't have the memory of what it was like those eighteen years you were gone." He motioned for her to precede him and followed her the rest of the way to the house.

At the back steps, she turned to study him with a concerned expression. "Life is full of risks, Ardan." She left him gaping at her, as she entered the house without a backward glance at him.

For a long moment, he stood in the backyard area, listening to the chickens *cluck*. Shaking his head to clear it of his momentary melancholy, he took off toward the café. He thought it better to return the churn and then not have to think about Mrs. Finnegan again for a while. He rapped on the back door, shifting from foot to foot with impatience for her to answer it. When she did, his breath caught, and he forgot his ire.

She wore an apron; a spot of flour dotted the end of her nose, and her eyes had lost their guarded look. She appeared happy.

"Mrs. Finnegan," he croaked out in a husky voice, clearing his throat. "It took some time, but my sister Maggie 'n' I were able to clean your butter churn."

A smile burst forth. "Oh, thank you," she said.

He sniffed the air and then shook his head. "I thought you'd be in the midst of baking something." At her perplexed look, he waved at her flour-dusted attire and appearance.

"Oh, I'm preparing everything for tomorrow. I'd forgotten how much I missed being in a kitchen." She took a step back, allowing him to enter. "If you could set the crock back in the larder, that would be helpful."

Ardan did as she asked and then returned to the kitchen, noting she had one area set up for baking and another area for working with vegetables and meat. "A very organized space," he said with approval. "Well, missus, I hope you enjoy the rest of your day."

She stepped in front of him and flushed. "If you could help me with one more thing?"

"Aye?"

"I have a trunk of belongings that I would like to bring upstairs, but it is heavy. Could you carry it up there for me?" She entered the dining room area and then pointed to the trunk pushed against a wall.

Ardan hefted it and motioned for her to lead the way. He followed her up a narrow staircase that led from the kitchens to the upstairs. Once inside the door to the living space, a hallway led to four rooms. Three were bedrooms, and one acted as a sitting room, while no kitchen was upstairs. "Which room?"

She peered into each room, all covered in a layer of dust, and shrugged. "I don't believe it makes much difference."

"If I could suggest, I'd choose a room toward the rear. You'll have more peace in the evenings from the street noise." She nodded her agreement with his suggestion, and he set the trunk in a large room

29

with two windows. He yanked open the windows, the slight breeze blowing away the stale air.

"I hadn't realized this needed cleaning too," she said, as she held a hand to her head, and her shoulders sank. For a moment, her determination appeared deflated, and it looked like she was on the verge of tears.

"The last to live here were the Tompkins family, and they moved out over a year ago," Ardan said. "Irene was a fabulous cook, which is why no kitchen is up here. She would have always prepared the family meals downstairs." He swiped his dusty hands on his pants leg and turned for the stairs. "I'll leave you, missus. Good luck."

She followed him downstairs, watching him as he left. "Thank you, Ardan," she called out.

He waved but didn't look back.

～

The following morning, Deirdre was a bundle of nerves. The café opened for breakfast at eight, and she feared no one would come. She feared too many would come. Could she fix enough food to feed everyone who arrived hungry? She had bacon and fried potatoes warming in the oven, eggs ready to scramble, and fresh baked bread ready to cut. She had determined the men could have a simple breakfast on her first morning preparing it.

Taking a sip of tea from the pot she made for herself, she let out a deep breath. The large carafe of coffee was filled, waiting for Buford to serve the men. Hopefully there was plenty of everything, and they'd never run out. Pasting on her impersonal smile, she waited for Buford's reaction. When he stared around the kitchen, speechless, she nodded with satisfaction.

"I only needed two days," she said with pride. "And now we will have satisfied customers. The coffee is there, ready for you to serve to the waiting men. There will be scrambled eggs, with bacon, fried potatoes, and fresh bread for breakfast."

"We usually serve more than one offering," he grumbled, as he picked up the polished carafe and the towel next to it.

"Not this morning." She met his gaze. "I'm certain none will leave dissatisfied." When he gave a grunt of frustration at being so ably managed by her, she turned away, so he wouldn't see her smirk.

Soon she was busy scrambling eggs, washing pans, and preparing food for the midday meal. More bread was in the oven, and a sheet cake was almost ready to be baked. She was uncertain if any had a sweet tooth but knew dessert would bring a tidy profit, as the men were reminded of home.

At the knock on the back door, she grumbled at the interruption. "Come in," she called out, stirring the bowl of cake batter once more before pouring it in a baking pan.

Three women entered her kitchen.

"I beg your pardon, but who are you?" she blurted out. "I'm not in need of staff." She looked around. "Not yet, at least."

The oldest of the three smiled at her with a sparkle of mischief in her hazel eyes. "I'm Mrs. O'Rourke, but you should call me Mary. These are my daughters, Maggie and Aileen." She pointed to a young woman who looked just like Mary, except for the startling blue eyes the young woman named Maggie shared with her brother Ardan. The other woman looked nothing like the two of them, nor like Seamus O'Rourke. She was short, plump, with plain brown hair and eyes.

As though noting her confusion, Aileen murmured, "I married Kevin recently, and I'm part of the O'Rourke family now."

Deirdre paused in what she was doing, recalling that Mary O'Rourke had referred to both of them as her daughters. She shook her head, finding it difficult to imagine anyone so readily accepting outsiders into her family. "As you can see, I'm occupied and not free for a social call."

Mary laughed. "Oh, we're not here to call, although I believe I'd like to swap recipes with you some day. Your kitchen smells marvelous." She took an appreciative sniff of the scents wafting around her. "We're here to work."

Setting aside the cake pan filled with batter, Deirdre swiped at her forehead. "I fear I don't understand what you mean."

"Ardan mentioned your upstairs is a right mess. Dusty and filled with cobwebs after over a year's vacancy. We're here to give it a polish for you." Mary motioned for Maggie and Aileen to fetch their pails and cloths.

"Oh, I couldn't ask you to do that. I …" She broke off at Mary's intense stare.

"You didn't ask, dear. We offered." She patted Deirdre on her arm. "You'll have to adjust and understand 'tis our way. Now, if you would be kind enough to save us a little somethin' for a treat later, I'm sure we'd appreciate it." Mary followed her girls upstairs, and their footsteps, giggles, and soft voices could be heard as they worked.

Deirdre stood another moment in shocked silence before forcing herself to return to her tasks.

Ardan watched his mother, Maggie, and Aileen that evening at supper, as they chattered together about their successful day and all they had accomplished. "What did you do?" he asked.

"We cleaned Mrs. Finnegan's house," Maggie said with an impish smile when he gaped at her.

"I didn't tell you about it so you'd bother her," he said, his appetite disappearing at the thought of his family bursting into Deirdre's space on her first day cooking at the café. He closed his eyes, as he forced himself to think of her as Mrs. Finnegan. "She has enough work with her new job without worryin' about the lot of you."

His mother stared at him with blatant disappointment in her gaze. "Ardan Malcolm O'Rourke, never is there a bad time in life to show another charity." She nodded as he flushed and ducked his head. "I believe she will be pleased with all we accomplished."

Ardan looked toward his mother but saw her attention focused on his father, who had gripped her hand. Maggie and Aileen ignored him too, and he felt at sea amid his family.

"What did you three do for the lass, Mary?" Seamus asked, as he sent a warning glance in his eldest son's direction.

"We swept, dusted, polished, and cleaned her rooms from top to bottom. I'm certain she will feel much more at home now," Mary said with pride.

"We hung curtains from almost every window," Aileen interjected, giggling at something Kevin whispered in her ear.

"An' we made sure she'll sleep on fresh sheets tonight," Maggie said. "She'll be very comfortable in her new home. Although I'd imagine she's quite lonely up there, with so much space."

Seamus chuckled at his youngest daughter. "Well, Maggie darlin', 'twas built for a family, not for a woman livin' alone. And, from what I heard today from the men eatin' at the café, she won't be a widow for long. She'll be a newly married woman."

Ardan watched as his father eyed Declan, and Ardan's focus turned to his brother. At age twenty-five, Declan had made known his desire to wed and to start a family. Although he had the O'Rourke black hair and blue eyes, he had a riotous mass of long hair and a bushy untrimmed beard. He appeared more like a backwoodsman than a business associate and son of Seamus O'Rourke. Tonight, Declan's hair was pulled back, and his beard appeared to have been trimmed. Ardan wondered at his brother's attempt to tame the wildness of his appearance.

"Are you interested in her, Dec?" he asked his brother in a low voice. Declan sat across from him and beside a chattering Eamon and Finn.

"She can cook, and I hear she's fine to look at," Declan said with a casual shrug. "I might as well make her acquaintance. There'll be no disappointment if nothing comes of it, as she's not promised to me."

"You know you're not still angry at Kevin." Ardan's voice held a tinge of warning.

"I know," Declan said, as he glanced at his brother chatting with his wife. "It's more the disappointment of still being alone."

Ardan ate more of his dinner and then murmured, "Someday you'll meet someone who fills your mind and spirit to the point where you can't remember a time when you didn't know her. And your conversations now about being satisfied by a pretty smile or a good cook will seem ludicrous." He saw Declan stare at him like he was mad, and then he shook his head as he focused on his meal.

Ardan feared he had already met the woman he had just described to Declan. The difference was, he had no desire to marry and no wish to have his life turned upside down by a woman who would only end up breaking his heart.

Deirdre trudged upstairs, holding a cup of tea. The last customer had left a little after 8:00 p.m., and she had finished cleaning the kitchen by nine. She rubbed at her sore back and knew she'd have to speak with Buford about hiring help. She couldn't keep up this pace.

Thinking fondly of her café in Baltimore, she sat with a groan on one of the stuffed chairs in her living space. She'd had two cooks and a dishwasher, while she had spent her energy cooking pastries. She took a sip of her tea, opening her eyes to look for a low table to set it on.

Gaping at the spotless room, she set her tea on a lace doily by a small table placed by her chair. She racked her memory, but she was certain that table had not been here this morning. Every surface in her living area had been polished and cleaned, and a fresh lemony scent permeated the room. One window was ajar, and the curtain fluttered in the breeze. *Curtain?* She shook her head in confusion. She'd had no curtains on any of the windows this morning.

Heaving herself to her feet, she checked each spotless room, coming to a stop when she reached her bedroom. Her trunk, which she had left overflowing and ajar this morning, was closed and against one wall with a colorful cloth over it. The maple bureau shone after its polishing, and a vase with dried flowers was set on top of the pale-blue cloth. She moved toward it, her fingers rubbing over the fine linen.

In the mirror, she saw her bed with fluffed-up pillows and a new quilt on top. She sat down, hugging a pillow to her chest, as tears coursed down her cheeks. Never could she recall receiving such a wondrous act of friendship. Especially not from women she did not know.

"How will I ever thank them?" she whispered to herself.

Yawning, she kicked off her shoes and rose, closing the new curtains that hung over her windows. She changed into her nightgown and slipped under the sheets. Sniffing at them, she realized they were freshly washed, as the hint of sun and lilac soap clung to them. With gratefulness filling her, she fell into sleep.

Three days later in her midmorning lull, Deirdre knocked on the back door of the O'Rourke house. She had tried the front door, but no one answered. Desperate, and with only a few more minutes of free time, she decided to try the back door. She waited, but no one came to the door. With stooped shoulders, she returned to the café, intent on providing another delicious meal for the men who walked through the door.

She stopped short upon entering her kitchen to find Ardan sitting on one of the stools, staring at an oatmeal cookie in a glass cookie jar, as though it were one of life's greatest temptations. "You may have it, if you like," she murmured. She giggled as he jumped at her voice. "It's the least I can do to thank you for sending your mother and sisters over to help me."

Ardan didn't reach for the cookie and flushed with guilt. "I can't take any credit, Mrs. Finnegan. I told them of the state of your rooms, and they decided on their own to offer aid."

She smiled. "Still, you told them. Thank you." She motioned for him to stand in a corner as she donned an apron and began walking around the kitchen. "I was looking for your mother and sisters, but they weren't home."

"Why?" Ardan asked, his arms crossed over his chest, as he watched her graceful movements.

"I wanted to see if Maggie would like to help me in the kitchen and if one of your younger brothers would work here washing dishes." She began to mix the batter she had dumped together and raised an eyebrow. "Could you ask them?"

"I fear if you ask one brother, you'll end up with two or three. They run in packs." His voice was filled with fond affection.

"Two would be a tremendous help," she said. "I'm exhausted, and I can't keep up this pace. In my café, I never had to do it all alone. It's not possible to feed this many men and do all the prep and cleaning."

Ardan frowned and nodded. It appeared he would march out the door to find one of his siblings. Instead he approached the sink and began to scrub the pots and pans piled up within.

"No, Mr. O'Rourke," she sputtered. At his dark glower over his shoulder, she said, "Ardan, please. I never meant for you to do such work."

"If it's good for one of us, it's good for all of us. That's what my da used to always say when we complained about our chores." He set aside a pot and began on another.

"What else did your father always say?" she asked.

Ardan smiled at her and faced the sink to focus on scrubbing the pan clean. "That none of us were more important than the other. That we were all precious and deserving of respect." He smiled. "Da was an evicted Irishman. Lost his land during the famine." He paused. "*Our* land," Ardan whispered. "He never believed—because we were Catholic, poor, and Irish—that we were inferior to others. He's always had a tremendous pride in who he is."

"And he's given that pride and sense of self to you," Deirdre said. "You're fortunate."

"Aye," Ardan said with a smile, as he reached for a cloth to wipe dry the small mound of pots and pans, so those could be put away, and he could then start on the pile of dishes. "Did you not have that?"

Deirdre shrugged. "No." Her clipped response brooked no invitation to inquire further into her past. However, her reluctance to reveal anything only fueled his curiosity.

"I wonder if 'tis true what some of the men are sayin'," he noted with a broad smile, as he followed her silent instructions on where to place the pots and pans. "That you're the Queen of the Fairies, come here to tempt us with your cooking and to prevent us from finding success anywhere far away from you."

"Get away with you," she said with a laugh. "I'm no fairy, and I'll never pretend to be one. If the men are enchanted by my cooking, it's because they've had to make do with food fit for the pigs until now."

"Well, yes, since Mrs. Tompkins left," Ardan said in agreement.

Standing with her hands on her hips and fighting a smile, Deirdre asked, "Did you accuse Mrs. Tompkins of being a witch or a mystical being because she could cook?"

"Of course not," Ardan said. "She was twenty years older than you, married, and not half as pretty." He winked as she sputtered out a laugh, and then he moved to the sink to continue his task of washing dishes.

After she set cakes into the oven, she moved to dry the dishes he washed.

"You've been doing all this work yourself the past days?" he asked. At her proud nod, he swore under his breath.

"There's no need to be upset that a woman can be independent," she snapped.

"If you believe that's why I'm angry, you're an *eejit*," he said, as he wiped his hands on his pants and faced her. "You're workin' yourself into the ground while Buford sits an' chats with the lads out front. He should be workin' as hard as you, for he wouldn't have a successful business if you weren't here." He paused. "Buford *is* going to pay for your hired help?"

She shrugged at his implied question. "He said, if I wasn't up to the task of doing all the necessary work, I would need to subsidize them from my share of the profits. That he hasn't needed to pay for more than one cook in the past."

Ardan rested one hip against the counter. "And look where that got him," he muttered. "Bloody *eejit*." He stormed past her and down the back steps, the door slamming shut behind him.

She watched his swift departure, absurdly upset that he hadn't eaten one of her oatmeal cookies. Unable to spend any more time on his mercurial moods, she focused on the evening's meal, thankful for the help he had provided her. And his company.

At least once a day the following week, Ardan strolled by the café in a casual manner, surreptitiously scanning the interior as he passed it to see the number of customers inside. He always noted they were contented with the fine fare prepared by Deirdre, enthusiastic and effusive in their praise of her cooking. He paused one day, unable to stop himself from sighing with pleasure as the scents of roasted chicken and rosemary wafted on the breeze. He yearned for a taste of one of her homemade cakes but refrained from entering the café.

One day, nearly a week after he had last seen Deirdre, he paused near the café, before turning away with a regretful shake of his head. He barged into someone walking on the boardwalk, and he reached out reflexively to keep her from tumbling to the ground. "I beg your pardon," he said. "Niamh?" he asked, as he stared at his oldest sister, the third oldest O'Rourke. "What are you doin'?"

She watched him with a curious expression. "I could ask you the same," she muttered, as she tightened her grip on her one-year-old daughter, Maura. "I thought to go on a walk with Maura. See if there are any ships for her to watch. An', if no ships, I'll bring her by the livery to see if Dunmore or Cormac will let her pet an animal."

"Don't let her too near the water," Ardan warned, as he reached forward to tickle his niece's cheek. "How is it she grows so much each time I see her?"

Niamh shrugged, a smile finally lighting her eyes as she beheld her precious girl. "I don't know. But, aye, she does." After a moment, she focused again on her eldest brother. "Are you well, Ardan? You seem out of sorts." She paused as she looked from him to the nearby café. "And all too focused on the café." When he muttered under his breath about 'interferin' family members,' she grinned. "Or should I say, all too interested in a certain woman in the café?"

"Don't start," he said, unable to hide a grin. "Mrs. Finnegan works too hard and needs help," he muttered. When Niamh looked too interested, as though she would pursue that topic of conversation, he shook his head and said, "You know I'll die a bachelor, carin' for my wee nieces and nephews."

She laughed. "Ha! They'll be carin' for you in your decrepit old age. And, as of now, you only have one niece." She kissed Maura's head, as Maura played with a strand of Niamh's loosened auburn-colored hair. When Maura held out her arms to her uncle, Niamh passed her daughter to Ardan. "Seems she is charmed by you, even if the new cook isn't."

Ardan rolled his eyes, as he bounced Maura in his arms. "Forget your mum's foolishness. She wants to see us all married an' as happy as she is." He paused when Niamh froze at his words. "Niamh?" he asked, as he kissed Maura's small fingers that patted at his face. "Are you well?"

She shrugged, staring at the river. "Of course I am. And, if I know disappointment, I only have myself to blame." She stilled her movement away from Ardan, when he rested a hand on her forearm.

"No," he said in a soft voice. "'Tis Connor's. He's workin' with Cormac, aye?" Ardan referred to Niamh's husband, Connor Ahern, a man who preferred to spend his time in the saloons and at the gambling tables rather than working with his brother, Cormac, driving oxen.

"Not just now. He finds the work … too strenuous for him." She flushed as she looked at her feet in well-worn shoes. "Don't worry about me, Ardan. I'll find a way to ensure we are well cared for."

Shaking his head, Ardan fought swearing in little Maura's presence. "'Tisn't your job, Niamh, to find a way. Your husband should care about your well-being."

Niamh shrugged and stared bravely at him. "I would hope you

choose more wisely than I did, Ardan," she whispered, as she eased Maura back into her arms. "For I'm discovering just how long a life-time can be when married to …" She broke off without finishing her sentence, but the sentiment, *the wrong man*, hung in the air between them. "I'll see you soon," she whispered as she brushed past him.

Ardan watched her go, his fascination with Deirdre and the café momentarily eclipsed by his concern for Niamh.

CHAPTER 3

Every day for the past week, Deirdre had looked to the back door when supplies were delivered, but Ardan didn't appear and had never returned. One of his brothers always came by and made the deliveries, showing her what Ardan would have looked like as a boy without as many responsibilities as he had now. His brothers teased her and told her funny stories, but they never expressed any concern for her or her business.

Like Ardan did.

She stood at the sink, during a lull in cooking, elbows deep in washing dishes and silently chided herself for missing Ardan. She barely knew the man. Even though he had shown her kindness and consideration, it did not mean he had any regard for her. She scrubbed extra hard at a stain on a plate and silently chastised herself. She refused to have any feelings for him.

Her musings did nothing to dampen her disappointment at his absence from her life. She had hoped he would speak with his family about her needing help and that they would appear again without her having to seek them out. After a week of backbreaking work, she acknowledged she had to find time to discuss her need for helpers with Mary or Seamus.

At the tap on the café's back door, she dropped the plate back into the sudsy water and dried her hands on a towel. "Yes, come in," she called out, as she turned to the door. "Ardan," she breathed, her gaze roving over him. Although she had thought of his brothers as a younger version of him, she doubted they had ever carried the weight of responsibility as he did. They were younger brothers, protected by their older siblings and father, and had the lightness of spirit to prove it. "Did you bring supplies today?"

He shook his head and frowned at the sight of her at the sink. "No." He moved toward her.

She took a step away from where she had been working, her eyes huge as she saw the anger in his gaze.

"Do you have another apron?"

"Apron?" she repeated. After a moment, she spun and pulled open a cupboard, extracting one, showing it to him.

As she watched him shuck his coat and waistcoat, his strong muscles bunching and relaxing under his shirt, he grabbed the apron from her. She blurted out, "Why do you want an apron?"

"I'm not busy at the warehouse. I can help you with dishes. Miserly Hunt has no right to squirrel away the profits, when you are the reason why he's having any success."

She flushed at the determination in his gaze and the pleasure his words evoked. "I ... This isn't proper," she whispered.

"Buford should have paid for at least one of my brothers to help you. And you most likely still need Maggie to aid you with the cooking. But, for now, you have my help. Free of a costly wage."

Rubbing at her forehead, she shook her head from side to side, as though attempting to figure out a riddle. "I don't understand." Her eyes filled with tears as she saw him dive into work.

"I hate bullies, and, against my will, I like you," he said.

She jerked and took a step away from him. After turning, as though looking for something for one of her recipes, she swiped at her cheek to clear it of the tear that fell. His words had cut through her fragile confidence and the ease she had felt with him. "Am I that awful?" she asked in a small voice.

A dish clattered in the sink. *"Awful?"* he asked. Wet hands touched her shoulder, and he gave them a soft squeeze. "No. It's because you aren't that I have trouble thinking of anythin' or anyone else. You're under my skin, Deirdre, an' I find that hard to accept." With another squeeze, he moved away.

She took a deep breath, inhaling his spicy aftershave and a musky scent she knew was all Ardan. After another steadying moment, she pivoted to see him working diligently, as though he hadn't turned her world upside down. She forced herself to act as though nothing momentous had occurred and moved to bake a special cake for the evening's dessert and more bread.

"What are you servin' for the midday meal?" he asked.

"Stew," she said. "I've decided the midday meal will be a simple one, and the men don't seem to mind."

"Of course not. It's edible," Ardan said, as he looked at her over his shoulder. "Would you mind if I had a bowl after I finish? I'll miss the meal at my mum's, and I'd rather not explain why." He flushed as she stared at him with curiosity. "They always have a lot of questions, aye?"

She shrugged. "I wouldn't know what that's like. I never had much family."

"No?" he asked, as he rinsed and then rewashed a dirty pot. "Where is your family?"

"All dead," she said in a clipped tone. At his shocked stare, she shrugged. "I have no one."

Ardan looked as though he'd been poleaxed at the thought. "I can't imagine," he breathed. "Even after we lost mum, we still had each other." He paused, his brows furrowed. He returned to his work, quiet for minutes as he diligently washed and dried dishes.

"How is it your family can spare you again?" she asked. She squeaked and turned to the connecting door at Buford's bellow for bowls of stew.

Ardan looked at her and shook his head, as she set down her mixing bowl and moved to dish up and serve the stew. "No, lass. Let the man come in and ladle it up himself. You've prepared it. He can serve it."

She paused in her movement toward the stove and beamed at him. "You're right. I'm so tired that I'm not thinking straight." She moved back to the bread she was kneading and to the cake she needed to finish mixing and smiled calmly at Buford as he stormed into the kitchen.

Flushed red and with eyes on fire, Buford failed to notice Ardan standing in the corner washing dishes. "I told you to get those bowls of soup ready, woman," Buford snapped. "Why are you still elbow deep in that muck?"

"This *muck* is what is garnering you acclaim, Mr. Hunt," she said in a sweet voice, although her cognac-colored eyes gleamed with anger. "Do you know how many times I've heard the men talk about finally eating good bread? Or that my desserts remind them of their mama's?" She waited for him to apologize. "I'm too busy to be serving the food as well. That's your job. I've prepared the stew. Ladle it out and put a slice of bread beside each bowl."

"You lazy wench," Buford sputtered, as he watched her continue her work without making a move to comply with his demands.

Flushing at his verbal abuse, she shook her head. "If that is how you think of me, I will need to take my baking and cooking talents to another location. I'm certain I will have as much success elsewhere. Although I'm doubtful of yours." She pulled her hands from the dough, swiped them on a cloth, and took a step away.

"Now don't get hasty," Buford stammered. "Just a little meaningless banter between partners."

Glaring at him, Deirdre remained silent.

"So, if she were to call you a miserly, manipulative bastard, you'd take that all as good fun?" Ardan asked. He smiled as Buford gaped at him, finally noting his presence. "Buford, always a pleasure to see the real man behind the facade."

"O'Rourke, what are you doing here?" Buford Hunt demanded. "You have no right to be on my premises without my permission."

Ardan chuckled. "Imagine the townsfolk's amusement to learn you were so threatened by my presence washing dishes that you had to throw me off your property." He met Buford's irate glare. "Mrs. Finnegan needed help with the most basic of chores because you are too closefisted to ensure she has appropriate help to keep her kitchen running smoothly."

Buford puffed out his chest. "As I've said before, and I'll say again, if she's such a poor manager of her time and her kitchen, I should not have to suffer the expense to clean up after her."

Ardan leaned against the counter, his arms over his chest, ignoring the consistent calls for service from inside the café's dining area. "With your other cooks, did they ever bake bread? Or cookies? Or a cake?" he asked. Answering his own questions with a shake of his head, he said, "They barely served an edible stew, which is why you rarely saw an O'Rourke here when we were desperate for a meal before my mum returned. Now you have three different meals a day, along with desserts and bread. That requires aid, you fool."

"The Tompkinses did it without outside help," Buford said, a stubborn tilt to his jaw as he moved to the stove to ladle out bowls of stew.

Ardan rubbed at his temples and shook his head. "You really are an idiot, and I'm surprised your business has lasted as long as it has." When Buford glared at him, Ardan said, "How can you not remember that Harold ran the front, Irene cooked, and her grandchildren cleaned? They were always tryin' to sneak away to play, but they had their chores. Irene had plenty of help."

He paused as he met Buford's stubborn stare. "An' the town wasn't as busy then. We weren't in the middle of gold rush fever. You should continue to pray that Mrs. Finnegan doesn't depart for one of the larger towns in the Territory to earn greater fame, as she deserves."

Buford let out a huff of frustration as he stormed out of the kitchen, carrying bowls of stew. He came and went numerous times, feeding the hungry men. Finally he was heard telling a tale in the café, and Deirdre knew he wouldn't return for a while.

Deirdre turned to face Ardan, unable to fight a smile. "Thank you," she whispered. "I've been too tired to fight his bullying."

Ardan winked at her. "Anytime, Deirdre. Anytime."

45

~

That evening, Ardan watched as his mother cleaned the family's kitchen, chatting and laughing with Maggie. His eldest brothers had scattered, and Da was in the living room, reading a novel aloud to Niall, Oran, and Bryan.

The simple scene reminded him of long-ago times, when they had lived in a tiny cottage in Ireland. He and his siblings would circle his mum's skirts, eager to help her and to earn a pat on the head or a word of praise. She was never stingy with her approval, and he remembered her gentle approbation always made him want to do more and to be better. After watching her with Maggie for another long moment, he rose and moved to the sink and met his mother's startled gaze a moment before he pulled her into his arms.

"Ardan?" she whispered, as she wrapped her arms around his waist and held him close.

"Can you give us a moment, Maggie?" Ardan asked his sister, barely noticing when she slipped from the room. "I'm sorry, Mum," he whispered in her ear as he fought tears. "Forgive me."

She leaned back, his face cupped in her palms, as she gazed deeply into her eldest son's eyes. "There's nothin' to forgive you, Ardan." A tear coursed down one cheek. "Do you know the pride I feel every time I see you? To think you're my son?" She reached up and stroked back a lock of his hair. "I remember the first moment I held you in my arms, swaddled in a rough wool blanket. You already had Seamus's black hair and blue eyes, and I feared you'd have nothing of mine."

"Mum," Ardan whispered.

"But you did. You had my compassion and keen sense of right and wrong. And I hate that you've felt wronged by me." Her eyes overflowed as tears coursed down her cheeks.

Ardan nodded, unwilling to lie to himself or his mother any longer. "I was so angry," he rasped. "At fate. At you. How could I have mourned you for eighteen years, and yet you lived? You had another family. Did we mean nothing to you?" He took a deep stuttering

46

breath as he saw the pain in her gaze evoked by his words. "My head understands what happened, but my heart still feels betrayed."

"I didn't betray you. I could never betray you," Mary said, as she gripped his face and stared at him with a fierce urgency. "Please tell me you understand that."

After a long moment, he nodded. "Aye, I finally do. I've seen how you are, and 'tis as though you never left us. Which has almost made it worse because all those years without you didn't have to be that way. I didn't have to rock Niamh to sleep for a year as she called out for you. I didn't have to watch Da staring out the door, as though waiting for you to appear. I didn't have to live with Colleen ..." He shook his head and closed his eyes.

"Oh, Ardan," Mary whispered, as she pulled him down and held him close. "There was a horrible misunderstanding, and I was separated from you for nearly eighteen years. But we're together again, and we'll never be separated again."

"I have trouble believing that," he whispered. "I have trouble believing in forever."

"Time will prove I'm right," she said, as she continued to hold him close. After many minutes, holding her eldest in her arms, she said, "I want you to understand one thing." She backed up, so she looked him in the eyes. "Although I had another family, and I love my boys Lucien and Henri with all that I am, they never took your place. Or any of you. Each of my children is a special and a wondrous and a unique gift. You all lived on in my heart forever." She paused and then asked in a hesitant voice, "What changed today, Ardan?"

"I realized how strong you had to be to continue forward and to still be the generous loving mum I knew as a lad." He paused and then whispered, "I realized today we were never alone. We had each other. I had Kevin to share things with, and Da had all of us. You only had Maggie, a baby, who never knew us. You had no one to keep the memories alive." His eyes shone with passionate intensity. "An' memories are precious."

Her eyes glistened with unshed tears. "Aye, they are, Ardan."

"I'm glad you're back, Mum," he said, as he pulled her close for one last embrace. He held her as she cried in his arms, giving thanks for second chances.

~

Deirdre sipped at her cup of tea, as she played with the week's menu. She worried the men would become bored with the simple fare she cooked, but it was impossible to obtain fancy spices at this time. She jotted down a note to see if she could have the O'Rourkes order her spices for the upcoming year. Her breath caught at the idea she might still be here in a year. That she might have found a home.

"Well, don't you seem pleased with yourself," Buford said, as he stomped into the kitchen. He glared at the tidy space and the scent of bread in the oven.

"And why shouldn't I be pleased, Mr. Hunt?" Deirdre asked, as she took another sip of tea. "I've been here nearly two weeks, cleaned up this atrocious kitchen, and turned your floundering business into a roaring success." She smiled at him as he gaped at her. "What part of that should upset me?"

"You have no right to allow that upstart O'Rourke into your kitchen," he said, flushing with misplaced indignation.

"As you just said, for all practical purposes, it's *my* kitchen. He's a friend, and, as a friend, he saw that I needed help and willingly rendered aid. I'm hopeful one of his brothers and his sister will begin to work with me. As a kitchen expense. Not one that I need to pay for."

Buford looked at her, his gaze filled with shrewd intensity. "You're emboldened now because you have the support of the O'Rourkes."

"No, I know you are trying to cheat me of my profits due me." Her cheeks flushed at the scornful idea. "I understand this building is yours. This kitchen and its supplies and wares are yours. But you'd have nothing if it weren't for me doing all the cooking—and with much greater success than any of the other cooks who worked here in the past year since you bought the café." She met his glower as she rose from her seat. "Thus, the bargain we struck is fair. And I expect you to keep to it, or I will walk away now, and you will be left with nothing but a shell of a business that earns you a pittance." She stood tall with her red-gold hair in a long braid down her back, her eyes shining with sincerity.

"Unnatural woman," he rasped, as he turned on his heel and stormed out.

She let out a deep breath, a smile bursting forth as she hoped it had meant he agreed to her demands. Soon she was back to work, unable to gloat over her victory as her cooking continued at an unrelenting pace.

Later that morning, she answered a knock on the back door, fighting hope and expectation that it was Ardan. When it was a woman who looked like Maggie but had hazel-colored eyes, Deirdre frowned. "Yes?" she asked.

"Might I speak with you?" the woman asked. She was half turned away from her and held something in her arms.

"If you can come in and talk while I work," Deirdre said, motioning for the woman to enter. "I'm Deirdre Finnegan." Deirdre froze when the woman stepped inside and set down a child with reddish-gold hair and blue eyes for a moment. Deirdre gripped the counter, hearing a buzzing noise as she feared she would faint. "Who are you?" she rasped.

"Are you all right, Mrs. Finnegan?" the woman asked, as she found a stool and urged her onto it. "I'm Niamh Ahern, and this is my wee daughter, Maura."

"Maura," Deirdre gasped, as she looked at the little girl who was again in her mother's arms, drooling over the finger she'd stuffed into her mouth and resting her head against her mother's shoulder. "You look like an O'Rourke. Like Maggie," she said, as she attempted to regain her composure. With a nod of her head, she gratefully accepted the glass of water Niamh pressed into her hand.

"Aye, my da's Seamus O'Rourke," Niamh said.

Deirdre noted she didn't mention Mary, and she bit her tongue.

"What might I do for you? Forgive me my foolishness. I fear I've been working too hard."

Niamh let out a sigh of relief and smiled. "'Tis why I'm here. I heard you need help, an' I'd like to offer what aid I can." She bit her lip as she fought embarrassment. "Although I can't work without pay."

Deirdre focused on Niamh and not the baby, who had the power to devastate her. "There will be a salary, although I'm still uncertain as to the amount. Mr. Hunt and I haven't decided on the specifications. However, as you can see, I am in desperate need of assistance." She cleared her throat. "The one problem I foresee," she said, causing Niamh's relieved smile to dim, "is that this is no place for a child. You'd need to find someplace for your child to be during the time you are working here."

Niamh kissed Maura's head, her hold on her tightening. "We're never apart," Niamh murmured. She cast her gaze around the room, frowning when she saw no readily available space where her daughter could play. "Are you certain?"

Deirdre nodded. "Yes. For reasons of practicality and my own well-being, I can't have a child in my kitchen when I am cooking." She paused as she saw Niamh bite her lip, as though undecided what to do. "I had thought to ask your sister, Maggie, to help me."

"No!" Niamh said, reaching forward to grasp Deirdre's arm. "I'll find a way. And I'll be here tomorrow, without Maura. Thank you, Deirdre." Niamh spun on her heel and clambered down the back steps, the back door *thunk*ing shut behind her.

Deirdre stood frozen in place for many minutes, lost to her memories of a different time. She sniffed the air and, rather than smelling the baking bread and the lye of the kitchen soap, the sweet scent of her daughter's skin after a bath filled her lungs. Rather than the bubbling stew on the stove, she heard the gurgle of her laughter. Rather than a corset, tied so tightly she was nearly out of breath, she felt her daughter's arms wrapped around her neck, her sweet breath on her cheek, as she whispered a secret about butterflies and moonbeams. Swiping at a tear, she opened her eyes and forced herself to bury her memories as she returned to work.

Deirdre sat in the shade on the back steps, relishing the warm air that had yet to turn hot. She had a few moments to rest during the midmorning lull, and she looked forward to the arrival tomorrow of Niamh O'Rourke. Niamh *Ahern*, Deirdre silently corrected herself. Although Deirdre enjoyed her time with Ardan, she was intrigued by Niamh's reluctance to speak of her mother.

Silently chastising herself for her fascination with the O'Rourkes, Deirdre attempted to focus on something else. However, her gaze continually strayed down the lane toward the back of the O'Rourke warehouse and store, hoping to catch a glimpse of Ardan.

She jolted when a scornful voice boomed at her from her right. "I hadn't thought the new cook would be so foolish."

Deirdre looked at the woman, about her height, dressed in a fashionable eggplant-colored satin dress. A glower seemed to be a permanent part of her expression, and smiling seemed a foreign concept to her. "I'm sorry. I fear I haven't met you."

"Of course you haven't. You've been too busy cozying up to the likes of the O'Rourkes." She snickered at the thought. "You'll learn of your folly soon enough, miss."

"I'm *Mrs.* Finnegan, and I believe I'm capable of making my own impressions about the townsfolk." Deirdre stood, grateful she was on the second step, as that made her taller than the woman. Otherwise they would have been eye to eye.

"If you believe that, then you truly are an idiot." She waved at the café. "Only a simpleton would agree to work for a man like Buford Hunt. He'll promise you the world and never keep his word."

Deirdre watched the stranger closely and shook her head. "Is that the truth or your bitterness toward all men shining through? For I believe I will be treated fairly by Mr. Hunt." She said a silent prayer that she had reason for her faith, but she refused to show any doubt to this dreadful woman. "Who are you?"

"I am the estimable Mrs. Janet Davies." She preened as she said her name. "Unlike some who arrived here believing a man would be waiting with baited breath for him to marry her," she snickered again at Deirdre, "my niece was actually betrothed to an O'Rourke before she arrived."

Deirdre shook her head in confusion. "I'm afraid there are too many O'Rourkes for me to know who they are or their stories. However, congratulations on your niece's nuptials. I'm certain they'll be very happy." When Mrs. Davies flushed with indignation, Deirdre bit her lip and stifled a giggle.

"Happy? *Happy?* How can such an abomination of a family ever make my niece happy?"

Deirdre shook her head. "I'm afraid I don't understand, nor do I have the time to untangle your complicated relationship with them. I wish you a good day, and I hope you find some solace in the fine weather." She returned to her kitchen, locking the back door behind her, lest the woman followed her inside.

When she heard Mrs. Davies muttering to herself before walking away, Deirdre heaved out a sigh of relief. "What a singularly unpleasant woman." However, her interaction with Mrs. Davies only increased her fascination with the O'Rourkes, a fact she attempted to ignore.

Returning home midafternoon, Ardan paused at the entrance to their kitchen to see Niamh present with Maura. Mary was at the stove, working diligently on the family supper, and Maggie was nowhere in sight. He considered tiptoeing out the door again, but Maura saw him and gave a squeal of delight at the sight of him.

"Maura, love," he *coo*ed as he entered, plucking her from Niamh's arms and into his. He kissed her head before kissing his sister's cheek. "Niamh, are you well?" His alert gaze roved over her, searching for any sign that her useless husband had harmed her. Ardan ached for a reason to fight that man. However, other than Ardan's recent conversation with Niamh that her husband had no desire to work, confirming Connor as a drunken layabout with no ambition, Connor Ahern had given Ardan no reason to knock him senseless.

"I'm well, Ardan," Niamh murmured, her eyes glowing at the easy affection he showed her daughter. "Wee Maura is so lucky to have an uncle like you, Ardan. You're always so happy to see her." She smiled ruefully. "You're so good with her, not holding her as though she were a sack of potatoes."

Ardan frowned, wondering at her compliment, grimacing as he considered the possibility of her subtly criticizing her worthless husband.

Niamh maintained an impassive expression and said, "I've come to ask for a favor."

"Oh?" Ardan tickled Maura's belly. "What do you need me to do?"

Niamh flushed, her gaze flicking to their mother. "Not you, Ardan." She looked at Mary, who stood with their back to them. "I need your help, Mum."

The wooden spoon clattered to the stovetop at Niamh's softly spoken words. After a moment, where a stuttering breath was heard, Mary turned to face them. "What?" Mary asked, her hazel eyes luminous with unshed tears.

"I need to ask a favor," Niamh whispered. At Mary's nod, Niamh cleared her throat. "I need work. I know you wanted Maggie to work for the Finnegan woman, but I need it." Niamh lifted her chin in challenge, but, when neither her mother nor eldest brother showed any sign of contradicting her, Niamh's shoulders stooped forward, and her bravado evaporated.

"Maggie was only going to help her because she likes the woman. Not because she desired the work," Mary said. "I believe Maggie's interests lie outside the kitchen." She waited with her hands crossed over each other at her waist. "What favor do you need?"

"Deirdre doesn't want Maura underfoot. Wants a kitchen free of children. I can't work there and worry about Maura. Connor ..." She shrugged, and Ardan and Mary nodded their understanding. "Will you watch Maura while I work?" Niamh wrung her hands in front of her.

Mary's breath caught at her daughter's request. "You'd trust me with your daughter?"

Niamh nodded. When Ardan moved to hand Maura to Mary, Niamh nodded again. "Yes, Ardan."

Maura fussed for a moment in Mary's arms and then settled. She sniffed at Mary's neck before resting her head and falling half asleep.

"Oh, I'd almost forgotten," Mary whispered, as her hands traced patterns over her granddaughter's back. "What it feels like to have them snuffle at your neck." She kissed Maura's head and swayed her hips side to side as she hummed to her. "There's a wee girl."

Niamh stood transfixed as she watched her mother with her daughter. "Thank you, Mum," she whispered. She reached for Maura, snatching her daughter from her mother's arms and earning a yowl of protest from her slumbering child. "I'll be by in the mornin' with her." She rushed from the room, her voice soothing Maura as she cried.

Ardan stood watching, as a mixture of emotions played over his mother's face. "Are you well, Mum?"

Mary shrugged and turned back to the stove. She picked up the wooden spoon and then slammed it down so hard that it cracked. When her shoulders shook with sobs, he gripped them and turned her to face him. "Mum?" he whispered, pulling her into his arms.

He held her as she sobbed in his arms and stared at his father with a helpless expression when Seamus entered. "I didn't upset her. I promise," Ardan said, as his father glared at him. He eased her from his arms and urged her to go to his father.

He heard his father whisper soft words of praise to her and encouraged her to cry all she needed. Arden slipped from the room, giving them the privacy they required.

⌒

When Mary finally calmed, Seamus never asked her what had upset her but continued to hold her close.

"I'm filled with such rage," Mary whispered, as her fingers dug into her husband's back.

"*Shh*, love, there's no need for it." He ran his hands over her, attempting to ease her of her sadness. "It only brings more heartache."

"Why did I have to be separated from you and our children? Why did I have to suffer through years without you?" she gasped, her hands holding him tightly to her. "Why must my own daughter resent me and believe I would find carin' for my granddaughter a burden?"

"Oh, love," he murmured, holding her to him. He said nothing further for he knew Mary needed to make her peace with each of their children in her own way. Although he wished he could soothe their pain and have them be the large happy family he had always envisioned with no undercurrents of resentment or doubts, he knew that wasn't yet possible. "Time will heal this pain, love."

"How much time, Shay?" she whispered into his chest. "How much time before they forgive me?"

"They forgive you now," he said in a soft voice, as his large palms traced over her back. "'Tis more they don't trust fate not to steal you away again, and they are cautious to accept you're here to stay. Be patient with them, love."

Mary sighed, rubbing her face against his chest, relaxing under his gentle touch. "You should have seen Niamh, Seamus. When I held Maura and relished feelin' her wee snuffle against my neck, 'twas as though Niamh recalled the times that she did that. The times I carried her in my arms, and we whispered words to each other. And she didn't want to remember."

Seamus made a soothing noise. "No, love. 'Tisn't that she doesn't want to remember. 'Tis that the remembering hurts too much. Of all the children, Niamh mourned you the fiercest. They all needed their mother, but Niamh felt adrift as the only girl." He sighed. "I did what I could for her, but I was never you."

Mary backed up a step and stared into his gaze filled with anguish. "Oh, Shay, I never doubted—not for one moment—how much you cared for them. That you loved them with your whole heart."

"Aye," he said with tear-brightened eyes. "But the missing of you nearly drove us all mad."

She sighed and burrowed into his embrace, taking comfort in the fact they were reunited and never to be separated again.

~

A few days later, Niamh bustled around the tidy café kitchen. She chopped vegetables for a stew, made pots of coffee, sliced bread, and washed dishes. Basically anything that was called for so that Deirdre could continue to bake and to prepare meals. Somewhere during the past day, she and Deirdre had begun to talk, and they now chattered away as though they were old friends. Niamh hadn't realized how much she had missed a woman's company.

Deirdre paused a moment, sipping from her ever-ready cup of tea. "So, you arrived in Fort Benton with a man in pursuit of you?" Deirdre asked.

Niamh paused and sighed. "I fear it wasn't as romantic as I made it out to be. Connor and his brother were on the same steamboat, an' Connor showed an interest. I was a silly girl, with a loving family, an' I longed for adventure. An' I thought it romantic that a man promised to another would be so enchanted by me that he'd forget his first love." Her eyes clouded at her words, as though she had revealed too much.

Deirdre took a sip of tea, noting an undercurrent of bitterness and regret in Niamh's words. "What happened?"

Niamh shrugged and pasted on a cheery smile. "The steamboat couldn't make it all the way here. We had to dock at Cow Island." She made a motion, as though indicating the landing site over a hundred miles from Fort Benton.

Deirdre nodded, as the same had occurred to her earlier this summer.

"Connor an' I snuck away in a stagecoach, without any of my brothers or my da. Only his brother," she murmured. Her gaze was distant. "When my family arrived in Fort Benton a few days later, Da knew nothin' was to be done but to agree for us to marry."

Deirdre took a deep breath. "Your father seems a proud man. Did he like being fooled?"

Shaking her head, Niamh moved to the stew to stir the pot. "No, but he feared I was with child already." She shook her head. "My da's a good man. But I went against everything he had instilled in me. To be cautious. To always have him or one of my brothers with me. And he couldn't imagine subjectin' a child to the stain of bein' born out of wedlock. So we married."

"And now you have a child," Deirdre said.

"Aye, but Maura came later. *After* I realized Connor recognized that my father was a man destined for success and hoped to live off my family's prosperity." She flushed. "I beg your pardon for soundin' bitter."

Deirdre shrugged. "I wondered why you would be desperate for work, when you had a living husband and your family is the most esteemed in town. You're committed to make it on your own, aren't you?"

Niamh stood facing Deirdre, her body filled with a tenacious determination. "Aye," she said. "My husband far prefers the saloons or the gamblin' tables to workin' with his brother. Cormac is the hard worker. Connor is the layabout dreamer."

"Cormac," Deirdre muttered. "Is he the man who drives the oxen carts?"

"Aye, the bullwhacker," Niamh said. "The younger brother, although you wouldn't know it by how he acts." She sighed. "What made you come to Fort Benton?"

Deirdre took another sip of her tea and rose to start mixing ingredients for rolls for dinner. "Oh, a desire for adventure. A yearning to leave all that was familiar behind."

Niamh shook her head, as she studied the woman who appeared to be about her age, but she suspected was a few years younger. "Nay, you never run from the familiar if it's bringin' you comfort." When Deirdre remained silent, Niamh smiled. "'Tis all right, Deirdre. We all have our secrets."

~

A few nights later, Ardan left his house and wandered over to the café. He looked inside to see a few stragglers remained at the tables, and he sauntered around to the back door. Tonight, she had left it open to allow the cooling night air to enter. He paused on the bottom step as her soft, sweet voice carried on the breeze. Closing his eyes, he listened until she finished the slow song and moved on to another he recognized as *"Darling Nelly Gray."*

"A cook and a singer," he teased from the doorway. At her squeal of surprise, he chuckled. "I hadn't thought one person could have so much natural skill."

She flushed and rolled her eyes as she grinned at him. "The baking I learned. The singing I inherited." She motioned for him to enter, and she swiped at the countertops, not laboring over a dishpan of dirty dishes.

"Niamh's helpin' you then," he said.

"She's a godsend," Deirdre said. "Not only is she an excellent cook but she never complains about doing all the other tasks that keep a kitchen running." She sighed with contentment. "How are you?" At his careless shrug, she pointed to a stool and moved to the icebox. "Come. Have a glass of milk and a slice of my cake. You've yet to try anything I've made."

"There's no need to go to any fuss, Deirdre," he complained, although he had already sat and was eyeing the cake with lascivious intent.

She laughed. "You can't fool me!" After cutting him a generous slab and pouring him a glass of milk, she sat beside him. She frowned when he grimaced at his first bite of the yellow cake with powder-sugar glaze. "You don't like it?" She sat back, perplexed at such a possibility.

"No," he said, as he grabbed his plate and held it away from her, as though she were about to snatch it from him. "'Tis a little piece of heaven itself, and I don't understand how you can sell it for so little."

He saw her flush with pleasure at his words and smiled at her before taking a sip of milk.

She relaxed, enjoying watching him eat her food. "I had to improvise. I don't have all the spices I'm used to here. If I'm to be here next year, I'll need your father to order spices for me."

Ardan instinctively tensed at her mention that she might *not* be here the following year. He lowered his fork, as he feared any food might get stuck in his throat. "Where would you go?" he asked, clearing his throat. He took a sip of milk and attempted to act nonchalant as he fought panic.

She shrugged, appearing not to notice the dismay her words caused. "I'm not sure. If things don't work out with Mr. Hunt, perhaps I'll go to Helena or Virginia City." She rose and moved to ensure the remaining cake was covered. "Nothing's keeping me here."

Ardan choked, biting back words he knew he had no right to say. Finally he rasped, "You'd be missed."

She stared at him a long moment, her gaze ensnared by his as he rose and slowly approached her.

"The men would lament the loss of my cooking for a few days," she said in a quavering voice, in an attempt to elicit a chuckle or a smile.

He shook his head, his expression serious. "I'm not talkin' about the men. Or Buford the buffoon. I refer to Niamh. To my mum." He paused as he came to a stop in front of her, his hands reaching forward so his fingertips caressed hers. He watched her swallow. A flush rose up her neck, to her cheeks, until she seemed to glow in front of him, and his breath caught at her beauty. "To me," he breathed.

He leaned forward and was inches away from kissing her when he heard heavy footsteps approaching and lurched away. He spun to the sink, dumping clean pots into it so he had something to do with his hands and to ignore Buford at the same time. Paying no attention to Buford's prattle, he finally noticed the room was quiet.

Looking around the kitchen, he found Buford was absent. But so was Deirdre.

Ardan walked to the door leading into the café, noting Buford out front, locking the door. All lanterns had been extinguished for the night, and the curtains covered the windows. He turned into the kitchen, latched the back door, and walked on his toes up to the second floor. He peered into the living room, coming to a halt at the sight of Deirdre staring out at the Missouri in the waning evening light.

"'Tis always a beautiful sight," he said. He smiled as she yelped and faced him.

"I thought you'd leave," she whispered. At his shake of his head, she watched him with wide eyes as he approached her. "Why are you here?"

"We have unfinished business," he said in a deep, impassioned voice. A satisfied glint flashed in his gaze when he saw her shiver at his words. "Don't act as though you don't feel this, Deirdre."

"Just because I feel something, it doesn't mean anything has to happen," she said. However, she had inched away from the window, moving in his direction.

He waited, not wanting anyone from the street below to witness him upstairs with her. "Come here, lass," he cajoled. His blue eyes shone with passionate tenderness. When she was a pace away from him, he raised his hand as though to pull her to him. Instead, he traced his fingertips over her arm to her wrist and then back up again to her shoulder. "I want to feel you in my arms, Deirdre. But I want to know you want to be there too," he whispered.

Her gaze was filled with a tumultuous yearning as she arched into his touch. "I shouldn't," she breathed. "But I'll dream of you tonight, no matter what we do."

"Lass," he rasped, cupping her silky cheek in one of his callused palms.

They each took the last step separating them, their arms entwining around each other's necks, as he lowered his mouth and she stood on her toes. Their lips met, tongues tangled, and he pulled her tight against him as he spun her until she was pressed against a wall. The kiss deepened, with his hands roving over her clothes, caressing and soothing aches she hadn't realized she had.

60

When he broke the kiss, he smiled as she gasped for air but did not arch away from him. Instead she leaned into his touch as he kissed down her neck. "You've skin like satin," he rasped as he nibbled at her earlobe. "God, how I want you, Deirdre."

He stilled as he felt her stiffen at his softly murmured words. "Lass?" he whispered. "*Shh,* you're safe. You're well," he said, as he eased away from her, his hands running over her arms again as they had in the kitchen. "I won't hurt you."

She stared at him with wide eyes, panting and gasping as tears coursed down her cheeks. "No," she rasped. "Never again. I will not care again. I will not!" She pushed at him. "Go! Leave my home. You're not welcome here."

"Deirdre?" Ardan asked, raising a hand to run over her head to soothe her. It was a movement he'd seen Da do numerous times with Mum, and it never failed to soothe his mum. Instead Deirdre batted at his hand, refusing his touch.

He took a step back, pushing his hand through his hair as he looked around her living space, at a loss for how things had ended so poorly. "I ask your pardon for letting you know of my desire." He clenched his hands at his side. "But I will never ask your forgiveness for, nor regret, kissing you." After one long torment-filled stare, Ardan spun on his heel and left her home soundlessly.

When he stood a fair distance from her house, he paused to stare at the stars. When that failed to calm him, he closed his eyes and took deep breaths. The memory of holding her in his arms would not abate. The feeling of her soft skin, her moan as he deepened the kiss, filled him with unremitting desire. "Feck," he muttered, as he let out an uneven breath. After all the promises he'd made himself, how had this woman turned his life upside down in only a few weeks?

Deirdre sank to her knees as Ardan left. His words, *I will never ask your forgiveness for, nor regret, kissing you,* echoed on endless repeat in her mind. She heard the passion in his voice, the lovely lilting hint of Ireland. She smelled his subtle cologne and the scent of sweat, musk, and soap that was all Ardan. The feel of his strong hands holding her. Molding around her curves as though she were beautiful.

"Why?" she asked the quiet room. After a moment, anger began to replace the agony, and she rose, retracing his steps to lock the back door and then the door at the top of the stairs. She clung to her anger so as not to have to confront the tumult of emotions he had wrought.

"You'd leave me too," she said through her tears, as she moved to her bedroom, stripping off her dress. "You'd abandon me too."

A sob escaped, and her anger proved no match for her anguish as she fell onto her bed, curling around a pillow. Memories of her husband, Alonzo, flooded back. His bright smile, filled with love and adoration on their wedding day. His promises for a wonderful future, as they opened their café. His determination to fight for the Union, ignoring her fears.

She cried and cried, repeating the litany, "No matter what they say, they never stay," until she finally tumbled into a restless sleep.

CHAPTER 4

The following morning dawned bright and hot. No breeze stirred the air, and even the songbirds had quieted, as though the heat had exhausted them too. Ardan worked in the warehouse, sweat dripping down his back and off his forehead. He relished any work to keep his mind off the previous night's encounter with Deirdre. Pausing, he swiped at his brow with his shirtsleeve, unable to think of anything other than the moment he took Deirdre in his arms to kiss her. The absolute joy in his soul to hold her close to his heart.

Ardan turned at the noise with an expectant smile, irrational hope filling him that the woman bursting into the warehouse was Deirdre. At the sight of Niamh, his smile faded, and he turned back to what he had been doing. Staring at a box, as he acted like he was cataloging something.

"Ouch," he yelped, as she slapped him on his arm. "What was that for, Niamh?"

Her eyes gleamed with ire, as she stood with her hands on her hips.

He knew her well and knew she was itching to belt him again.

"How could you, Ardan? I thought you'd be a good friend to her, and all the while you saw her as another lonely widow?"

"What?" he gasped, as he rubbed at his arm. His arm didn't hurt, although her words dug into him like spikes, and he wanted something to do with his hands.

"You sweet-talked her and then tried to ease her into bed?" she whispered in an irate voice.

He flushed red, righteous anger filling him. "Listen closely, Niamh. I didn't interfere with your ill-formed choice of husband. I'd be thankful if you granted me the same courtesy."

She shook her head as she stared at him in disillusioned wonder. "I thought you noble. Good. Like the type of man I would want Maura to choose."

"And I am," he said in a low voice. "I did nothin' more than kiss her, Niamh. I'm not some man who goes around findin' widows to seduce. Don't you know me better than that?"

She stepped closer, meeting his anger and disappointment with her own. "And didn't you know better than to toy with a woman mourning her husband? Or did you believe that you, the wonderful eldest O'Rourke brother, would be such a consolation that she shouldn't have need of her grief any longer?"

Ardan shook his head and backed up a step. "I can't believe you, Niamh." His blue eyes shone with pain and regret as he stared at her. "You've known her a few short days, and yet I'm the devil in all this?" He turned away for a moment before facing his sister again. "One day you will realize that your discontent with your present situation does not give you the right to abuse the rest of us. We'll only take so much, Niamh, before we've had enough."

She flushed beet red before storming from the warehouse, leaving Ardan alone, lost to his thoughts.

～

Ardan sat on an empty crate, his gaze distant, as his mind swirled with Niamh's angry accusations and the thought that he had done irreparable damage to his friendship with Deirdre. He closed his eyes and sighed at calling what he felt for her so insipid a term as *friendship*. However, he instinctively shied away from calling it anything more. Although he yearned to go to the café, to tease her and to talk with her, as he had done for the past few weeks, he knew that what had occurred the previous night had changed everything. For the first time in his life, he had acted rashly without considering the consequences.

However, he knew what he had told her was true. He would never apologize for and would never regret kissing her. The moment had been wondrous, while it lasted. Frowning, he wondered why it had ended so precipitously. Didn't Deirdre like knowing he found her attractive? That the man kissing her was moved to near madness at having her in his arms?

Kevin and Declan approached, and Kevin kicked Ardan's foot. "What'd you do to Niamh to have her spitting nails at you? I've always thought you were her favorite—but not today."

Ardan rolled his eyes at the second oldest O'Rourke. "You know you've always been her favorite," Ardan said with a half smile, although his heart wasn't in their ritual teasing.

"What happened, Ardan?" Declan asked. His attempt at taming his wild appearance had failed, and his hair and beard were as unkempt as ever. "I know it can't have anything to do with Maura."

"No," Ardan said, with a quick shake of his head. "Never." He rubbed at his forehead. "Niamh's upset because of somethin' to do with Deirdre—Mrs. Finnegan." He waited as his brothers jabbed elbows into each other's sides as he stumbled over her last name.

"And what would have upset the fine Mrs. Finnegan?" Kevin asked with a twinkle in his hazel eyes. "Could it have something to do with the fact I saw you stumblin' out of her place long after the café was closed last night?"

"Feck," Ardan muttered, swearing under his breath. "I hope few others saw that, or they'll think she's fair game."

The teasing faded from Kevin's expression, and he focused on his brother. "Are you all right, Ardan? You've had a dalliance here and there with a widow in the past, and it's never affected you." He frowned as Ardan rose and paced away from them, until he stood staring out the back window of the warehouse.

"I never want to marry," he said in a low voice. "Never want to wait, as the days pass, for her to leave me."

He heard a *thud* but ignored the sound, his attention focused on a scene only he could see. "'Tis why I've never wanted a serious relationship. A kiss here or there. A wee flirtation but nothin' that would ever lead to heartache." He breathed softly as he added, "Heartbreak."

Kevin strode silently over, so that he leaned against the wall, facing his brother. "What happened?"

"I thought her the most annoyin' woman that day," Ardan murmured with a smirk, as though reliving when he had first met her. "But the most intriguin' too. I never wanted to stay away for long. And I wanted her to succeed. 'Twas as though her success was mine, aye?"

Declan joined them, standing on the other side of Ardan. "She has succeeded, Ard."

"I realized last night, as I kissed her, that I wished I never had to kiss another woman." He met Kevin's gaze. "I remember teasing you about Aileen. Thought I'd never feel this way—the superiority I felt because I was above such emotions." He let out a stuttering breath and shook his head.

"There's no use fightin' what you feel, Ard," Kevin said with urgency. "Embrace it. Marry her and have children. Live a good life with a woman you care for."

Ardan shook his head and massaged his nape. "'Tisn't that simple, Kev. Never is." He sighed. "She doesn't want me. She yearns for another."

Kevin gasped and then reached around Ardan to smack Declan. "How could you, Dec?"

Ardan grabbed both of his brothers before they started scrapplin' with each other. He gave them severe stares before bursting into laughter. "Only you, Kev, could make me laugh today. No, 'tisn't about Declan. Sorry, Dec, but I doubt she even knows who you are." He released his brothers, and he saw Declan righting his clothes and glaring at Kevin, as though Declan were a wronged man. "She mourns her husband who died in the Civil War. Wishes him back."

"*Shite*," Declan muttered. "There's no battlin' a ghost."

All three brothers sighed, as they remembered their father's second marriage to Colleen. Although a nice woman, she had never filled the void left by Mary. Colleen had never mistreated them, nor done anything wrong, but she had never fit into their family either. Too many nights, the children had sat in tense silence as Colleen fought tears and as Da found an excuse to leave the table early to avoid an argument. When they did fight, the argument always returned to the basic problem that Seamus would never love Colleen as he had loved Mary. Shouts of "Why must you love a ghost more than you love me?" had rung throughout their small home, while Ardan held a whimpering Niamh, and Kevin and Declan covered Eamon's and Finn's ears so they wouldn't hear so much.

After Mary returned to them a month ago, Seamus readily admitted Colleen had been correct: he'd always loved Mary in a way he could never love Colleen. Ardan knew it to be true when he saw that the special sparkle had returned to Da's eyes now, and joy seemed ever present again in their home.

"I refuse to be a Colleen," Ardan said. "No matter what I feel."

Kevin sat in deep thought. "Do you think 'tis more than that?" When Ardan and Declan stared at him as though he were daft, he said, "Aileen told me that she had the sense your Deirdre mourned much more than a husband."

Ardan kicked at the wall and then stood tall. "It doesn't matter, Kev. For the first time in my life, I was willin' to try. But I refuse to always be someone's second choice. If I'm going to brave lovin' a woman, I want what Mum and Da have. What you an' Aileen have. A shared madness."

∼

S eamus sat on the edge of his bed with his head in his hands and shoulders stooped. The conversation he had overheard that day played repeatedly in his mind. Closing his eyes, he was thrust back into the living hell that had been his second marriage.

Although he had hoped marrying Colleen would bring succor from the constant ache of missing Mary, it had instead intensified his longing for his first wife. Colleen, a good and loyal woman, never believed she had the right to her own opinion, even with his urging her to speak up. She was never free with her affection either. No pat on the arm, stroke over his head, kiss on the cheek. Mary had unconsciously done those and more, and he hadn't realized how much he needed small signs of affection each day.

Then there were the fights. The horrible accusatory words she'd spew at him as she sobbed. He never had any defense because everything she said, everything she accused him of, was true. Yes, he'd married her to help with his six children. God knew, Seamus couldn't manage to work and to raise them all on his own. Yes, he still loved Mary. And he'd love her more, love her better, forever.

He sighed, rubbing at his temple, at the headache blooming there. At the soft kiss to his head and the gentle caress to his temple, he sighed. "Mary," he breathed, reaching out for her and drawing her close. He buried his face in her belly, his arms wrapped around her back. A sob burst forth that he could no longer contain, and his hold on her tightened.

He felt her hands and fingers caressing him. They ran through his hair, over his shoulders and upper back as she arched over him, as though to make herself a vessel for his grief. After a short time, he calmed, rubbing his face back and forth over the soft cotton of her dress. "Forgive me, love," he rasped.

She backed away a step, cupping his face. Her thumbs rubbed away the moisture of his tears, and she stared at him with concern. "What is it? Can I help?"

He stuttered out a laugh and pulled her close again, sighing with pleasure as he wrapped his arms around her and felt the rise and fall of her breaths. His soul sang with joy to feel her arms readily cling to him and stroke him to soothe him. "You already do. Just by being here."

Finally he released her, and she moved to sit beside him on the bed. She continued to hold his hand, her fingers playing over his palm and then intertwining with his fingers. "Can you tell me what brought this on?" she whispered. "Did I do something?"

He shook his head and then shrugged. "Yes, and no." He closed his eyes. "I realized today I failed my boys, and I never thought to feel such agony. Not since you died." His blue eyes shone with regret and impotent rage when he braved meeting her gaze. "I never realized how much I damaged them by marrying Colleen. Because I loved you too much."

She stilled before taking a deep breath. "Will you share with me how it was?" She paused. "I've told you about Francois, but I've never wanted to hear about Colleen. The thought of you with another was always too painful." She took a deep breath. "The thought that you could have loved another …"

He gasped and shook his head as he reached for her, cupping her face so she would meet his ardent gaze. "Never, Mary, never." He waited until she saw the veracity in his vow. "That is what made our marriage a living hell. I could never care for her as I did you. A half-love could never be enough, and Colleen realized that. And was heart-broken by it."

Mary smiled. "Is it terrible of me to be relieved you never cared for her as you did me?"

He shook his head and grinned at her. "No, love," he whispered as he kissed her, "no, *a ghrá*." He called her *his love* in Gaelic. "I never said those words to her. They were yours alone." He closed his eyes. "But therein lay the problem. She knew I never cared for her the way a husband should have. She accused me of only wanting a drudge to clean and to cook. Of wanting a nursemaid for my children. At the worst, she'd scream at me, begging me to love her as I loved you." He nodded as Mary watched him with wide-eyed dismay. "And the lads overheard."

"Oh, Seamus, 'tisn't your fault," she soothed, as she ran her hands over his shoulders. "You're human. You did what you had to do for our children, and I'll be forever grateful for that. And for you." She scooted forward until she sat astride his lap, wrapping her arms and legs around him in an all-body hug. "You sacrificed so they might have a woman who could be their mother."

"No, no one could ever replace you," he whispered, as he held her close. "I realized too late my folly in marrying her."

"*Shh,*" she whispered, running her hands over him. "Never regret your time with her, for she gave you three beautiful sons. And whatever our lads are going through, they will overcome it. They are strong, fine men because of the constancy of your love. Never doubt that, Shay, *a chuisle,*" she whispered, calling him *her heartbeat* in Gaelic.

"Oh, Mary, how did I survive without you for so long?" he whispered as his hold on her tightened.

"What matters is we are together again. And I'm never letting you go."

Seamus called Ardan into his office, as he reviewed the list of supplies he readied to send on one of the last ships of the season. He handed it to Ardan, his astute gaze taking in his son's disheveled appearance. Although he had a long way to go to ever look as wild as Declan, Ardan was beginning to have a mountain man appearance. "Do you need a trip to the barber?"

Ardan raised an eyebrow and shook his head. "No, I can shave myself. I've been lazy," he said, as he ran his palm over his fine scruff of beard. Unlike his father's, which was mostly white and gray, Ardan's was pure black and highlighted his chiseled jaw. His astute gaze roved over the list. "Appears complete to me. The only concern I'd have would be that there may be new mining tools or supplies we won't know about because we aren't in a bigger city to learn about them."

Seamus nodded. "Aye, I know. 'Tis why Declan has said he'll travel to the steamboats at Cow Island and ride south. He'll travel with Cormac, as he brings a load of pelts and furs to the waiting boats."

Ardan ran a hand through his hair, now nearly chin length. He hadn't cut it since he left Saint Louis in March. Perhaps Da was right, and he needed to visit the barber. "I'll miss Declan. It'll be hard to be separated from him for nearly a year."

"Aye," Seamus said. "We need to have a better system for ordering supplies, where one of you lads doesn't have to be absent for the majority of any year." He tapped his pencil on the top of his desk. "And I worry about Declan being alone in the city. He'll get into mischief with no one to look out for him." Seamus waited to see what Ardan would say, frowning when Ardan rose and paced to the window overlooking the empty lot beside their warehouse. Seamus had purchased it with the belief their company would need room to expand. "Ardan?"

"I should say I'd go an' watch over him. But I don't want to," Ardan said in a low voice. "I've no desire to be away again. Not now."

Sitting back in his chair, Seamus studied his eldest son. "Why not?"

"What if she leaves again, an' I'm not here to say goodbye?" he whispered. He turned to face his father. "I want what time I can have with her."

"Marry the lass if you can't abide her leavin' you," Seamus said with a frown.

Ardan flushed at his father's words but shook his head. "I won't lie and say I don't worry that Deirdre will leave. I do." His gaze was filled with pent-up anguish. "I meant Mum."

At his whispered words, Seamus shot to his feet and approached his son. He gripped Ardan's shoulders, squeezing them fiercely as he looked into his eldest's eyes. "She's not leaving, Ard. Not now. Not ever. You must believe in her. In me."

Ardan shrugged helplessly. "I don't believe it. Not yet."

"Forgive me, lad," Seamus rasped. "I failed all of you, an' I don't know how to ever make up for my mistakes."

"No, Da," Ardan protested. He took a deep breath and scratched at his beard. "You did what you had to do to ensure we were always

71

together. I never worried we'd be separated or sent to an orphanage, as so many children born into a large family did."

"Never," Seamus vowed, as though his son had spoken the worst blasphemy. For Seamus, family was sacred.

Ardan nodded and cleared his throat. After taking a deep breath, he said, "Mrs. Finnegan is wantin' some spices. You should have Niamh get a list of what she'd like, so Declan knows to order them."

Seamus released Ardan's shoulders, understanding his son had no further desire to discuss his fears today. However, Seamus continued to hope he could help Ardan whenever needed. "Then you should speak with her. Niamh is busy enough with her work there without worrying about an order we want to send south."

When Ardan stared at him for a long moment, Seamus said, "Face her, son. Nothing good comes from avoiding what you fear. Or what you desire."

That evening, after he knew Niamh had left for the day, Ardan knocked on the back door of the café. He waited as he heard Deirdre's soft singing end and the sound of her heels *click*ing as they approached the door. When she poked her head out the door, he pursed his lips but remained quiet.

"Ardan," she whispered. "You're here."

"Aye," he said. "I'm on an errand for Da. Might I come in?" He waited for her to open the door and stepped inside. Unable to help himself, he closed his eyes at the scents wafting around him. The welcoming aromas of bread, of cooling cookies, of roasting chicken. He fought the yearning to come home to just such a scene every night with his own family after a day's work. Opening his eyes, he found her staring at him, and he flushed. "I forgot how good it always smells in here."

"How is it you look so different, and it's only been a few days since I've seen you?" she asked, blushing after she blurted out her question.

He ran a hand over his beard self-consciously. "Da said I should visit the barber."

She shook her head, her hands clasped together, as though fighting the urge to reach out and to caress him. "No, you look quite handsome as you are." When his eyes flared, and he took a step closer to her, she jolted and spun to pick up a plate of cookies. "I tried an experiment today," she said, attempting to ignore the undercurrents flowing between them. "I think the men liked it." She set out a cookie in front of him. "I missed chocolate, so I put cocoa in the batter." She motioned for him to eat it.

He took a small bite and nodded. "Delicious." His gaze never left hers as he ate the treat.

"I think it's the vanilla." She waited for him to say something more, for him to tease her or to praise her, but he simply stared at her. "What was it you wanted?" she asked, taking a step away from him.

Reaching for items in his back pocket, he extracted paper and a pencil. "Da wants you to make a list of the spices you'll need next year. Declan's headin' to Saint Louis soon to work on restockin' our supplies. We want to make sure we have what you'll need." He paused as he looked around the kitchen. "Assumin' you'll be here next year." When she remained quiet at his comment, he sighed. "Perhaps you should say how much flour and sugar you'll need too."

She rubbed at her head and frowned. "Must I have this for you tonight? I'm afraid it will take some time, and I might forget a spice."

Ardan shook his head. "I'll return tomorrow or the next day." At her nod, he walked to the door, pausing when he felt her hand on his arm.

"Ardan," she whispered, her cognac-colored eyes large and luminous. "I ... Why can't things be as they were between us?"

He raised his hand to cover hers, his large palm caressing her work-roughened hand. "I don't understand what happened, Deirdre. I care for you, but I will not force you to spend time with a man you don't like."

"Ardan, that's not it," she whispered.

His blue eyes flared with pain. "I will not compete with a ghost."

He lifted her hand from his arm, freeing himself from her hold, and eased from her kitchen, leaving her staring after him.

~

He left, she thought as she watched him depart. With a sigh, she locked the door and headed upstairs to her too-large living space. This was a space meant for a family. Not for a single woman. She sat in the comfortable chair she had claimed as her own, pulling a throw pillow against her chest as she leaned her head against the back of the tall chair.

Closing her eyes, she pictured Ardan as she had seen him today. His jet-black hair growing long. His strong jaw, now covered in a beard her fingers itched to touch. His gorgeous blue eyes, tormented and filled with longing as they stared at her. She held a hand to her lips, remembering the kiss they'd shared. The passion and pleasure she'd felt. The security she always felt in his presence.

These past days without him had been horrible. Buford had somehow learned of her disagreement with Ardan, although she suspected he didn't understand the reason behind it, and Buford felt entitled to now threaten to again garnish Niamh's wages from Deirdre's portion of the profits. She wished she'd had the sense to have him sign a written agreement with her. Although she knew few would ever side with a woman in a legal dispute.

For a moment, she let her mind play out a fantasy. That Ardan was her husband. He came home to her every day after work, helping to tidy the kitchen before joining her upstairs. They laughed and talked, discussing their days and the news trickling in from the outside world. When they tired, they retired to their bedroom, where they shared passion too. Soon they'd have children, and the empty space would feel like a home. She scrunched her eyes closed, fighting such imaginings.

"Oh, why do you tempt me so?" she whispered into the night, her yearning for the dream to be true nearly outweighing her fears.

Three days later, Ardan had not returned, and Deirdre fretted that Declan would leave without her order for spices. After finishing up that evening, she picked up her list and walked to the O'Rourke house. Although nearby, it was a block off Front Street and in a much quieter area. She paused a moment as she approached the large home, taking a deep breath, as she had not realized how the persistent noise from the rowdy men in town had affected her.

After a moment, she picked up her skirts and walked to the back door. From what Niamh and Ardan had said in their conversations, she knew the front door was rarely used. Knocking on the back door loudly, she waited as the door opened.

Blinking in confusion was a man who looked remarkably like a younger version of Ardan, now standing before her. "Might I help you, Mrs. Finnegan?" he asked. "You may as well come in and join us."

He motioned for her to enter, and she heard numerous voices chattering before she entered the kitchen area. A long dining room table with chairs and benches filled with O'Rourkes was set closer to one wall, and they were passing food, laughing, and telling stories as they prepared for their evening meal. At her abrupt appearance, the conversations stopped.

"I beg your pardon for intruding," she stammered. "I shouldn't have come." She spun to race away, pausing with a gasp as a strong arm gripped hers.

"No, Deirdre," Ardan said in her ear. "You're very welcome."

She watched as Ardan turned her to the group, staring at them with avid curiosity.

"Most of you know of Mrs. Finnegan, but this is Deirdre." His family nodded at her, and Ardan smiled his thanks when Kevin scooted closer to Aileen so there was room for Deirdre on the bench, while his mum set another place setting. "Come," he urged Deirdre. He sat beside her, passing the simple fare to her. "I fear it won't match what you cook each day."

"Oh, it will be lovely to eat something I didn't prepare," she said with a smile to Mary and Maggie. She noted Niamh sat away from her mother, with Maura on her lap.

"Ah, but you didn't contradict me that your food was better, did you now?" Ardan asked with a wink.

She flushed and focused on the simple meal of boiled potatoes and roasted chicken, as the conversation continued to float around her. When she had finished her meal, she began to fidget.

"What brings you by, Mrs. Finnegan?" Seamus asked, as he accepted Maura from Niamh. He kissed his granddaughter's head and tickled her belly, as she played with a button on his coat. "If I recall properly, you informed me that, if there were justice in this world, you'd never be forced to speak to the likes of me again."

Deirdre flushed. "I fear I have a temper and say rash things at times." She relaxed when she saw the teasing in Seamus's gaze. "I brought the list of spices and supplies I need ordered for next year."

"Grand," Seamus said. He rose, approaching her with Maura in his arms. "I'll trade you." Before she could protest, he had snatched her list, and she sat with a babbling Maura in her arms.

"I ... This isn't ... She should be ..." Deirdre stammered out incoherent words as Maura patted at her face and smiled beatifically at her. Rather than a blue-eyed cherub in her arms, she saw a little girl with cognac-colored eyes, filled with curiosity and love. Deirdre's gaze swam with tears, and she gasped, "I can't do this." She pushed Maura into Ardan's arms and rose, tripping over the bench and her skirts in her urgency to flee.

"Deirdre!"

She heard Ardan call her name, but all she focused on was her escape. Her mind roared at her to flee the room. To flee their pitying stares. To flee the oppressive memories. "No, no, no," she rasped, as she stumbled down the back steps, past the chicken coop, and to the darkened field behind their house. Her foot snagged in a gopher hole, and she fell to the ground, her knees and palms abraded by the rough earth.

Welcoming the pain, Deirdre fought her panic. Fought remembering. Fought feeling anything. When a hand stroked her back, she screeched, "Don't touch me!" Instinctively she knew it was Ardan. "Don't …" she gasped, as she fell forward, her face in the grass as she keened. Soul-shattering cries and sobs burst from her.

"Deirdre, love, you're not alone," Ardan whispered. He didn't touch her again, but he continued to talk to her, to whisper words of comfort as she cried.

She felt his presence beside her as he sat down, and she yearned for him to hold her. To soothe her agony. With jerky movements, she crawled into his arms, needing his support to ground her.

"Have a good cry," Ardan soothed, as his arms banded around her, holding her close, as he rocked them side to side, his strong hands caressing her back. He kissed her head as he would his niece, Maura, continuing to murmur soft words of support. "You're safe. You're well."

She shuddered as he kissed her head, burying her face in the crook of his neck. "I'm sorry," she stammered out in a broken voice. At his murmur that she had nothing to apologize for, she said, "Your family must believe me a crazy woman."

"No, love," he whispered as he held her. "They believe you to be like the rest of us. Human and trying to find your way." He kissed her head again.

"I feel so safe when I'm with you," she whispered, her admission provoking another sob. "And I hate that illusion."

His hold on her had tightened with her whispered confession. "Why is it an illusion?"

"Because you'll leave. Just like they did," she said, her voice fading away, as she fought drifting to sleep. "And I couldn't bear to be left behind again."

Ardan held her, momentarily stuck dumb as she voiced his own deepest fear. When he realized she had fallen asleep in his arms, he rose, carrying her securely back home. As he approached his father's house, he saw Kevin and Declan sitting on the back steps, waiting for them.

Kevin shot to his feet at the sight of him carrying Deirdre. "Is she all right?"

"She's exhausted. She fell asleep," Ardan murmured. "I'll bring her home. Ensure she is well tonight." He turned for her home, stopping when Declan called out to him.

"Wait, Ard," Declan said, disappearing inside. After a moment, Declan returned with Maggie, holding a small bag. "If you plan on spending the night there, Maggie should too. There's already enough talk in this town about Mrs. Finnegan. You don't want to add more."

Ardan studied his brother a moment in the faint light shining from the house, as he hadn't heard any gossip. However, he realized few would be willing to gossip about him to his face. "Is this all right with you, lass?" he asked his sister.

"Of course," Maggie said. "I like Deirdre. And I can't imagine why little Maura would send her into a crying fit."

Ardan didn't say anything but motioned for his sister to follow him. The back door to the café was unlocked, and he ushered Maggie inside, ensuring she locked it behind them before he carried Deirdre upstairs. When they reached her living quarters, Maggie lit two lamps, leaving one on Deirdre's bureau before she moved to the living room. Ardan stared at a slumbering Deirdre in his arms and sat on her bed, unwilling to release her from his hold just yet.

"Oh, lass," he murmured, as he brushed away fiery strands of hair. "What am I to do with you?" Kissing her on her forehead, he called out softly for his sister. When she poked her head in, he asked in a murmur, "Can you slip off her boots?"

Maggie complied, each one landing with a muffled *thunk*. She set them underneath Deirdre's bureau and stood back when Ardan rose with Deirdre still in his arms. Maggie pulled down the covers and watched as Ardan settled her underneath them, fully dressed, with the covers tucked up tight around her neck. "She'd be more comfortable if we were to remove her corset."

Ardan shot her a look. "First, she'd never forgive me were I to see her with so little clothes on without giving me permission. Second, there's no need to start more rumors than necessary." He kissed Deirdre's head, squeezed her shoulder, and backed away. "What?" he asked, grimacing at the defensive note in his voice when he saw Maggie staring at him.

"Someday I want a man to care enough about me to treat me as you do Deirdre," she said. "I'll sleep in the far bedroom. If you were to fall asleep on top of the covers here, I don't know how anyone would be the wiser." She rose on her tiptoes and kissed his cheek.

"Imp," he muttered, his voice filled with affection.

She giggled and slipped from the room.

Ardan remained, staring at a slumbering Deirdre. Finally he gave in, blowing out the candle. Tugging a throw blanket around himself, he curled onto the bed beside her, counting her breaths, and thankful for each moment he knew she was well.

Bright light filtered through the curtains. Shouts from outside drifted up to her window but mingled with a dream. Rather than in Montana, she was in Maryland. In her husband's arms, the night before he left. Men celebrated, drank, and found willing women, as they knew they would soon leave for duty to fight for the Union. Refusing to focus on the certainty of their separation, Deirdre spun dreams for Alonzo and her to share when he returned. About the farm they would own after they sold their café. Of the children they would have. Too soon, the pounding on the door interrupted her time with him, and she knew he would leave her. Deirdre groaned as the pounding intensified.

"No, don't go," she whimpered, as the strong arms around her released her. "Please, don't leave me alone again." A soft reassuring murmur came. A kiss to her head. And then she was alone. Pulling the blankets up, she covered her head, crying to have lost her love. Again.

Again? She pushed through the wisp of her dream, fighting to awaken as the bed dipped beside her once more. Strong arms secured her against his chest once more, and she breathed in deeply of the spicy, musky sent. Her mind rebelled at that, as her husband never smelled like this. "What?" she gasped, as she pushed and struggled to free herself and wake up. "Where am I?"

"*Shh*, love." A deep, melodious voice with the soft burr of Ireland soothed her. "You're well. You're safe."

"Ardan," she said, as her eyes opened, and she took in his worried expression. She traced a finger over his beard, noting that, although she had slept like the dead, he appeared to have barely slept at all. "Why are you here?"

"I was worried about you."

She jerked back. "You're in my bed?" She yanked on the covers, but he rested on them, so they didn't budge. Her panic abated when she saw they were both fully dressed. "I don't understand. I don't remember." She felt panic returning, attempting to swallow her whole again.

"*Shh*, love," Ardan repeated, cupping her cheek and staring deeply into her eyes. "You're well. Maggie an' I are here to care for you, and Buford understands you are ill today an' will not be cookin' in the café. Niamh an' Mum will do what they can, but 'twill be limited."

"No!" Deirdre gasped, pushing away from him and vaulting from the bed. "I must work. I must earn my way …" She screamed with pain as she tried to walk, tumbling to the floor.

"Deirdre!" Ardan leaped over the side of the bed to kneel beside her. "What happened, lass? What hurts?"

"My ankle," she gasped. "Oh, I can't walk on it at all," she whimpered. Without thinking she leaned into him as he eased his arms around her and carried her back to her bed.

"'Tis swollen," he said, as he ran his fingers lightly over it. "You must have hurt it when you fell last night, racin' from the house."

"Why would I have—" Her eyes widened, as the memory of the night before rushed back, and she paled and then flushed. Tears threatened, and she took gulping breaths, as a subtle quivering began. She barely noticed as he rested beside her on the bed, pulling her into his arms. She nestled her head against his shoulder, fighting for control.

"Let go, Deirdre," he whispered, as his hands tangled in her unkempt hair, slipped loose from the knot at the nape of her head after a night's rest. "Let out this sorrow."

She shuddered as he tenderly kissed her forehead. Clamping her eyes shut, she attempted to cease the tears from falling, but they would not be stopped. A keening sob burst forth, an echo in her memory from the previous night, and she clung to him.

Absently she heard him speak in a soft voice. Something about *ice, a doctor, time,* and *cherished.* Words from the present jumbled together with memories from the past, and her hold on him tightened. "Don't let me go," she rasped. "Please."

"Never," he promised, his hold on her equally fervent but never evoking discomfort.

Finally her grief waned; her tears abated, and she lay on him, gasping and shuddering. "Forgive me. That was unseemly."

"None of that," Ardan said in a low disgruntled voice. "That was honest and pure, Deir," he whispered, shortening her name to sound like *dear.* "Don't hide yourself away again. Please."

She hid her face against his chest, flushing. "I'm mortified."

He ran his hands over her back, his soft touch soothing her. "Don't be, love. You have every right to your sorrows. As we all do. Da is devastated he hurt you."

She shook her head, the memory of holding Maura in her arms evoking a sweet agony. "I never wanted to hold another child again. Smell her sweet baby scent. Hear her gurgle of laughter." She swallowed a sob as she choked out, "Have her pat my face and giggle up at me."

"Your lass died," Ardan said in a matter-of-fact voice that still held tremendous sympathy. At her nod, he groaned and buried his face in her hair. "I'm so sorry, love."

She took comfort from his acceptance of her grief. Resting in his strong arms, she allowed herself to mourn all she had lost. Her husband. Her daughter. Her home. Her dreams. For a moment, she gave herself permission to dream of a life with a man like Ardan. Of hearing him call her *his love*—and mean it. Right now she was too emotionally exhausted to fight off her yearnings. "I'm so tired," she whispered.

He kissed her head and eased out from under her. "I know. Grief causes the worst exhaustion." He met her startled gaze at his understanding. "I asked Maggie to see if there's still ice in the ice house. Last I heard, they were runnin' low. If 'tis the case, we won't have anythin' to help you with your ankle. The doctor should be on his way." At the soft knock, he looked to the ajar door. "Maggie."

She entered with a shake of her head. "There's no ice and no doctor. He left to attend an ailing passenger at Cow Island." She bit her lip. "I ran into Dunmore. He said he has experience with hurt ankles and would like to help, if permitted."

Deirdre ran a hand over her skirts, ensuring her legs were covered and earning a sardonic look from Ardan. "If Mr. Dunmore is willing to aid me, I'd appreciate it."

"It's just *Dunmore*, ma'am," a deep voice called out from the hallway. "No need for formalities."

Deirdre stifled a gasp and then nodded at Maggie for the man to enter. For a moment, Deirdre noted Maggie moving to the corner of the room and watching the stagecoach driver's every move with fascination. Dunmore was a tall lanky man that only a fool would believe easy to fight. Deirdre had a sense he'd be a menace in a brawl. Dunmore had a steely determination about him, and his blue-green eyes appeared to discern the reality of the situation with ease. He relaxed at seeing Ardan present, and his strong hands took off his hat, revealing long russet-colored hair sliding free over his shoulders.

He approached the bed and nodded at her, his gaze focused on her ankle. "May I, ma'am?" At her nod, he reached forward to examine her ankle.

The minute he touched her swollen joint, she gasped, her whole focus on the agony her grief had allowed her to temporarily ignore. "Oh, that hurts."

Dunmore moved her foot one way and then the other, watching her reaction closely. "You tripped last night?" he asked.

"I don't know what I did," she whispered. "All I know is that I fell."

"In a gopher hole," Ardan said.

Dunmore grunted at that knowledge and then stood. "I know I'm not a doctor, but it doesn't appear to be broken. I think it's a sprain, but that will still take plenty of time to heal." He turned to face Deirdre. "If possible, ma'am, I'd rest as much as I could and keep it raised." He looked to Maggie. "If you and your mum have any, I'd brew willow bark tea for the pain."

"I have some downstairs," Deirdre said. She acted as though she would rise, only falling back to the bed when Ardan placed a hand on her shoulder to keep her in place.

"You're not goin' anywhere today, Deirdre. Perhaps not tomorrow either," Ardan said.

"Thank you, Mr. Dunmore," Deirdre said. "When I'm feeling better, I'll make a treat, just for you." She watched as he smiled shyly at her and slipped from the room—but not before he cast a covetous glance at Maggie. Deirdre groaned as she sat up, leaning against the pillows. "Aren't you needed at the warehouse?" she asked Ardan.

"No, but I can tell you need some time alone. Perhaps Maggie could help you change, an' then I'll return to see how you are." He kissed her forehead and left.

Deirdre watched him, fighting the sensation of feeling bereft at his absence. A feeling she had never wanted to experience again.

A rdan wandered downstairs to find his mum and Niamh cooking in Deirdre's kitchen. He paused in the doorway, noting the tense silence between the two women. Although he had trouble believing his mother was never leaving again, his love for her had never been in doubt. Niamh, though, swaddled herself in a deep resentment and refused to allow any of their mother's tenderness to free her of her bitterness at the years of separation.

"Mum, Niamh," he said, as he entered. He smiled at them, seeing his mum's relieved expression at his presence. "Thanks for helping Deirdre today."

"'Tis the least we could do after causing her such anguish," Mary said. "Poor Seamus is beside himself."

Niamh slammed down a pan and glared at her mother. "You're not to blame Maura, Mum. She did nothin' wrong."

Mary stared at her daughter in confusion. "No one did anything wrong, Niamh. 'Twas a horrible misunderstanding." After a moment she shook her head. "No, 'twas time for that poor woman to face what she hid from. An' I'm glad we were there to help ease her through it." She stared at her eldest. "I'm glad you were there, Ardan."

He nodded at his mum but focused on Niamh. "No one is blamin' wee Maura, just as no one blames Da. Deirdre's feelin's were goin' to bubble up at some point, Niamh."

Niamh turned to glare at him, her hazel eyes glowing with an emotion he couldn't understand. "I see you're forgiven now that you've acted like her knight in shinin' armor." Her voice was laced with bitter disdain.

Shaking his head as he and his mum shared a concerned look, he crossed his arms over his chest. "What's happened, Niamh? You've been pricklier than usual but never mean. Now you're cruel, an' you seem to relish it."

She sobbed and ran from the kitchen, a paring knife still in her hand. Ardan watched her go but didn't race after her. "Feck," he muttered and then whispered his apology for swearing in front of his mother.

She waved away her concern at that and focused on him. "Are you well, Ardan?" She stepped up to him and ran her hand over the hair at his temple, brushing it back into place. "You seem more at peace and yet more troubled at the same time. Quite a contradiction."

He gave a soft laugh and pulled his mother into his arms for a hug. "I've missed you, Mum, so much," he whispered.

"I know, my boy. Just as I know you wait for me to leave again." She cupped his face. "You must understand, the next time you say goodbye to me is when I die." She saw his eyes widen in terror. "*Shh*, my sweet boy. You know we all must face such a future. My hope is that it is many years from now."

"Aye," he rasped.

"You must cease allowing your fear of being left alone sometime in the future to keep you from enjoying life, from loving, *now*. For *now* is all we have, Ardan." Her eyes filled with tears. "Do you believe I would ever have given up a moment I had with you or your siblings or with your da, if I'd known I'd be separated from you for so long?" She shook her head. "Never. The joy I knew with all of you fed me for the many years I was away."

"I thought you were bitter toward Da," he said.

"I was when I first saw him again," she admitted. "But that was to protect my heart against further pain. As you are trying to protect yours. But I quickly learned that road only led to more loneliness and a life I'd already determined I didn't want. A life devoid of the happiness and joy I'd known with all of you."

She cupped his face as she looked deeply into his eyes. "Be courageous, my Ardan. For you were always meant to be bold and brave."

He pulled her close, holding her for a long moment.

Maggie heard a door slamming downstairs and looked out the back window of Deirdre's room. "Niamh's angry again," she murmured, as she puttered around Deirdre's room. She had helped Deirdre change from yesterday's clothes into a comfortable night-gown and brought over a pan of water and a towel so she could wash her face.

"Why should she be angry? I thought all you O'Rourkes got along?" Deirdre asked, as she rested with her foot elevated. She shifted around, as though searching for a comfortable position.

Maggie left the room and returned with pillows from the other bedrooms and used them as supports for her leg. "Oh, Niamh doesn't like Mum and me," she said with a careless shrug. "She hasn't since we came back."

"*Back?*" Deirdre asked. "Where did you go?"

Maggie pulled over the chair from the corner of the room until she sat near Deirdre's side of the bed. Careful not to jostle her ankle, Maggie propped her feet atop the bed, making herself comfortable. "Haven't you heard the story about us? It's what the townsfolk most like to gossip about." Her eyes gleamed with interest, as she watched Deirdre.

"No," the older woman said with a flush. "I've not had time to make many friends. Just your brother and sister, and that's because they've helped me in my kitchen." She grimaced. "I do everything I can to avoid any interaction with Mrs. Davies." She grinned as Maggie snickered. "And Buford is too busy chatting with the men out front to spend time talking with me."

Maggie giggled again and shook her head. "That's not why he ignores you," she said with an amused grin. "He knows Ardan will pummel him if he mistreats you, and he has no desire to lose the favor of the O'Rourkes. Or be on the wrong side of a fight with us." Her voice was filled with pride as she talked about her brothers. "They're fierce fighters when provoked and very protective of those they care about."

Deirdre paled and then flushed, her eyes widened in alarm. "No, Maggie, you misunderstand. Your brother is a friend. Nothing more."

Shaking her head, Maggie rested in the chair. "One day you'll have to admit the lie of what you say. For the little I know about Ardan, I understand he's never acted this way toward another woman." She waited for Deirdre to speak, but, when she remained quiet, she said in a soft voice, "Treat him gently, if you don't want anything from him."

Deirdre closed her eyes, suddenly swallowing back more tears. "I don't know what I want right now, Maggie."

The young woman shrugged and laughed. "Why should you? You've just met him." She bit her lip. "Mum always said to be patient and to not rush love." After a moment, she added, "Although I don't know how you'll ever get to know him, if he's in Saint Louis, and you're here."

"Saint Louis?" Deirdre asked, clutching the blanket around her. She tried to curl onto her side, but the motion provoked too much pain, and she had to remain on her back.

"Declan's traveling there soon for supplies, and I know Da worries about him traveling alone. Ardan and Kevin spent last winter there together, so it makes sense to me that Ardan would go back again this winter."

"Be gone the entire winter?" Deirdre asked in a near breathless voice.

Maggie nodded and then shrugged. "But you were asking about Niamh and why she would be angry with Mum." She sighed, as she wrapped her arms around herself. "She doesn't much like me either." At Deirdre's puzzled expression, she grinned. "It's baffling, isn't it?"

After a pause, Maggie said, "Mum and I were separated from my father, my brothers, and Niamh for almost eighteen years. From the day of my birth." She nodded as Deirdre gaped at her. "They had just arrived in Montreal after their voyage from Ireland, and Mum gave birth to me in a shack filled with others sick with typhus. Da visited us while Mum slept but had to go home to take care of my siblings. When he returned, Mum wasn't in her cot, and he was told by a nun who barely spoke English that we'd died and had already been buried in a mass grave."

"Oh, no," Deirdre gasped, her hands covering the lower half of her face, as she stared at Maggie in horror.

Maggie nodded. "All the while my da mourned my mum, moved the family, and made plans to leave the city, Mum waited for him with me in a nearby shed. Another nun had moved us there to protect Mum and me from the typhus."

"Oh, what a tragedy. But he found you soon afterward. He learned of his mistake," Deirdre said.

"No, not until about a month ago, when my mum walked into the family store here and saw my brothers, Eamon and Finn. And then she saw my father." Maggie's smile faded, as though remembering a trying time. "I didn't know anything about him because she never spoke of my father. Or my siblings. I never knew I had brothers and a sister who were older than me."

Deirdre was silent a long moment and then whispered, "Why doesn't Niamh like you?"

87

Maggie shrugged. "I don't know. Perhaps she was used to us being dead. Or being the only sister." She sighed. "But we're back, and I've never seen Mum so happy." She gave a self-deprecating smile. "It's a relief to be free of Jacques."

"Who's Jacques?"

Maggie sat up with a start as boot steps sounded in the hallway. "That's enough chatter about the past." She smiled at Ardan as he entered the room, kissing him on the cheek. "I'll check in with Mum, while you talk with Deirdre. Bye, Deirdre!" Maggie raced from the room, her footsteps echoing down the stairs.

Ardan stared at Deirdre, his blue eyes lighting with joy at the sight of her. However, an ever-present concern lingered, as he looked after the quickly departed figure of his sister. "What did you say to make her run away?"

"I didn't say anything. I just asked who Jacques was." At his groan as he sat with a *thud* in the chair vacated by Maggie, she flushed. "I didn't know I was doing anything wrong. She mentioned him."

Ardan's head jerked up, as he stared at her with wonder. "Maggie mentioned the man?" When Deirdre nodded, he sat in confused silence for a long moment. "She's not whispered his name in weeks. Not since we tricked him and sent him away."

Deirdre reached her hand out to him, stroking his hand clenched into a fist. "Why would you need to send him away?"

"Maggie's an O'Rourke, aye?" he said in a low voice. "She should be spirited and proud. Never afraid." His jaw hardened as he stared at Deirdre, and his eyes glinted with anger. "When we found Mum, she was livin' with her brother-in-law. A man who relished abusin' her. And he coveted my sister."

"Jacques?" Deirdre asked in a voice barely above a whisper. At his nod, she gasped. "Poor Maggie."

"We saved her as he tried to break into her room," Ardan said. "I carried her home, bruised and soul weary. Soul wary," he amended.

"Frightened of her own shadow. And never believin' she had a rightful place with us."

"Things have changed in the past weeks, Ardan. She's curious and bright and secure in who she is."

He nodded. "Aye, as long as we are near, she is the impish, boisterous sister I always imagined. But, if she were alone with someone she did not know, she'd freeze up and become a stranger." He rubbed at his head. "I hate Jacques. I hate what he did to my mum and my wee sister."

"He won't hurt her again?" Deirdre asked.

"By the grace of God," he whispered. "He's far away, in Virginia City. I pray, every night, he's buried under a pile of rocks." When she stared at him wide-eyed, he asked, "Does that lower me in your estimation, Deirdre? Because I pray for another man's death?" He waited a long moment for her to answer.

"No," she said in a nearly inaudible voice, "because I pray for the same."

"What?" He canted forward, gripping her hand. "Why?" He waited for her to share her story, but, when she remained silent, he sighed. "One day I hope you trust me enough to share your fears." He raised her hand and kissed the back of it. "I'll leave you to rest, Deirdre."

CHAPTER 5

Three days later, Deirdre woke and stretched. She stilled, waiting to hear Ardan's deep voice beside her, as he whispered words of encouragement and endearment to her, but he must have already risen because the space beside her was cool and empty. Although she knew it to be scandalous, he and Maggie had continued to stay with her the past nights, and each evening, after Maggie went to bed, Ardan would slip into Deirdre's, holding her tightly against his chest. Rarely would they speak.

Generally his presence lulled her into a dreamless, contented slumber, a feeling of safety and security enveloping her. Once he sang to her a soft song in a language she didn't understand, and it acted like a lullaby, easing her into a deep sleep.

She rose and put pressure on her foot and ankle. Although her ankle was sore, it didn't ache nearly as badly as the previous day. The rest and the willow bark tea had worked their magic. She flushed as she thought about the previous days, where Ardan had carried her to the privy whenever necessary, ignoring her words of protest, and had insisted she feel no embarrassment.

Why was such a man interested in her? she asked herself. With a small huff of frustration that her interest was equally as piqued, she shuffled around her room. She pulled on comfortable clothes but remained in her slippers, as she feared tightly laced boots would be more than her ankle could handle.

As she slowly descended the stairs one step at a time, she was met with the sounds of laughter and numerous voices chatting. Deirdre paused at the entrance to the kitchen, mouth agape at the scene in front of her. Gone was her organized kitchen, with everything tidy and in its place. Instead it looked as though a tornado had blown threw. Chaos seemed to reign here, as it did in the O'Rourke household, although she suspected it was a controlled chaos, as bread cooled on racks and plenty of food awaited the men in the café.

Around the central butcher block table, the O'Rourke family sat, eating breakfast. Seamus glanced up to see her peering at them from the doorway. "Lass," he called out, dropping his fork to his plate and striding to her. "You're up an' about. You should have called for Ardan. He would have helped you down the stairs." He eased her onto a stool beside one of the brothers Ardan had called the twins, with the wild-looking brother named Declan on her other side. Ardan sat across from her. "We can't have you injurin' yourself the first day you're feelin' better."

Deirdre stared at the family in wonder, as Mary and Maggie worked by the stove. "I can help," she said with a grimace. "Although I shouldn't stand for the majority of the day."

"You'll sit and not injure yourself anymore, if you have any sense," Seamus said, earning a nod of agreement from Ardan.

Deirdre stared at Ardan, but he broke eye contact and focused on the plate of food in front of him. When Maggie brought her a plate heaping with eggs, bacon, bread, and fried potatoes, she whispered her thanks. After Deirdre had only had a few bites, she jumped at the booming, disapproving voice of Buford Hunt, as her fork rattled to the floor.

"So, you finally decided to grace us with your presence, did you?" Buford asked with a glare, his hands on his hips.

"Buford," Seamus and Ardan said at the same time, in the same warning tone.

"Don't *Buford* me," he snapped, as he looked around the table of O'Rourkes. "I have no idea what I did to suffer your presence in my café."

Deirdre watched as Seamus and Ardan exchanged a long look before Ardan spoke. "We are here as a friend to Mrs. Finnegan. As you are well aware."

Seamus nibbled on a piece of bacon, as though he didn't have a care in the world, although his gaze was filled with warning. "It's what friends do for friends."

Buford shook his head in disgust and marched toward Deirdre. He roughly gripped her arm, hauling her upright and toward the kitchen's back door. "We need to have a chat, partner to partner," he hissed.

Deirdre stumbled, due to the awkward movement and due to the pressure on her ankle. "Stop. My ankle hurts," she gasped. She yelped as she was about to be towed down the rear steps into the alleyway in a rapid manner. When she had come downstairs this morning, she had descended each step like a child, both feet on one step, with a long pause on each as she balanced and eased her way down. She stumbled, nearly falling to her knees as her ankle gave out.

"A likely story," Buford muttered as he pulled on her to stand up.

Deirdre shrieked again as she was tugged away from Buford and hauled up into Ardan's arms. Declan followed Buford down the stairs, the twins on his heels, and she heard him muttering something about a lesson. "Put me down. It isn't proper," she whispered to Ardan, although she buried her face in his neck and breathed deeply of his scent. Instantly she relaxed, as she was held in his protective embrace.

"Did you miss me this morning?" he breathed into her ear. At her subtle nod, he chuckled. "Good." He kissed her head and settled her on her stool again. "Eat, love." He returned with a clean fork for her and winked at her, as he sat in Declan's vacated seat.

She stared at her food and then at the fresh cup of tea set in front of her by Mary. "I don't understand," she whispered. As the O'Rourkes stared at her, she cleared her throat. "Why are you all here?"

Seamus smiled at his wife and daughter. "Mary an' Maggie needed to be here to work in the kitchen. We missed them at home. An' none of the lads like to cook. So we came to be where they are. Besides, we're decent at dishwashing." He looked pointedly at a group of his youngest sons. They groaned but stood to begin washing. Soon they were jabbering and laughing, as they washed and dried plates, pots, and pans.

Deirdre looked at her still-full plate of food. "What did Declan mean about teaching Mr. Hunt a lesson?"

"No one likes a bully, love," Ardan said. "An' Buford's becoming too big for his britches, thanks to your fine cookin'." Ardan rose, accepting plates from his mother, and made his way into the café area. His voice, laughing and cajoling with the men there, echoed into the kitchen.

"He's a natural at whatever he does," Deirdre whispered to herself. She saw Seamus with a speculative gleam in his eye, but he smiled innocently at her before she could ask him about it. "I can't continue to count on your kindness."

"Of course you can," Mary said. "'Tisn't much different than plannin' to cook for this horde." She ran a soothing hand down Deirdre's back. "You're still not well enough to be on your feet much yet. 'Twill take a few more days, and you shouldn't rush it. You can see we're handling things well."

Deirdre's eyes filled, and she ducked her head. "Yes, quite well."

Mary sat on one of the empty seats beside her and frowned. "Why the tears, lass?"

"You make this look so easy. And it was so hard for me," Deirdre whispered, the truth sputtering out of her, as Mary stared at her with a kindness which she was unaccustomed to.

"You think this is easy?" Mary asked with a wry smile. "You haven't heard my husband mutterin' about his sore hands as he kneads my shoulders and feet each evening after a full day here." She looked around. "Besides, you did all this work, with only Niamh's help, while I've had Niamh, Maggie, and at least four of the lads at a time to clean up after me." She wrapped an arm around Deirdre's shoulder, urging her to rest her head on her shoulder. "You've done well, but you've done so much on your own, lass. 'Tis all right to lean on those who care for you."

"It's been so long since I haven't been on my own."

Mary made a soothing noise and patted her back. "Well, we've adopted you, so you'll never be alone again."

"**M**um?" Ardan asked, as he entered the kitchen, his delighted smile at the tall tale he'd just heard fading at the sight of Deirdre crying on his mother's shoulder. "What happened?"

"We all need a little cry now and again," his mother said with a smile and a shooing motion. He feared he was hovering, but he wanted to ensure she was well. "Deir?" he whispered.

"I'm fine," Deirdre cried, as she continued to lean against his mother's shoulder.

"Leave the lass be, son," Seamus said. "She needs time with a woman like your mum. I fear she's had too little time bein' coddled."

Ardan grabbed his cup of tea and sat beside his father. "The lads have been outside a long time," he murmured to his father. At his father's tilt of his head, Ardan rose. "I'll check on things."

"Aye, an' I'll keep an eye on the café," Seamus said, rising and entering the café with a booming voice and a tale at the ready.

Ardan stood on the back steps, watching as his brothers talked with Buford. Although Buford didn't look as though he'd just had a run-in with three O'Rourkes, he clutched his side and breathed carefully, as though his ribs were bruised. Ardan winced and hoped his brothers hadn't broken a rib. For, if they had, he knew the O'Rourkes would have to start working regularly at the café. He shrugged. He wouldn't mind having an excuse to be at the café daily.

"Buford," Ardan called out, as he descended the steps. He smiled as the man cowered away a few steps. "Ah, so you finally have sense. You understand better than to harm Deirdre again."

Buford spat on the ground and glared at Ardan. "She has you under her spell. You think she's telling you the truth about who she is, but she ain't. No woman who can cook and work like she does just waltzes into a town without calamity stalking her."

Ardan stood with his legs spread wide and his gaze filled with amusement, as he stared at Buford. "Perhaps that's *your* tale of woe, Buford, but it isn't mine. An' I doubt 'tis Deirdre's."

"You believe you're unlike every man taken in by a pretty face and a smile," Buford said with a shake of his head. "You'll learn your folly soon enough, boy." He turned on his heel as though to walk away.

Ardan grabbed his arm. "I want to make sure you understand Deirdre is to be treated with respect. Always." He waited for Buford to nod before he released his arm. When Buford stormed away, holding his right side, leaving the café untended, Ardan looked at his brothers. "I've brought more chaos to the family."

"Nay," Declan said. "We haven't had enough to do at the warehouse. 'Twill be fun to chat with the men as they eat an' to hear their stories." He slung an arm over Ardan's shoulder and gave him a squeeze before dropping his arm. "Does the lass understand how much you care for her?"

"I don't know, Dec." He stared at his brother with unguarded fear in his gaze. "I never thought to feel this way."

Declan smiled and gave him a small nudge with his shoulder. "'Tis about time, Ardan. You deserve to be happy."

Ardan stared at him in wonder. "How can you have such faith it will not end in a tragedy?"

Declan shrugged. "Life is filled with risk, Ardan. And all your attempts to protect yourself will only lead to loneliness." He pointed in the direction of Kevin and Aileen's small cabin. "I've come to realize I want something like they share. Just having a woman to cook, clean, and warm my bed would never be enough." He paused. "Not after seein' Mum and Da together again."

Ardan nodded. "No, 'twould never be enough." He slapped his brother on his shoulder and walked beside him into the café to rejoin his family and to ensure Deirdre was well.

∾

Aileen poked her head into Deirdre's room and smiled to find her resting on her bed, reading a book. "It's good to see you have sense. I fear an O'Rourke sibling would be up and about, harming their ankle, no matter how much it hurt."

Deirdre set aside her book and smiled at Aileen. "No. It's too painful to do too much today. I hope it improves so I can do more tomorrow." She motioned for Aileen to join her in her bedroom and smiled when Aileen sat on the chair near her bed. "I have never thanked you for your hard work cleaning my home when I first arrived."

Aileen waved away the thanks. "It's the least we could do. And Mary wanted to ensure you felt welcome." She shrugged. "Besides, a man like Buford would never have thought such a task important."

Deirdre rolled her eyes. "He didn't believe a clean kitchen was essential for the success of his enterprise. Why would he consider the cleanliness of my home?" She shared a sardonic smile with Aileen. "I'm sorry if I'm keeping you away from the women of your family."

Aileen shook her head. "Not at all. I'm busy with my own endeavors." At Deirdre's curious expression, she flushed. "I'm married to Kevin, and we have a small home."

Deirdre squirmed around on the bed, until she'd settled on her side and her ankle was comfortable. "I imagine that takes some time."

Aileen laughed. "It takes no time at all! It's a tiny home, and we rarely even eat there. We always eat at the O'Rourkes, and, as you can imagine, Mary and Maggie always cook. I'm afraid I'm becoming spoiled." She ducked her head, as though ashamed.

Deirdre looked at her with confusion, before snorting with incredulity. "Your aunt is Mrs. Davies, isn't she?" At Aileen's nod, Deirdre sighed. "I imagine she's filled your head with such nonsense. You aren't spoiled because someone else delights in doing a task you find onerous. I'm certain you do other things that help the family."

Aileen flushed. "My aunt believes I'm a scandalous woman and despairs of me. Although I try to avoid her whenever possible." She shrugged. "My aunt is not charitable."

Deirdre nodded. "I fear I've had a few unpleasant conversations with her, and I've no desire to further my acquaintance with her." She paused before asking in a hesitant voice, "Why would she believe you scandalous? Marrying Kevin O'Rourke would not make you so."

"Well, my aunt wanted me to marry Declan, not Kevin, and was scandalized when Mary spoke out against my marriage to Declan at our wedding ceremony. The priest was most entertained. Thankfully Kevin and I wed soon afterward." Her blush deepened to a dark crimson. "But my aunt's most despairing of the fact I have my own work." She smiled with pride. "Kevin rejoices in it, and I know the income will help us during the slow winter months." She paused. "But there are those in town who are uncharitable."

"I don't understand," Deirdre murmured.

"I'm a seamstress. And I don't discriminate against my clients." At Deirdre's persistent frown of confusion, Aileen said, "I work mainly for the Madam at the Bordello. Few other female clients need my talents."

"Oh my," Deirdre breathed, her cognac-colored eyes widened with shock and delight. "How marvelous!" She giggled. "I imagine your aunt is furious at you."

Aileen chuckled and nodded, her smile one of satisfaction. "Yes. Although I'm not working with Madam Nora to spite my aunt. I genuinely enjoy the work, and Madam Nora is a nice woman." She shivered. "Although I give thanks every time I leave there that I have a home to return to. That Kevin is waiting for me."

Deirdre leaned forward and gripped her hand. "Are you telling me that you've been inside the Bordello?"

Aileen's smile widened at Deirdre's fascination. "Yes, I have a tiny workshop there, where I mend the girl's dresses or make them new ones. You'd be surprised how often their dresses need mending." Her eyes widened at the comment, before she and Deirdre erupted in gales of laughter.

"Oh, I can't imagine," Deirdre, whispered. "And the O'Rourkes don't mind you working there?"

Aileen shrugged. "They are practical. They know I am devoted to and love Kevin and that the extra money will only help us. Seamus knows lean years will come, and he wants us to be prepared for them. He's terrified of suffering what they did in Ireland."

Deirdre shivered and nodded. "Which is understandable."

Aileen's smile was filled with mischievousness as she met Deirdre's gaze. "Besides, Seamus is good friends with Madam Nora and knows her to be a kind woman. He used to spend many evenings with her before Mary returned." She laughed as Deirdre gaped at her. "As a friend, never as a customer. Kevin told me that his da needed someone to turn to. Someone to speak with, when he felt the loneliness overwhelming him."

Deirdre sighed and curled her arms up under her head. "Mary knows of such a friendship and accepts it?"

Aileen shrugged. "You'd have to speak with her, but she is always friendly toward Nora when she sees her. And Mary has never spoken a word against me working there. She understands my need to have something other than my marriage and Kevin's family."

A comfortable silence filled the room, as both women were lost in thought. Finally Deirdre murmured, "They seem a remarkable family."

Grinning at her, Aileen said, "Yes, they are. And I'm fortunate enough to call them mine."

Ardan slipped into her room to find the lamp still shining on her bureau. It cast a soft glow over her beautiful features and made her hair shine more red than gold. "What's put a frown on your face, lass?" he asked, as he kicked off his boots and undid his coat and waistcoat. With a sigh, he climbed onto the bed and pulled her into his arms. "Ah, heaven," he whispered, as he breathed in her subtle scent of lilacs.

"When are you leaving?" she asked, the tension in her body slowly easing as he cocooned her with his warmth.

"Where would I be goin', lass?" he asked with a chuckle. He smiled as his warm breath on her nape evoked a shiver.

"To Saint Louis. With Declan." Her hand rubbed over his arm wrapped around her waist, evoking a small shudder.

"Would you miss me, were I to leave?"

"You know I would," she said with a sigh, as she moved around so she could face him. "Are you leaving? Am I to be separated from you until next spring?"

He studied her earnest gaze, filled with longing and trepidation, her worry easing part of his fear that his feelings were one-sided. Ever-so-slowly, he raised a hand to trace his fingers through the baby soft hair at her brow, before leaning forward to kiss one cheek and then the other. He smiled as he breathed, "No, love. I've no plans to travel with Dec, although I do worry about what mischief he'll get into while he's in Saint Louis." He kissed his way to the sensitive skin behind her ear, earning a startled gasp as her hands rose to grip his shoulders. "Declan has too much curiosity an' not enough common sense at times."

She arched into his touch. "Common sense can be overrated."

He chuckled as he nibbled at her earlobe. "I agree."

Pulling at his hair, she ran her fingers through his beard, her soft palm and thumb caressing his lips. Her eyes glowed with passion and joy at the ardor in his gaze. "My ... Ardan," she whispered, leaning forward to kiss him.

He groaned, tugging her to him so she lay atop him. He deepened the kiss, his arms banded around her, as they shared their passion for each other. Soon he eased her to his side again, his hands caressing her head, shoulders, and arms. "*Shh*, love," he murmured. "You know I desire you, but we have no need to rush anything. We have plenty of time."

She reached for him, wrapping his arm securely around her. "Time has always been the one thing I've never had enough of with those I ... care about," she said, as she caught her breath.

"I'm not going anywhere, Deirdre. As I hope you've surmised, I've no desire to leave right now."

"Right now or ever?" she asked.

He shook his head, his gaze filled with longing and a subtle chastisement. "Don't tease me with what you aren't willin' to give. 'Tisn't fair." He saw her face fill with regret, and he stroked a hand down her back. After taking a few deep breaths, he murmured, "Tell me, love. Is this what you imagined when you thought to answer the advertisement my da posted?"

She gave a grunt of laughter and shook her head. "Of course not. I had hoped, by answering the advertisement, I'd meet a pleasant-enough man who never stirred any emotions." She paused, flushing. "I had hoped to never ... care about anyone ever again."

He rolled so they lay side by side, facing each other. "Deirdre," he breathed. "'Tisn't a way to live." He flushed. "You should never live a life devoid of love."

She stroked his face. "Nor should you, Ardan."

He nodded and pulled her close. "Let me hold you, *a stoirín.*"

The following morning, Ardan sat on his parents' stoop, enjoying the shade and the cooler temperatures before the July heat arrived after midday. He would have preferred to sit on Deirdre's steps and listen to her sing as she cooked, but he feared his presence at the café was becoming widely remarked upon. His mum and Maggie had just walked over to the café to join her in the kitchen, and he knew they would enjoy their gossip session without him listening in on the stoop.

With a sigh, he admitted to himself that Deirdre was becoming an integral part of his life, and he fought panic at having developed such strong feelings for her so quickly. He rubbed at his head in frustration at the thought of ever losing her.

Glancing in the direction of the café, he frowned as he saw Niamh approaching. "Niamh," he said, his voice cool, although welcoming.

"Ardan," she said. She held Maura on her hip. "Da will watch Maura this mornin', while I help in the café." She shifted a squirming Maura to her other hip.

"Come here, darlin'," Ardan said, rising and holding out his hands to his niece. His gaze held a silent challenge for his sister, as though daring her to defy him from offering comfort to his niece. After a long moment, Niamh eased Maura into Ardan's arms. He tickled his niece's belly, earning a giggle and a delighted squeal. "There's my precious girl," he crooned. Smiling, he looked at Niamh and frowned to see her watching him with unveiled disdain. "You can't possibly still be upset with me, Niamh."

She shook her head. "You'll never understand what it's like."

With a frown, he kissed Maura's head and stared at his sister with a perplexed expression. "To marry a man such as your husband?" At her pained expression and quickly averted gaze, he murmured, "I pray every day I make a better choice than you did, Niamh."

She stared at him with disillusionment. "No matter what, it's always my fault because I chose him. Everythin' that happens, I deserve." She closed her eyes, as she wrapped her arms around her waist and turned away from her brother's too-perceptive gaze. "Aye, I suppose 'tis only fair. I was impetuous and foolish. One must always pay for one's mistakes."

For long moments, the only sounds were the distant calls of men, the *cluck*ing of the chickens, and the persistent *chirp* of a robin. She took a deep breath and turned back to face her brother, her expression carefully blank.

"Niamh?" he asked. "What are you payin' for?" He reached forward and gripped her hand. "You know we'll always support you. You and Maura. No matter what."

She nodded, fighting tears. "Aye, but some battles can't be fought for you." She forced a smile as she saw her daughter snuggled on her brother's shoulder. "Will you pass her over to Da? She has a change of clothes and nappies in my old room here."

"Aye," Ardan said. He watched as she walked away in the direction of the café, frustration roiling through him that his relationship with his sister remained fragile. When Maura patted him on his cheeks, he chuckled. "Aye, little one. 'Tis too beautiful a day for worries. Come. Let's find your granddad, for I know he has all kinds of stories for you." He turned, walking up the steps to enter the house to find Seamus.

～

A few evenings later, Ardan sat alone in the café's kitchen, long after the café had closed, sipping at a cup of black tea. He grimaced at the bitter taste and fought the urge to add milk and sugar. He eyed the sugar bowl and gave in to his desire to taste tea the way he loved it. After adding a healthy spoonful of sugar and a dollop of milk, he stirred it with a spoon, before taking a sip with a satisfied sigh. "Heaven," he breathed.

After emigrating from Ireland—and even before, due to the potato famine—he had learned to do without so much of what brought him pleasure. A full stomach. Milk and sugar in his tea. His pillow. Anything so that his siblings would not know more discomfort than they already did. However, now that they were successful, he realized he could indulge a few of his desires.

"Never heard a man so enthralled over a cup of tea before," Cormac Ahern said with a wry grin, as he stared at Ardan from the back door of the café. Broad shouldered and as tall as Ardan, Cormac rivaled Declan with his wild appearance. His long brown hair fell in waves past his shoulders, and his sky-blue eyes sparkled with mischief.

"First proper cup of tea I've had since I was a boy," Ardan murmured. "Would you like one?"

Cormac chuffed out a soft laugh. "Not unless you have a dram of whiskey to add to it." At Ardan's shake of his head, Cormac sighed and accepted the cup of tea with only sugar. "Your da said I'd find you here."

Ardan nodded, his alert gaze wholly focused on Cormac. Although he was loyal to the O'Rourkes, Ardan always felt a sense of reserve emanating from the man. As though he were waiting to see how things shook out. "What's the matter, Cormac?"

"Could be nothin'." He blew on the warm tea. "Or it could be everythin'." After a long moment, he said, "I met an interesting man when I was at Cow Island. He's waiting his turn to get a stage here, but I suspect he'll be here in a day or two. Perhaps tomorrow." Cormac rubbed at his thigh. "Ran my oxen hard to get here before he did."

Ardan shook his head in confusion. "Why?" He took a sip of tea, fighting a deep sense of unease.

Swiping at his face streaked with dirt, Cormac had apparently searched for Ardan before seeking out a bath, after his latest trip to the improvised port downriver. His eyes flashed a warning as he said, "Man claims that he's Silas Fiske and that he's been wronged. That his sister-in-law, a Deirdre Fiske, stole his property and ran away from him, after agreeing to marry him." He nodded as he met Ardan's widened stare. "I made sure to inform the man no Deirdre Fiske was in our town, but I know some fool will mention Deirdre's cookin'."

"What else did he say?" Ardan asked. He grimaced at the desperate urgency in his tone.

Cormac scratched at his too-long brown hair and pulled it away from his face. "This Silas, who has the face of a bulldog and the manners to match, said that Deirdre was a tiny woman, reddish hair, and eyes the color of a good liquor."

"Feck," Ardan rasped.

Cormac lifted his tea, as though it were whiskey, toasting his friend's assessment of the situation. "I had no reason to keep the dandy from comin' here. Although I doubt he'll last a winter. He's a bit ... pampered."

Ardan rose and paced to the stove and then back again. "Why warn me, Cormac?" He studied the man who had always been an enigma.

"You're family of sorts. I know you don't like Connor, but you've never treated him poorly. Even though you've had every reason for how he's let Niamh down." At Ardan's intense stare, Cormac rasped, "Makin' his own wife work, rather than earnin' an honest livin' with me. It's disgraceful." He shook his head in disgust, as he thought about his older brother, Connor.

Ardan nodded. "She loves him. There's no need to add to her heartache."

Cormac shrugged and rose. "I don't know what you can do, but I hope what I told you helps." He slapped Ardan on the back and slipped from the kitchen.

Ardan latched the door and headed up the stairs. Although Deirdre's ankle was better, he had continued to sit with her until she fell asleep. Something inside him needed to be with her during her unguarded moments, and she hadn't protested. He pushed open the door to her upper rooms, shutting and locking it behind him. "Deir?" he called out in a soft voice.

"In the bedroom," she murmured.

His breath caught at the sight of her in her nightgown, slipping under the sheets. "You're beautiful, lass," he breathed, his worries momentarily forgotten.

"And you're daft," she said, mimicking the soft burr of his voice. She waited for him to settle beside her on top of the covers, frowning when he remained apart from her. "Ardan?"

He pulled the chair over to sit beside her. He clasped her hand, tracing patterns over her soft skin. "I've just heard disturbing news that I don't understand. I need your help." He paused. "I need you to be honest with me, Deirdre. Whatever is coming will be faced better if we are honest with each other. And if I'm prepared."

She frowned at him and shook her head. "I don't understand, Ardan. What's coming?"

"No, love. *Who*." He paused, looking deeply into her eyes. "A man named Silas Fiske." He kept hold of her hand as she jerked at the name. "And he's looking for a woman named Deirdre Fiske." He paused, waiting for her to speak, but the only sound was her breath, sawing in and out of her. "He says he is a man played false by a woman. Robbed by the woman who was to marry him."

"He lies!" she gasped, as a tear coursed from each eye. "How did he find me?" she asked. "I used my mother's name. Not Alonzo's."

"Alonzo was your husband?" Ardan asked.

She closed her eyes and nodded. "Will you come and rest beside me? Hold me while I tell you what I should have told you before?" She met his gaze, frowning to see it guarded and filled with uncertainty. "I promise you, on everything I hold sacred, I will not lie. I will not paint myself a martyr."

He nodded, kicked off his boots, and rested along her back. He wrapped an arm around her belly, tugging her against him, as he buried his face in her neck. "I believe you." He shuddered at feeling her in his arms again. "Are you promised to him?" he whispered. "Will you leave with him?"

She wriggled against him, moving so that she turned and faced him. Raising her hands, she cupped his cheeks, her fingers playing through the beard he trimmed but didn't shave off. "No, my Ardan," she whispered, seeming to falter as though she were about to say *my love*. "Never."

He took a deep breath. "I'll listen and not interrupt you." He rested one arm on her hip, the other was tangled in her hair. "I will not judge you."

"I came from Ireland, on a ship in 1848," she whispered. "I was seven." She focused on his steady gaze, as though his calm presence grounded her and gave her strength to speak of her past. "My parents died on the ship, and I arrived in America, starving, completely alone, and with no one caring if I lived or died." She paused. "I went to an orphanage and then to work for a wealthier family."

She shrugged with embarrassment. "Anyone with money would have seemed wealthy to me. I wore rags. And I'd stopped talking after the death of my parents."

She paused for so long, Ardan whispered, "What happened?"

"The family had two sons. One was handsome but always seemed a bit full of himself. The other was good-looking enough but kind. We became friends. He talked with me, teased me, and treated me like a friend. He taught me to read, even though his parents thought it was something a beggar from Ireland had no need of." She flushed at the bitterness in her voice. "After unpleasantness at their home, and against his parents' wishes, we ran away to marry." She smiled at the memory. "He had money saved from a trust from his grandmother, and we settled in Baltimore. I was a decent cook, and he was always cheerful, so we started a café. We were happy."

Her eyes clouded. "Too soon the Civil War broke out. He wanted to do his part. Insisted the war would be over in a matter of months. He never imagined the rebels would have the supplies or the will to fight for years." She sniffled. "He died in 1863 during the Battle of Vicksburg."

"Oh, love," Ardan whispered, kissing her head.

"I kept the café running, but it was hard. When he left, he didn't know I was with child. I thought to surprise him when he returned in a few months. The months turned to years, and he never returned to meet our Lydia. And then she died too. From rheumatic fever." Tears coursed down her cheeks.

"And this man?" He swiped at her tears. "This Silas?"

"He's Alonzo's brother. He returned from the War, wounded and bitter and insistent that I was his because I'd been Alonzo's. He wanted my café. My home. Me." She shuddered. "I encouraged him to visit his parents in Philadelphia, who had already mourned the loss of one son, and, while he was away, I sold the café and fled. I remembered your father's advertisement for a mail order bride and decided to travel here. Who would think to follow me to Fort Benton? Who would want to?"

"He must believe you worth quite a bit of money to have traveled all this way to find you," he murmured.

Her laugh held no humor. "I spent almost everything I earned from the sale of my home and business on the ticket to come here. I had only a few dollars in my pocket when I bluffed my way into a job with Buford. I'm not worth much, Ardan."

He made a noise of disagreement, clasping her face between his fingers. "Never speak of yourself like that, my love. You are priceless. Your worth doesn't come from the money in your pocket or the family or the connections you have. It comes from who you are." He touched her heart. "From how deeply you can love."

"Ardan," she breathed, "I don't want to hurt you." Another tear coursed down her cheek.

"Then don't," he said in a soft voice, as he leaned forward and kissed her. "Be brave with me. Face your fears with me. For we have the same fears, my love. But I know I don't want to walk this earth without you by my side."

She sobbed, pushing herself forward into his embrace.

He sighed, holding her close, although he couldn't help but notice she didn't say the words back.

She didn't promise to always walk beside him too.

CHAPTER 6

All hell broke loose the next day. Ardan sat at the butcher block table, watching as Niamh and Deirdre worked. Although they usually chatted about customers or ideas for recipes, today they were silent, only Deirdre's humming breaking the monotony of their chores. At the slam of the café's front door, Deirdre stiffened, and Ardan sat up straight.

"Why does the sound of a slammin' door always make you nervous?" Ardan asked. He couldn't wait for her response as shouting reverberated through the café to the kitchen, and he rose to investigate.

He walked through the largely vacant café, as it was midmorning, to see a peg-legged man gesticulating as he spoke in a haughty voice, as though suffering to speak to someone so inferior to him. Ardan remembered only too well that tone and accent from the short time he had spent in New York City with his family. Ardan had hoped any acquaintance with that type of man—who believed himself superior to all he met—had ended when the family moved from New York City. Ardan sighed as he studied the dandy and realized such men would inevitably find their way to Fort Benton too.

Ardan stared at the man in a dust-covered black suit with a cranberry waistcoat and flamboyantly tied neckcloth that served no purpose other than decoration. Shaking his head, Ardan wondered how long he'd last in his fancy clothes as the day warmed. "Buford?" Ardan asked as he approached.

Buford, flushed red as a beet and on the verge of a stroke, stood toe-to-toe with the newcomer. Ardan suddenly realized if he was annoyed with the yelling man, Buford, a Southerner, would be irate. "He claims he can steal her away."

"No one is stealing anyone," Ardan said. "Who are you, and what do you claim?" He stood tall and calm, although he fought an internal panic.

"I'm Silas Fiske, and I'm here for my recalcitrant sister-in-law, Deirdre Fiske. Although I've heard she goes by the worthless beggar name of Finnegan."

"'Tis a proud name," Ardan said, emphasizing his accent, as though daring the man to contradict him.

"It's the name of an inconsequential immigrant who should never have had the temerity to marry into a family such as mine." He stood tall, forgetting his disability, and nearly toppled backward as he lost his balance. He flushed with mortification as Ardan grabbed him to keep him from tumbling to the floor.

Buford stood tall, pushing out his small paunch until it bumped into Silas, causing him to stumble back a step. "I don't know a Deirdre Fiske."

Silas snickered. "But you do know a Deirdre Finnegan. You recently hired her to run your backwater café after she couldn't get a respectable man of this town to marry her. She's as pathetic as ever and just as unlovable."

Ardan gripped Silas by the collar of his shirt, lifting him to the tippy toes of his boot. "I'd remember that you're the newcomer to this town and that few will agree with your vile opinions." He met Silas's glare with a gaze filled with ire. "Deirdre is a respectable member of our community, and you are the unknown. Your fancy accent and pompous clothes mean little here." He released Silas and took a step back.

Silas ran a hand down his jacket and stared from Buford to Ardan in disdain. "Money always talks, even in such a trivial town as this." He pointed to the door at the back of the café, leading to the kitchen. "Will you allow me to speak with her, or would you prefer me to accost her when she is unprepared and without such gallant defenders?" His voice dripped with disdain.

Ardan let out a long breath and then nodded. "Follow me."

Deirdre stood with her hands on the wooden table, her gaze focused on the doorway. She had heard them talking and then uneven footsteps approaching the kitchen doorway. "Silas," she whispered as her brother-in-law stepped into view. Although Ardan loomed behind him, she only focused on Silas and the covetous hatred in his gaze. "You're here."

He took a step toward her, his limp pronounced. He had a wooden peg leg from the knee down on his left side, after he lost part of his leg to gangrene in the Civil War, and his jaw tightened as she noted his limp. His dishwater-blond hair was greasy, his dark-brown eyes filled with fiery emotion. "Yes. Did you think a cripple couldn't travel? That I wouldn't follow you after you stole what was mine?"

She shook her head in confusion. "I'm the widow. I had the right to sell our property and to travel wherever I wanted to."

"Widows have little rights," Silas said. "I'm surprised you didn't know that. Did Alonzo leave a will?" he asked. When he saw Deirdre pale, he said, "You were entitled to, at most, one-third of his property. You stole the remainder from his family." He looked at her with derision. "I always knew you were a scheming thief."

"No," Deirdre whispered. "I was his wife. The mother of his child."

He gave a snort of disgust and rolled his eyes. "A likely story. My mother said she never met the thing. That you made such a claim so that you'd believe you would feel a greater entitlement to Alonzo's money and estate."

Deirdre shook. "No, I had a baby. A beautiful girl. Lydia." Her breaths emerged as gasps. "Who can travel in wartime?" She tried to focus on Ardan, staring at her with love and devotion, but she felt like she was in a dark tunnel, becoming narrower. Sweat broke out on her forehead, and her heart raced.

"You're a thief and a liar, and I'm here for restitution," Silas intoned. "If you can't pay back what we are owed, then I'll take you with me."

"No," Deirdre gasped, taking a jerky step away from the table. She only calmed when Niamh laid a soothing hand on her arm. "Never. I'll never leave with you."

"Not even to see Alonzo again?" Silas murmured.

Deirdre stilled, her eyes wide, as she felt her world spin. Shaking, she accepted the stool Niamh eased her onto and sat, thankful she had the fortitude not to faint. "He's dead."

"So you think," Silas said. "He was devastated to realize you'd sold everything and left. That you tried to escape from his family."

She shook her head side to side, as her hands wrapped around her middle. "Not your family. *You.*" Her mind raced at all Silas implied. "Leave. Leave me to think."

"Think about this, Deirdre Fiske," Silas said, using her lawful married name. "You abandoned your husband when he needed you. Never fear. He's heard all about your disdain of injured men from me." He tapped his peg leg. "He's in Saint Louis, waiting for you. Wishing his arms were around you. Instead you're here, in some backwater town, cozying up to an Irishman, peddling goods to miners." Silas shook his head. "Seems your heritage shone through."

Deirdre stared at Silas in horror, as he mockingly doffed his hat, pushed past Ardan, and stormed out.

After a moment of stunned silence, she dropped her head forward and waited for tears that never came. Instead she sat in a cocooned numbness, impervious to the voices around her. To Ardan's gentle strokes down her back. To anything but her renewed misery.

A rdan shared a long look with Niamh and approached Deirdre with caution. Although he wanted to offer her support in any way possible, he had no desire to hurt her. To cause her to further turn inward and away from him. "Deirdre," he murmured, "ignore the café today. Take time to think through what just happened."

He frowned as she rose, brushing past him as though he were an annoying gnat, and pulled out a bowl which she slammed down so hard it cracked.

"Love, you can't use that. It's broken."

When she burst into tears, he pulled Deirdre into his arms and rocked her. Hoping that Niamh would take over today, he glowered after his sister as she ran from the kitchen. Ignoring everything around him but the woman in his arms, he kissed her neck, held her close, and whispered his love for her in her ear.

"Don't," she gasped. "Don't say such things. Not now. Not now that I might …" Her voice broke, as tears continued to pour out. "I might have betrayed him."

His hold on her tightened, when she would have eased from his embrace. "No, love. Think. *Think*," he repeated. "Consider all Silas said and didn't say. Remember what your husband was like. Determine truth from lie."

She pushed at him again, her eyes ravaged from her crying spell. "I can't do that in your arms. I need time away from you." She shuddered out a breath. "I feel stifled." She stood frozen in the kitchen, her gaze downward, and her arms wrapped protectively around her middle.

"*Stifled?*" he repeated. Stumbling back a step, he focused on the clatter of footfalls up the back steps, thankful for the interruption. "Mum, Maggie," he breathed. He cleared his throat, wishing he could as easily calm his roiling emotions. He looked to Niamh with appreciation.

"We heard we were needed," Mary said with concern. "Are you well, Deirdre?" Mary asked, as she ran a hand over Deirdre's arm. "I can see you're not." She pulled the young woman into her embrace, holding her close. "Don't worry about a thing today. We're only too glad to help. Why, just today, Maggie an' I were bemoanin' we had too little to do."

That earned a chuckle from Deirdre, and Mary smiled. "See, lass? Nothin's so awful you can't laugh." She brushed at her cheeks. "All will be well. Give it time, and it will sort itself out."

Ardan watched his mother soothe Deirdre, as he had been unable to, and a kernel of resentment took root inside. He wanted her to turn to him. To find comfort with him. He ran a hand down his mother's arm, careful not to touch Deirdre again. "I'll leave you to work." He strode from the room, eager to find his brothers and father, to hear their words of wisdom.

Ardan sat on an overturned crate in the warehouse, staring into space, as he thought about her brother-in-law's arrival. Ardan resented she hadn't turned to him for aid. That she had sought comfort from his mum and her work rather than him. He had hoped his love would banish her fears and that she would see what was obvious to him: Silas was a snake, and there was little chance her husband was truly alive.

He closed his eyes, as he considered her predicament. He thought of Da. If he had suspected Mum were alive, Ardan knew his da would have raced to wherever she was purported to be to search for her. That was love. That was commitment. He pinched the bridge of his nose. How could he fault Deirdre for showing her first husband such devotion? He hated that he was so jealous of it.

He yearned for her loyalty. He rubbed at his heart, as he feared he would never have more of her than he already had.

The warehouse door burst open, and he sighed as Kevin and Declan burst in with worried expressions. "What is it?" he asked.

"You, you *eejit*," Kevin said, as he pulled out another crate to sit near him. Declan did the same, and they soon formed an informal circle. "Da told us you had trouble at the café."

"*Trouble*," Ardan scoffed with a shake of his head. He leaned forward, clasping his hands together, either in prayer or to prevent from striking out at something in anger. "I'm worse than a Colleen," Ardan moaned, as he rested his head in his arms.

"How could you be worse than a Colleen?" Declan asked, as he slung an arm over his brother's shoulder. "Nothin' is worse than fightin' a ghost."

"There's fightin' the hope the ghost lives," Ardan said, raising his gaze to see his brothers pale at his words. "Her brother-in-law arrived in town today. Claimed her husband lives in Saint Louis."

Kevin shook his head. "That's a load of rubbish, and you know it."

"Aye, I do. Especially because his first argument was that Deirdre owes him money. Then, when that didn't work, he claimed her husband never died. Seems he'll do whatever he must to entice her to leave the Territory."

Declan sighed and ran a hand over his face. "Why?" he asked. "Makes no sense, aye?" He shrugged as he met his eldest brother's gaze. "The lass is pretty, aye, an' has a wonderful talent in the kitchen, but why would that cause a man to chase after her?" He raised a hand, as though worried he had offended Ardan. "Does he love her like you do?"

Ardan shook his head. "No. He seems to only have contempt for her."

Kevin rose and paced around the otherwise empty warehouse. "Then why chase after her to Fort Benton? Why take months out of your life to follow a woman you don't even like?"

"I don't know." Ardan took a deep breath. "But I don't know how to fight against the hope I saw in her gaze. She wouldn't talk with me. She turned away from me, as though she were ashamed of our friendship." He bowed his head at having to use such a weak word to describe his relationship with the woman he loved.

"Hope is a tantalizing lure," Declan murmured, and his brothers nodded.

"She said I was stifling her," Ardan whispered. "How can she perceive my love that way?" His blue eyes shone with torment as he stared at his brothers.

"Oh, Ard," Kevin murmured, as he gripped his brother by the nape. "She's terrified and lashin' out. Doesn't know what to do. Give her space."

"Aye, an' time to realize all she's missin' by not bein' with you," Declan advised. "Soon she'll come to realize she's a fool."

Kevin paused, as he saw his eldest brother's misery. "The man just arrived. Surprised her. Give her time to work through all he said, an' I'm certain she'll see her way to the truth, as you have."

Declan gripped his arm. "Fight for her, Ardan. She's the woman you love. Don't give up on her."

Ardan nodded, his gaze bleak. "I will. I fear it won't be enough."

After the meals were served, the kitchen was cleaned up, and the café closed for the evening, Deirdre expected Mary, Maggie, and Niamh to depart. Instead they remained in the kitchen, sitting on stools, as they each sipped a cup of tea. Maura had come and gone a few times during the day to spend time with Niamh, but she was back again with her doting grandfather and uncles.

"I'm certain you have much more important things to do," Deirdre protested, as the women sat in quiet companionship with her. "Won't your men need a meal?"

Mary waved a hand. "They can fend for themselves for one meal," she said with a smile. "Although I know they'll all hope 'tisn't Ardan cookin' for them." She bit back a smile, as Niamh snickered.

"Oh, he's the worst cook!" Niamh said with a sigh, as she shook her head. "When we were young, he'd try to help out Da, before he married Colleen ..." Her voice faded away, and she flushed as she ducked her head.

"Seamus said he nearly burned down the house, trying to make toast one night," Mary said with a broad smile, as Maggie gaped at her. "Aye, 'tis hard to imagine, isn't it?"

"He mastered one soup, but, oh, we got so tired of eatin' the same thing." Niamh blushed. "Although we should always be thankful we had anything to eat."

"Yes," Deirdre whispered. "I might have been young, but I still remember the hunger that felt like it would eat your stomach out from the insides." She saw the understanding in Niamh's and Mary's gazes. Her eyes filled, and she whispered, "I don't know what to do."

Mary rose and wrapped her arms around Deirdre's shoulder. "Of course you don't. Today was a shock for you, and you need time to consider all you heard. For not everything spoken is the truth."

Deirdre sighed, as she leaned into Mary. "I feel horribly disloyal to Alonzo." She looked toward Maggie and Niamh, who stared at her with sympathy. She hoped it wasn't pity. "I should feel only joy at the news he lived."

"Ah, but does he?" Mary murmured. "Or is that a ruse to steal you away from those who would love and cherish you, only putting you at the mercy of a man who has little regard for you?" Mary ran a hand over Deirdre's head and then her shoulder. "Only you know the truth. It rests deep inside you, Deirdre."

Ardan slipped into her upstairs rooms that evening, after hoping all day she would seek him out. He paused at finding her staring out the rear window, tears tracking down her cheeks. "Love," he whispered. When she stiffened and backed away from his soft words, he froze from reaching for her. "How are you?"

Her tormented gaze met his, and she shook her head helplessly. "I don't know what to think. How can Alonzo be alive, and I not know it? For two years?" she asked, staring vacantly out the window again. "How could he ignore me for all that time?"

Ardan cleared his throat and took a tiny step in her direction. "Did you ever imagine that man Silas might lie?"

Deirdre shuddered and wrapped her arms around herself. "Only a truly vindictive man would say something so egregious. To a woman who's mourned." She lowered her head. "I feel so ashamed."

Stilling his forward movement, he felt a chill race down his spine at her words. "Because of me? Because of our friendship?"

As though in a trance, she whispered, "What must your family think of me? A married woman carrying on with another man?" She closed her eyes. "I'm no better than the women at the Bordello."

"No, Deirdre," Ardan rasped. He gripped her arm and turned her to face him. "No." His cobalt-blue eyes sparkled with the intensity of his feelings. "I will not allow you to sully what we've shared. What we have."

"What have we had, Ardan?" she whispered, her gaze filled with misery and doubt. "Why would you want an inconstant woman?"

Ignoring her gasp, he pulled her into his arms, intent on finding some way to soothe her. "We'll find a way through this. I promise." He ran his hands over her shuddering back. "You're not inconstant. Silas is a liar."

"I can't see my way to the truth," she whispered, rubbing her face into the soft flannel of his shirt. Taking a deep breath, she pushed at Ardan, forcing her way out of his arms. "I can't do this. Not if there's a chance Alonzo lives." She held up her hand, shaking her head. "No, Ardan. No."

"Deirdre, you know Silas lies." He reached for her again and stilled his movement when she backed away.

"I don't know what I know." She held a hand to her heart. "But I won't have peace until I discover the truth."

He paled as he watched her expression become resolute. "You're leaving me. You're returning with Silas."

She nodded. "Yes."

"No," he said, his voice cracking. He cleared his throat and blinked rapidly as tears threatened. "No," he repeated. "Leave with me. Leave with Declan. One of us will see you safely there and will ensure you come to no harm."

She stared at him with incredulousness. "Why should your family trouble themselves with me?" She shook her head. "Besides, I can't arrive at Alonzo's sickbed with another man in tow. What would he think of me, Ardan? If I were to show up with you?"

118

He gripped her shoulders, his touch gentle and reverent. "He'd think you were human. That you learned the lesson of that horrible war and learned to grab at happiness wherever you could."

"No!" she gasped. "No! Stop tempting me with what I have no right to desire." She pushed him back, severing his hold on her. "I will leave. With Silas. As is proper. There's nothing for me here."

He took a step toward her, his breath teasing the hair at her nape. "There's everythin' for you here, if only you were willing to fight for it." He waited a long moment for her to respond. When she refused to say anything more, he walked away, the door creaking as it shut behind him.

CHAPTER 7

During the midmorning lull the following day, Deirdre stood at the bank of the Missouri, watching as the river rippled past. Although she wished it were teeming with men working, so that something would distract her roiling thoughts, the levee was quiet, as no boats were docked. After the drought from the previous year had brought a lighter-than-average runoff and flow to the Missouri, all the recent boats attempting to bring passengers and cargo to Fort Benton and the Territory had to dock farther downstream.

Soon Fort Benton would be cut off from the outside world, as even those steamboats docking at Cow Island would head back to Saint Louis and would not attempt to return until next June.

She rubbed at her temple as her mind raced with her meeting with Silas the previous day. With her discussion with Ardan last night. All last night, she'd waited for Ardan to return. Waited to feel his arms around her again. To hear him whispering his words of reassurance in her ear. His love.

Instead she had slept alone for the first time since she had hurt her ankle in over two weeks. She had hugged a pillow, muddling through what Silas said and implied, her emotions roiling. What it would mean if Alonzo were alive.

How was she to know what to do? Her heart had raced at the possibility that her husband lived, while a sick dread filled her stomach.

How was she to leave Ardan?

Closing her eyes, she took a deep breath to steady herself. Reminding herself that her first loyalty was, and had to be, for her husband, she firmed her shoulders and turned from the river to walk to the hotel. When she arrived, she nodded to the owner, Mr. Foster. "Is there any place here I could speak in private with my brother-in-law, Mr. Fiske?" she asked.

Mr. Foster eyed her up and down and then nodded. "Of course, Mrs. Finnegan. You may use my office." He motioned for her to go to a room down the hall. "I'll see if Mr. Fiske is available to join you. If you wish, I may loiter in the hallway, should you need any assistance."

Deirdre nodded and wandered into the tidy office at the end of the hall, uncertain if her plan were sound, as she did not relish being alone with Silas. Ignoring her trepidation, she spun to face him, as he entered the room in an ungainly step. "Silas."

"I'm surprised you'd seek me out. Not after you wanted to throw me out of your kitchen yesterday." His brown eyes gleamed with curiosity, as he looked at her standing with perfect posture, while she gripped her hands together. "No need to act the perfect grieving widow. I had the entire evening to listen to how you've had an O'Rourke in your bed for the past few weeks."

She flushed and shook her head in denial. "That's horrible gossip," she gasped.

"Half the men I met informed me that Ardan O'Rourke doesn't leave your house until the next morning. Most often until he's had breakfast at your kitchen table." He looked at her with a scorn-filled gaze. "I had thought my brother's wid—wife would be more respectful of him. But then, I should have known better than to have optimistic expectations of you."

She raised her chin, her eyes glinting with unshed tears. "I have never dishonored Alonzo." Holding a hand to her heart, she whispered, "And to prove my sincerity, I will return with you to seek him out. No injury would ever prevent me from wanting him."

Silas snorted out a scornful laugh. "So you say now. What do you think Alonzo will say when he hears about your infidelity?" When she flushed, then paled and dropped her gaze to the floor in shame, his smile broadened, as he saw the effect his words had on her. "Do you believe the loss of a leg is the worst a man could suffer in the War?"

Shaking her head, she stared at him, a wild glint in her eyes. "Oh, please tell me how he suffered! What he suffered. I can't bear the thought of him languishing in pain and not being there to offer him some comfort."

He looked her up and down, his gaze filled with derision. "You've seen the men after the War. Horribly disfigured by their scars. So changed even their mothers wouldn't recognize them."

She paled at the thought. "My poor Alonzo."

"Save your histrionics for someone who believes in your sincerity." He motioned for her to follow him. "Come. We must make plans to leave here with all due haste. For all I know, Alonzo has already perished from his wounds. And from the belief you've forsaken him."

"No," Deirdre gasped. "That would be too cruel."

Allowing Silas to tow her along, she followed as they left the hotel to find a stagecoach driver to deliver them to Cow Island and the steamboats waiting to head downriver.

Dunmore poked his head into the warehouse, his alert gaze taking in the scene of Kevin and Declan playing cribbage, while Ardan stared into space. Although Dunmore had known it unlikely, he fought disappointment that Maggie wasn't visiting her brothers today. He had hoped to see the youthful joy in her gaze and her cautious smile as she stole glances at him. After a moment where he attempted to banish his improper fascination, he cleared his throat, and the brothers looked in his direction. "I hope I'm not interrupting," he said with a wry smile.

Ardan walked to him and shook his hand. "No, Dunmore, 'tis always good to see you. How was your recent journey?"

He shrugged. "Nothing unusual. Nothing to report." He saw Ardan's understanding that he had learned nothing new on his recent journey to Virginia City about Jacques Bergeron, who had abused Mary and Maggie. Although Jacques was Mary's brother-in-law, and a step-uncle to Maggie, he had treated them poorly during the time they had lived with him. The O'Rourkes hoped Jacques would remain far away. "I wish I could confirm his whereabouts, but he seems to have disappeared."

"Disappeared?" Declan called out. "There aren't that many places to travel to in the Territory."

"No, but there are enough," Dunmore said with a sigh. "I've asked those I trust to keep an eye out for him. We'll discover where he is before he has a chance to cause mischief again."

Ardan slapped Dunmore on his shoulder. "Thank you." He motioned around him. "As you can see, there isn't much work right now."

"Or there are too many of you trying to do the same work," Dunmore murmured. "I'm headin' to Cow Island in a day or two. As is Bailey."

Declan shivered. "God help anyone travelin' with that man. He's lucky he hasn't killed anyone yet with his run-down coach." His brothers murmured their agreement with his statement. Bailey preferred time in the saloon or the Bordello to time repairing his coach.

Dunmore nodded. "Interesting you should say that." He tipped his hat back, his blue-green eyes intense as they looked at Ardan. "I saw a man with your woman speaking with Bailey a little while ago. They appeared to be purchasing seats for his coach that is to leave tomorrow for Cow Island."

"No," Ardan gasped, paling at the news.

Dunmore nodded. "Seems they are eager to leave this 'godforsaken upstart town, filled with those who don't know their place.'" He shared an amused look with Kevin and Declan, as Ardan gaped at him in horror. "That's a direct quote from the peg-legged man she was with. Seems a rather cantankerous sort for such a sweet woman to consort with."

"He's her brother-in-law," Declan whispered.

Dunmore grunted and rocked on his heels. "Well, seems to me, he wishes he were somethin' more than that." Tipping his hat to the brothers, he sauntered out of the warehouse.

After speaking with Silas and the horrible Mr. Bailey, Deirdre returned to the café. Unable to focus on her work, she smiled her thanks when Mary, Maggie, and Niamh returned to help her. In the afternoon, as bread baked and a cake cooled, Deirdre slipped out the back door during a lull in work on the excuse she needed to use the privy. In reality, she needed a moment alone. She walked until she came to a halt by a small creek that led into the Missouri river. Although she had just made arrangements with Silas and Mr. Bailey, she fought panic.

How was she supposed to let Ardan go?

Bowing her head, she fought a sense of shame that she coveted another man while her husband might live. She fought guilt at the lie she had told Ardan that there was nothing for her here. Everything she dreamed of was here. What was she supposed to do? She swiped at her cheeks at the sound of someone approaching. Spinning, she let out a deep breath at seeing Seamus O'Rourke approach. "Mr. O'Rourke," she murmured.

"No need to show such joy at my appearance," he teased, although his gaze was serious as he watched her. "How are you, lass?"

She shook her head and shrugged, the ability to describe her tumult of emotions beyond her. "I don't know," she finally admitted.

"Ardan told me all that man had to say yesterday," Seamus said, as he stood in quiet companionship beside her. "An' I think there's quite a bit he left unsaid."

Deirdre stared at the older man in confusion. "I don't understand."

125

Sighing, Seamus stared at the fields of rolling grass, undisturbed by humans. "You know the story of my Mary and me. Of how we were separated by my foolishness and my inability to speak French. If I'd had the sense or the ability to ask more questions, we never would have spent almost eighteen years apart." He took a deep breath as though to calm himself. "Mary is wise. She tells me not to mourn overmuch the time we lost. For, if I do, it means I must mourn the lads I had with Colleen, and I could never regret Niall, Oran, and Bryan." He paused. "Just as I could never regret Mary havin' Lucien and Henri. I love them as though they were my own."

She stared at him with continued bafflement.

"What I'm tryin' to tell you, lass, is that, if I had known my Mary lived, there wouldn't have been a force on this earth that would have kept me from her. An' I pray, none that would have kept her from me."

Deirdre frowned as she thought through his words. "You believe Silas lies?"

"Of course. The man has the look of a schemer about him." He paused as he saw her think through his words. "What does he have to gain by tellin' the truth?" Seamus asked. "You're here, in a wild town in a Territory barely established, with a town sheriff of little authority and a judge hundreds of miles away. Few here care much for laws. I'm certain that man Silas is smart enough to know that the only way he can have restitution, if that's truly what the man is after, is by dragging you back to Saint Louis." He watched her closely. "And your husband won't be there waitin' for you."

Deirdre swallowed. "But Mary came back. After almost eighteen years."

"Aye," Seamus said. "An' I give thanks for that miracle every day. But 'twas a miracle. If your husband lived, he's been alive for over two years without a word to you. Why? Why wouldn't he have written to you? Why wouldn't he have come home an' held you in his arms as you mourned your babe?"

"Maybe he was a prisoner. Maybe he wasn't allowed to write," she said. Her words sounded hollow and weak even as she spoke them. "Perhaps he lost his memory."

Seamus waited a few moments for her to hear the ridiculousness of her last statement. Finally he asked, "Where is the letter from him now? If your man is truly too sick to travel here from Saint Louis, why wouldn't he have sent a letter with his brother? Why would he continue to torture you with his silence?"

"No," she gasped. "I won't listen to you try to fill my head with lies. With ideas that make a mockery of the sacred vow I took with Alonzo." Tears coursed down her cheeks. "I can't be what Ardan needs." She shook her head, as though in deep disappointment at Seamus. "I can't believe you'd encourage me to be unfaithful." She jerked away so he couldn't grip her arms.

"Lass, think," Seamus urged, his voice tinged with desperation. "Think of the two men. Who do you trust? Who truly cares for you?" He waited as Deirdre gasped and shook her head at him. "Please, lass," Seamus pleaded.

"No," she protested. "I will not allow you to make me false to my husband." She spun on her heel, racing away from Seamus and his tempting words.

The following morning, Deirdre lugged her trunk down the stairs and ignored Buford's glare as she dragged it behind her through the empty café. The O'Rourke women had not arrived to cook, and the kitchen was uncharacteristically quiet. When she stood on the front stoop, she shivered as the lock sounded behind her. "No turning back," she murmured to herself.

With another deep breath, she marshaled her strength and pulled at her trunk, battling tears that no one emerged to aid her. No deep baritone to send a shiver down her spine. No voice redolent with an Irish accent. Instead horses whinnied, while men spat wads of chewing tobacco and discussed the upcoming journey. Silas stood with his back to her, talking with a slender man with narrow shoulders. She recognized the other man as Mr. Bailey, the stagecoach driver.

Pausing halfway between the café and where the stage stood, Deirdre swiped at her forehead and looked at the small town. Although she had only been here a month, it already felt like home, and she dreaded leaving. With a will borne of desperation, she ignored glancing in the direction of the O'Rourke store. Instead she looked down the boardwalk in the other direction. Rather than continue her struggle with her trunk, she paused to see a well-dressed woman walking toward her.

This woman walked with a slow, purposeful gait, aware of but ignoring the appreciative glances of every man she passed. Her focus was on Deirdre. Frozen in place, Deirdre was uncertain why this woman would pay attention solely to her. As she neared, Deirdre noted the fine cut of her royal-blue silk gown, her shiny brown hair pulled back in a bun, and the determination in her brown eyes.

When the woman came to a stop in front of her, they were nearly the same height, although Deirdre felt overpowered and outmatched by the confident well-dressed woman. Deirdre glanced at her own dowdy cotton indigo dress, battling uncertainty. "Hello," Deirdre murmured.

The woman nodded and smiled. "Mrs. Finnegan," she murmured. "I have heard a lot about you." She looked at the scene over Deirdre's shoulder, and any delight in her gaze dimmed. "I had hoped you were more sensible than to be taken in by a charlatan."

Stiffening her shoulders and lifting her chin, Deirdre's cognac-colored eyes flashed with anger. "I'm certain you have no right to judge anything I do."

The woman laughed. "And I'm certain most would agree that a woman who runs the Bordello should never dare to speak with a respectable woman of this town." She shrugged. "However, I've never agreed to live by such limitations. And I fear, if I did so now, you'd make a grave mistake."

"I don't understand what you are saying," Deirdre said, although her gaze had widened upon realizing she spoke with Madam Nora, the famed owner of the most successful brothel in town.

Madam Nora smiled. "Yes, you know who I am. And, as such, you must know I hear the best gossip. Men are at their most indiscrete when they are … content." Her wry smile caused Deirdre to fight a giggle. "What I don't understand is why you are not heeding the counsel of the O'Rourkes."

Shaking her head, Deirdre said, "They are good people, but they are biased. They want me to choose Ardan, and I fear they will say what they must so that I will please them." Deirdre stiffened as Silas bellowed her name.

Madam Nora gripped her arm, preventing her from spinning away from her. "You need to think, Deirdre. Think hard before you make an irrevocable error. Who has always told you the truth? Who has supported you?" She paused as Deirdre seemed unconvinced by her arguments. "Why would that man come back for you now? Why would you believe what he has to say now?"

Deirdre gaped at her a long moment as doubts seeped in, but then Silas grabbed her arm and towed her away. "Thank you!" she called back to Madam Nora, as she stumbled along beside Silas. She tripped on a rut in the road and fell to her knees, crying out in pain as he yanked on her arm to get her to stand again.

Hands roughly picked her up, stuffing her in the stagecoach, and Silas crawled in after her. Four other men scrambled inside, and she pushed herself against the side of the coach to escape touching Silas. Belatedly she reached for the handle. "My trunk!"

Silas tugged the door shut, just as the stage rolled into motion, forcing them backward in their seats. "It's tied on the back." He clasped her arm so hard that he gouged bruises into her soft flesh. "Stop making a scene. You chose this."

Deirdre closed her eyes, willing him to stop touching her. When she failed to respond to his comment, he released her and sat back with a huff. Curling into the corner, she focused on everything but her reality. Images of the past month flooded back. Maggie and Mary laughing and teasing her as they worked with her in the kitchen. Talking with Niamh as though she were a sister. Seamus winking at her. Ardan kissing her temple. Running a soothing hand down her back. Massaging a kink out of her shoulders. Holding her as she cried.

RAMONA FLIGHTNER

She sighed as her every thought was of him. Although she tried to think of his family, she couldn't. Ardan filled her mind. And her heart. Clutching a hand to her chest, she relived each smile, each soft word, each caress. How would she survive without them?

Ignoring the chaos around her of men snoring, belching, and telling tall tales, she listened to the thunder of hooves as the stage rocketed down the road. Keeping her eyes closed, she contemplated what she knew to be true. Ardan's touch had always been filled with reverence, unlike Silas's. Ardan had never lied to her. Had never misled her. But Silas? … Silas was a snake. He'd always wanted her. She shivered as she remembered the angry visit from him after she had married Alonzo. His attempt to seduce her. To make her false to her husband. She shuddered as buried memories flickered through her mind, and she swallowed a moan of distress as she fought shame and anger at Silas's repeated attempts to sully her marriage.

With a deep breath, she forced herself to face the truth. Her husband was dead. Her beloved Alonzo, who had loved her so well and so devotedly, was dead. Silas was tricking her back to Saint Louis or Baltimore or Philadelphia for his own purposes. Alonzo would never have left her for years with no word. He had been a kind, good, loyal man.

A smile burst forth as she silently acknowledged she would return to Ardan. She belonged with him. Her smile dimmed at the prospect of being stranded at Cow Island, 120 miles from Fort Benton, with no means to return to him. Refusing to believe Mr. Bailey wouldn't take her back, she envisioned her reunion with Ardan. The joy in his gaze. The hunger and relief in his kiss. As she sighed with relief that her choice had been made, a horse squealed, the carriage flew through the air, and her last thought was one of regret.

She'd never told Ardan she loved him.

CHAPTER 8

Ardan worked moving crates from one side of the warehouse to the other, anything to take his mind off the fact that Deirdre had left without seeking him out. Without saying goodbye. "Feck," he swore, as he picked up a heavy box to lug across the room. He relished the hard work, as he had no desire to contemplate the heartache that would be his constant companion for months to come. He fought the inclination to travel with Declan to Saint Louis. He had no desire to look like a lovesick fool, but he feared he would appear as such, as he knew the temptation would prove too great.

He closed his eyes, after setting the box down, imagining her boarding the stagecoach. Talking with her brother-in-law. Him helping her inside. Ardan's hands fisted at the thought of such a vile man touching her, and he forced himself to relax, as he acknowledged that he had no rights where Deirdre was concerned. She had made that abundantly clear. She did not want him, nor would she ever want him.

"No," he whispered. His heart rebelled at his mind's imaginings. He knew she cared for him, but fear, hope, and lies had confused her to the point that she didn't know what to believe or what to do. He only wished she'd put her faith in him.

The warehouse door clattered open, and he spun to face the man who stood with heaving breaths. "Dunmore?" he asked. "What's the matter?"

"Stage accident," he said. "Bailey rode one of his horses back to inform us that his stage crashed a few hours outside of town."

Ardan strode to him, his gaze wide and wild. "Are there any casualties? Injured?"

Dunmore shook his head and shrugged. "There are injured, and there will most likely be casualties. I don't know who. Bailey, the coward, leaped off the top of his stage at the first indication of trouble, saving his hide and causing the crash to worsen, as no one was at the helm." He clamped his jaw shut with rage. "They're readying my horses. I have cloth, water, and other supplies. Get your brothers and come with me."

Ardan slapped him on his shoulder, bellowing for Declan and Kevin, praying he hadn't lost his love.

~

Ardan sat beside Dunmore on the front seat of his stage. The horses barreled down the deeply rutted road, but Ardan ignored the jarring ride. His one focus was on his prayer to find her well. To hold her again in his arms. To hear her soft voice as she whispered his name. He swallowed back tears as he prayed his dreams were not in vain.

As they turned a corner, Dunmore pulled up hard on his reins, coming across the crash, causing Ardan to grip the seat so as not to fall off. "Whoa," Dunmore called out to the horses, easing them to the side and away from the wreckage of Bailey's stagecoach. Crying and wailing carried on the wind, while the subtle scent of blood tinged the air.

Ardan launched off the top seat and raced for the carriage, resting on its side. He clambered up one of the wheels and wrenched open the door. The inside was empty, and he spun, staring at a dead horse attached to the reins. The other horses were tied to nearby bushes. He jumped from the carriage and followed the sounds of distress, moving toward the banks of the river. "Deirdre!" he called out.

After pushing through tall grass, he stopped to find three men laying on their backs with serious injuries, while four others sat on fallen trees, their arms looped through improvised slings or with bandages wrapped around their heads. A trunk had been dragged to them, and shirts and pants were strewn in an untidy mess.

"Deirdre!" he called again. "Deirdre," he breathed, when he saw her walking up from the riverbank, carrying a leaky bucket of water. When she shook her head, he stilled his instinctive desire to race toward her, and she hurried to the side of one of the injured men laying on his back.

"Tear that shirt into strips, Ardan," she said, as she dampened her skirt in the water and rubbed it over the man's face, murmuring soft words to the injured man. She held her hand out to Ardan, accepting with a silent nod of thanks the clean cloth he placed into her palm. She pressed the cloth to the man's leg, whispering her apology as the man whimpered in pain.

Ardan stared at the man, belatedly realizing a tourniquet circled his leg, but blood continued to spurt from his wound, saturating the previously pristine white cloth. He ripped more of the shirt apart and continued to hand cloth to Deirdre, although he knew their efforts would be futile. However, he refused to leave Deirdre here alone to nurse these men.

With an impotent glare of fury, Ardan watched Dunmore, Declan, and Kevin approach. Soon they too had begun to tend the injured men, although none were doctors. When the man Deirdre tended gasped his last breath, Ardan rested a hand on her quivering back.

"You did what you could, love," he whispered.

"It's never enough," she rasped through her tears. "Never enough." She rubbed at her cheeks with her arm, her hands coated in blood. After a moment, where she bowed her head and appeared to say a silent prayer to the recently deceased man, she rose and stumbled to the next man who needed tending.

"Deirdre, let us care for them," Ardan urged, resting a hand on her arm.

"No!" she said, as she poured water over her hands to clean them off a little. "I must help. I must." She pulled free of his touch and knelt beside Dunmore and then Declan, but each of the three most severely injured men soon died from their wounds.

Dunmore rose and pushed his hat back on his head, as he stared at the remaining passengers, sitting in shock nearby. "I should take the wounded back to Fort Benton." He looked at the sky and shook his head. "Doubtful I'll make it there in time to return here for you."

Ardan nodded. "Come for us early in the morning," he murmured, shaking the man's hand.

"I'll leave at first light," Dunmore said.

Ardan focused on Deirdre. "Where are you goin', love?" he murmured, as she stood with her back to him.

"I need to wash up, and I need a little time alone," she whispered. "I'll stay here. I won't stray." She looked at him over her shoulder, her expression shattered. "I promise." She backed away from him when he would have embraced her.

With a nod, he watched as Deirdre scurried away to return to the riverbank. After a moment, Ardan watched as Kevin and Declan helped Dunmore shepherd the injured men to the waiting stagecoach. One of them was her brother-in-law, Silas. He had a bandage wrapped around his head with a bloody spot in the middle of it, and he'd lost his peg leg. Declan and Kevin carried him to the carriage, and Ardan followed.

When he realized he had a moment alone with Silas, Ardan leaned forward and met the man's gaze. "I know Da would say I shouldn't speak with you now. That you're injured and should be given time to heal." He shook his head. "But I don't care."

Silas groaned and held a hand to his head.

Ardan paused and then said in a low voice, "In case your head is hurting you, I'll speak softly. Your attempt to force Deirdre to depart with you has failed. She now knows better than to ever leave with you again."

"You'd keep her away from her husband?" Silas opened one eye to stare at him with a hate-filled glower.

"No, I'd keep her away from you. If she wants to leave to search for Alonzo, one of my brothers or I will travel with her. But I'll ensure she's never at your mercy again." He stepped away when Dunmore returned with the last injured man. He ignored Silas's attempt to gain his attention and turned to face his friend. "We'll see you in the morning, Dunmore."

"Tell our family what's happened and why we are delayed," Kevin said.

"Aye, I'll be sure to tell Seamus. And your bride," Dunmore said with a teasing smile to Kevin, as he shook their hands before climbing to the high seat on the coach. He ably turned the coach around and was out of sight a moment later, leaving only a cloud of dust behind him.

Ardan nodded at his brothers when they handed him a shovel, and followed them to an area away from the riverbed. Soon each brother was busy digging a grave. They worked in a fluid synchronicity, and, after a short period of time, had three graves dug. Gasping slightly, Ardan wiped at his forehead. "Should we dig a bigger hole for the horse?"

Declan stared at him as though he were daft and shook his head. "I'm not movin' that creature."

Kevin nudged his shoulder and shared an impish smile with his brother. "Well, we could leave it where it is and wait for the wild animals to come graze on it. Should make for a restful evening."

"We dig a hole closer to the carcass, aye?" Declan stared at his brothers, waiting for them to nod. "It doesn't need a nice place on a hill with a view of the river, like the poor lads who died on the journey."

Ardan squeezed his shoulder and urged him to move toward the wreck. "Aye, I agree. Come. We still must bury the men and then work on the horse."

A s the daylight waned, the dead had been buried, and the O'Rourke men had prayed over them. The horse was in a shallow grave, although Ardan feared any rain would expose the carcass. As dusk approached, those who remained would have to make camp for the night. Ardan noted Declan and Kevin setting up a few canvas tents, and he motioned his thanks. He wandered the small area, looking for Deirdre. He walked to the area by the river, where the wounded had been tended and paused.

Ardan watched as Deirdre dampened a cloth in river water and then rubbed at her neck. Her indigo dress was caked in dirt, mud, and blood; and her hands, face, and neck were equally dirty. He paused as he saw her bend over to wash her hands. Rather than rinse them in the water, she began to scrub and scrub at them, her shoulders shaking with silent sobs.

Rushing to her side, he slipped and fell on the mud, sliding to her on his knees. "Deirdre," he murmured. When she canted in his direction, he wrapped an arm around her, pulling her back to his front. "It's all right."

"No, it isn't," she cried. "I couldn't save them. No matter what I tried, I couldn't … I couldn't stop the bleeding," she gasped out around her sobs.

"*Shh*, my little love," he whispered. "You did everything you could. Remember that, my darling. Take comfort in it."

She shuddered in his arms. "Just like with Lydia," she said in a defeated voice. "No matter how hard I tried. No matter what I did. Nothing would save her."

Ardan eased her back and turned her around so he could gaze at her. He cupped her face in his strong hands, his thumbs stroking over her cheeks, swiping at her tears, while he gazed deeply into her devastated gaze. "No, *a stoirín*, my darling," he said with an intense expression. "Remember all that you did. You saved lives today. And I know you would have saved Lydia's life if you had been able to." He paused as he caressed his thumb softly over her silky cheek. "I know you, and I know you did everything you could have for your daughter."

"How?" Tears pooled in her eyes and cascaded down her cheeks.

"Look at how you cared for these strangers." His gaze held a deep tenderness and an abiding love. "If you care for those you don't know with such zeal and passion, I can only imagine how you care for someone you love."

"I loved her so much," Deirdre rasped. "I hate that she's not a part of my life. That I lost her."

Ardan wrapped his arms around her, holding her close. "Nothing will ever take away the missing her. Nor the memories of the moments you had with her."

"Thank you," she whispered into his neck. "Thank you for not insisting time will make this better. Or that I will heal once I have a new child."

Groaning into her ear, he rocked her side to side. "Never, my darling. Never." He smelled her subtle lilac scent. "Such a loss will always be with you. But it doesn't have to define you." He sighed with pleasure as she snuggled into his arms, accepting the comfort he so readily offered.

"Where are the others?" she whispered.

"There wasn't room on the coach for all the injured and us. If we had crammed on board, their injuries might have worsened." He kissed her head. "You're stuck out in the wilds tonight with three O'Rourke men." His hold on her tightened as he felt her shiver.

"Will I have my own tent?"

He leaned away, brushing at her hair and face with his hands. "Aye, you can if you want. But I fear you will be frozen by morning if you don't share body heat with one of us." A smile bloomed as he saw her flush with embarrassment. "An' I hope the one you'd want to canoodle beside is me."

She rolled her eyes at him and then smiled. "Of course it would be you, Ardan. I can't imagine Aileen would be pleased if she knew her husband were cuddling another woman."

He pulled her close, cherishing the moments he held her in his arms. "Aileen's astute enough to understand the need to stay warm."

He kissed her head, and he felt her quiver. "An' she trusts her husband enough to know he'd never play her false."

She froze in his arms. "You believe I've done that to you. Your family believes that of me, don't they?"

His hold on her remained steadfast when she squirmed, as though she attempted to escape his embrace. "*Shh*, love, let me hold you. An' reassure you." He waited until she had calmed. "No, we don't believe you played us false. I never believed that." He paused. "I believe you were misled."

She pushed at him again and backed away a step. "Why did you come here?" She raised her somewhat cleaned hands to push at her dirty hair and cringed at the clumps of dirt and mud dried in it.

He stared at her for so long that she fidgeted and lowered her gaze. "How can you ask me that, lass? After the past month?" He waited for her to reply, before shaking his head at hearing his brothers calling out for them. "Come. We should join Declan and Kevin. Any discussion we need to have can wait until we are rested." He held out his hand, the stiffness in his shoulders relaxing as she took his offered hand and walked with him hand in hand to the small campsite created by his brothers.

After eating a small portion of bison jerky, Deirdre crawled into the makeshift tent. A blanket covered the ground, and two others were at the foot of the blanket-covered area. She assumed one was for her and one for Ardan. Already shivering as the temperature dropped quickly in the semiarid land after the sun set, she tugged one blanket around her, falling onto her side fully clothed.

"Idiot," she whispered to herself. Hugging the blanket tightly around her, as though to protect herself, she curled farther onto her side as she fought tears. All day she had battled a sense of incredulousness that Ardan and his brothers had raced to the wreckage site with Dunmore. That they had continued to show such concern for her. That she had her chance to tell Ardan how she felt.

She swiped at her cheeks as tears fell. Rather than running to him, telling him how much she loved him, she'd ignored him. And then cried in his arms about her daughter. She wrapped her arms around herself, as the reminder of her loss and the pain at loving and losing filled her very marrow. How she wished she were brave enough to love again.

~

Ardan stared into the flames of the small fire Declan and Kevin had made of the ruined carriage. Ardan knew Bailey would bellyache that they shouldn't have used part of his vehicle for kindling, but Declan, Kevin, and Ardan had agreed it was past salvaging. Ardan sighed, tossing in another piece of lacquered wood into the fire, watching with too-great intensity as the flames licked its sides before consuming it.

"What's the matter, Ard?" Kevin asked. They sat around the fire, leaning against rocks, their feet stretched out toward the fire.

"Deirdre," Ardan said. "I wish I could be what she wants."

Declan snorted. "The problem is, you are exactly what she wants. And that's what scares her." He played with a piece of prairie grass, chewing on the end of it, as he watched the glow of the fire highlight his eldest brother's torment.

Ardan sat up, sitting cross-legged and leaning forward. "What should I do?"

Kevin shrugged. "What you are doing. Show her your constancy, and her fears and doubts will ease." He made a sweeping motion with his hand. "Be honest with her, and push her to be honest with you."

Ardan sighed and eased to lean against the rock once more to stare at the stars. "When are you leavin', Declan?"

Declan shrugged. "In a week or two. Dunmore believes the last steamboat will leave in three weeks, later than Da expected. They want to give men from the gold fields time to travel to Cow Island to return to Saint Louis."

"Why?" Kevin asked.

"The captain earns a percentage of the total profit from the cargo. Some are willing to risk the ever-decreasing river flow for monetary gain," Declan said with a shrug.

"As long as you aren't stranded due to greed," Ardan said.

Declan smiled and shook his head. "Anyway, I'll be in town a few more weeks. 'Twill give me time to be in Fort Benton, in case you are smart enough to marry the lass." He winked at his brother as Kevin laughed. "I think I'm takin' Eamon and Finn with me."

"Both of them?" Ardan asked. "I thought Da didn't want us to be separated."

"He doesn't," Kevin said, "but Mum understands they are restless. She heard them bemoaning their fate of sittin' in Fort Benton all winter long while Declan has fun in Saint Louis."

"Only Mum could talk Da 'round," Ardan murmured. He sighed. "'Twon't feel like home 'til you're all back again."

Declan smiled slyly. "Unless you are a bumbling *eejit*, I suspect you'll have plenty to distract you."

Ardan smiled, saying a silent prayer his brother was correct.

Ardan eased into the tent, frowning to see Deirdre shivering under one blanket, with the other blanket folded up at her feet. "Why wouldn't you use both blankets, love?" he murmured.

"I thought one was for you, one for me," she said, her teeth chattering. "I never knew it could be so cold in the middle of summer."

"It's always colder out of doors and by the river." He sat beside her, kicked off his boots, and pulled up the second blanket, layering it over the first one covering her. He slid under the blankets and moved close enough so she would feel his warmth—but refrained from wrapping an arm around her waist.

"Hold me," she pleaded. "I'm so cold."

"At least I know you want me for something," he said, grimacing at the bitterness in his voice. He scooted closer, wrapping an arm around her belly, hauling her back against his front. When she groaned with relief, he buried his face in her hair. "God, I've missed this," he whispered.

"Me too," she admitted. "But nothing can change, Ardan."

His arm around her belly tightened, as though he were attempting to hold on to an ephemeral dream. "Why?" he rasped. "Why deny what we feel?" When she remained quiet, he asked in a low urgent voice, "Why won't you grasp at life and love and happiness after nearly losing everything, Deirdre?"

She shook in his arms, and he couldn't tell if it was from the cold or from her tears. "I can't have this conversation right now, Ardan. I'm too tired. Too vulnerable."

"Forgive me, *a stoirín*," he said, his deep voice laced with contrition. "I never would cause you more pain." He kissed the soft sensitive skin at the nape of her neck. "Sleep. There's plenty of time for us to talk."

He relaxed, relishing holding her in his arms as she calmed, and then she fell into a deep slumber. After many minutes, he followed her into sleep, dreaming of a future of uninterrupted nights with her in his arms.

CHAPTER 9

Ardan stood to the side of the café's kitchen, watching as his parents fussed over Deirdre. Although he had sat beside her during the return trip to Fort Benton, it had been a silent journey. Kevin had been inside the carriage with them, and Ardan had no desire to discuss his deepest emotions with the woman he loved while his brother was in attendance. Thus Ardan had attempted to find contentment holding Deirdre as she dozed, murmuring soothing words to her, and taking comfort in the fact she had not shied away from him yet today.

Now at the café, he watched as his da wrapped her in a warm embrace, while his mum fluttered around her, as though she were one of her own chicks, harmed in the accident.

"Oh, my poor Deirdre," Mary said, as she pulled Deirdre in for a hug. "When I heard there was a chance you were harmed, I feared I'd go mad with worry. I'm so thankful my boys raced to the crash site with Dunmore to ensure you were well." Her eyes shone with tears. "And to find you unharmed." Pulling Deirdre close, she rocked her in her arms, as though she were a wee babe.

"I'm fine, Mrs. O'Rourke," Deirdre whispered, although she clung to the older woman as though she were a lifeline.

"Oh, lass, I can only imagine what a shock it was to tend the injured and know some wouldn't survive. It takes a toll on us." She rubbed at Deirdre's wet cheeks. "Come. We have a bath waiting for you upstairs, and your trunk is unpacked."

"My trunk?" Deirdre asked, as her gaze flitted to Ardan in surprise.

He cleared his throat and shrugged. "It, *ah*, never made it onto Bailey's stagecoach." He shrugged. "Rather than have the townsfolk go through your things, we've kept it in safekeeping."

Her eyes widened at his words and then nodded a few times in comprehension, as she allowed Mary to steer her upstairs and out of Ardan's view.

When he could no longer see her but heard his mother murmuring to her in her soft soothing voice, he sat with a *thud* on a stool in the kitchen. Maggie entered, bustling around as she prepared food, and afterward Niamh arrived, handing Maura to their da as she aided Maggie. Soon a plate of food was set in front of Ardan, and he ate because he didn't know what else to do with himself.

"You seem out of sorts, lad," Seamus said, as he sat beside Ardan. They spoke in a low voice, and Ardan smiled in appreciation as his sisters began to sing, giving them the illusion of privacy. Although Niamh and Maggie had yet to forge a sisterly relationship, they shared a love of singing. Ardan had faith that soon Niamh and Maggie would find a way to span the divide of their animosity.

Ardan chewed the last bite of food and set down his fork. "I am. I don't know what to do. I had hoped the accident would show her the need to grab at life. To not let any chance at happiness pass us by." He rubbed at his head, his gaze shadowed with doubt and dread.

"Sometimes tragedy reinforces our fears," Seamus murmured, as he sipped at a cup of tea.

"Aye. I fear 'tis what happened with Deirdre. She's more afraid now than ever before. An' I don't know how to help her overcome it."

Reaching out, Seamus gripped Ardan's strong forearm. "By your constancy. By your love. Don't give up, lad."

"'Tis hard, Da, when the woman I cherish doesn't cherish me in the same way." His eyes shone brightly with unshed tears, and he ducked his head. "I wish … I wish for so much, but I know there is little to do. She must find her courage, or there is no hope for us."

"Be patient, Ardan. You've always been patient. 'Tis one of your best traits. Don't turn your back on that now."

Ardan nodded and rose. "I'll return later. Thanks for carin' for her, Da." He called out a few words of thanks to his sisters before he left to find hard work to tire himself out.

~

Deirdre sat on a bench on the boardwalk area in front of the café, sipping a cup of tea. The O'Rourkes insisted on giving her the day off after her ordeal. She had spent the time languishing in a hot bath, after scrubbing herself clean of all the muck and dirt, then taking a long nap. Finally she felt more like herself again. She watched the shadows fall on the distant cliffs, heralding the end of another day in Fort Benton. With a contented sigh, she closed her eyes and gave thanks she had returned.

"You seem mighty pleased with yourself," a snide voice barked, breaking into her silent musings.

Deirdre sat up straight, opening her eyes to meet the gaze of the glowering woman standing over her. "Hello, Mrs. Davies. I am well. Thank you for your concern after the terrible events of the past few days."

"Women like you never suffer timely deaths. You manage to evade death, like a cat with nine lives." Mrs. Davies held a hand on her hip, her burgundy dress fashionable, if a little faded after a mishap at the launderer's.

Deirdre wondered if she had damaged her own gown while working in her new job at the laundry. Although she had heard the gossip about Mrs. Davies accepting work at the laundry to help pay her bill at the hotel, Deirdre tried hard not to spread it. She did not relish demeaning others, unlike the woman standing in front of her. She stood, standing eye to eye with the older woman. "How horrible of you to wish me to suffer an untimely death. I've tried to ignore the uncharitable gossip about you, but I fear it is correct."

Mrs. Davies snorted at that statement. "As though the O'Rourkes don't find joy in belittling me every chance they can."

Shaking her head, Deirdre said, "No, I've never heard the O'Rourkes mention your name. Aileen spoke of you only one time. And for a family who tells stories of those they've loved and lost on a daily basis, I believe that speaks volumes. They have no wish to remember, or to honor, you with their stories."

Shaking with rage, Mrs. Davies struck out, slapping Deirdre across her face. "How dare you speak to me in such a manner? I am deserving of your respect. Of the O'Rourkes' respect. If it weren't for me, that pathetic second son wouldn't have a wife."

With eyes filled with loathing, Deirdre took a step back, her hand covering her cheek. "You have no business here at my café. And I refuse to serve you anything I cook ever again." She bristled as Mrs. Davies's cackling laugh carried on the wind.

"Your café? Your café?" she taunted. "You're too naive to even realize what they've done." At Deirdre's confused stare, Mrs. Davies leaned forward, her fetid breath washing over Deirdre. "While you were away, they bought the café. They own it now. You're their employee. Their servant." She saw the flash of panic in Deirdre's gaze at that word. "Seems little has changed in your life since you were a girl."

"You lie," she whispered, but a sinking sense of truth sank into her marrow.

"So you wish," Mrs. Davies taunted, as she spun on her heels. She called out over her shoulder before she strolled away, "I wonder what it feels like to only ever be wanted for your skill in the kitchen and nothing else?" With another vicious chuckle, she was soon out of earshot.

Deirdre collapsed onto the bench in front of the café, her earlier joy at her relaxing day and the cooling breeze eroded as easily as the riverbank during spring runoff. Her thoughts whirled, but she was no match for the doubts that crept in. Was this why the O'Rourke boys had raced after her? Because their father had bought the café, and they needed her as a cook? Could she trust anything Ardan said?

She bowed her head, fighting tears and anguish. Memories of working for years for a family who treated her with barely veiled contempt flooded back. The scathing comments, the jeering laughter, the slaps on her wrists and back when she was two minutes late with a meal. The long solitary hours in the kitchen as she prepared, cooked, and cleaned. Was this always to be her life? Lonely and forever dreaming of more?

Ardan entered the kitchen and locked the back door before making his way to her living space above the café. He fought the sense of rightness about the action. He stepped into the living room and battled the hope that this dream—returning home to her—would forever be his reality. A lit lamp on a side table cast light through the part of the room nearest the door, although the area near the window remained largely in shadow. He paused to find her standing near the window, with a shawl wrapped around her and her arms hugging herself. Suppressing the urge to rush to her and to enfold her in his arms, he remained in the middle of the room.

"Deirdre," he whispered. He frowned as his voice, his presence, seemed to distress her rather than soothe her.

"Why are you here?" she asked, her back to him, as she stared out at the prairie land and the sunset's changing colors from her rear window.

"Where else should I be?" he asked, taking a step toward her. He stilled when he saw the tension in her shoulders. "I had hoped you would come to me when we returned to town. That you would seek me out."

She rubbed at her forehead and let out a mirthless chuckle. "I suppose I should have. After all, I have a business now because of your family. Should we name it the *O'Rourke Café*? Am I little more than your employee? Should I bow and scrape before you?"

147

"Deirdre," he whispered in a hurt-ladened voice. "Why are you upset with me? With my family?"

She placed her hand on the windowsill, leaning forward and breathing hard, as though she were out of breath. "You have no idea what you ask."

He took a few steps in her direction, noting the polished furniture and the fresh wildflowers on a side table. All signs his mother and sisters continued to look after Deirdre too. "What do I ask that causes you such distress?"

She spun to face him, tears streaking her face, eyes swollen and nose reddened. "Do you have any idea what it did to me to learn that your family had bought the café? That none of you thought I was important enough to inform of the transaction?" She shook her head at him when he would have protested. "That I'm merely the cook. Why should I have any voice in the matter?"

"Deirdre, don't be foolish. It's not like that at all," Ardan said. He held up his hands to placate her, but she swatted at them.

"Don't touch me, and don't call me foolish! You're not the one who lived her life as no better than an indentured servant! You're not the one whose dreams have always been destroyed." She shook her head in dismay. "I thought *I* was creating something here. That *I* had control over my destiny." She sniffled. "I guess I am a fool to ever believe things would be different this time."

"Deirdre, please. You know how much I care about you." Ardan's gaze shone with torment, as she shook her head at his words.

"No! I can't care for you! I refuse to."

He took the last steps separating them, gripping her arms. "You mean, you're not brave enough. You're allowing your fear to rule you, rather than your hope and your love."

"How dare you imply I'm a coward!" she yelled, hitting him on his shoulder and pushing him back a step. "I'm brave. I'm here in this godforsaken town, aren't I?"

He shook his head, stepping closer to her, so they were only separated by a hairsbreadth. "No, that wasn't bravery. That was desperation. It wasn't courageous when you hoped to answer that ad with a determination never to love again. Never to feel again. That's not brave, Deirdre."

"You don't understand!" she screeched, hitting at his chest, while her lungs heaved in and out as she fought sobs.

Clasping her shoulders, Ardan stared at her with blue eyes glowing with passionate intensity. "You think I don't understand? That I don't know the agony of losing someone I love?" He stared at her with absolute disappointment. "Of course I do. And I was fortunate enough to regain her." His voice broke on *her*. "And I was blessed to have her wise advice again."

"You don't know what it is to lose your husband. Your child," Deirdre gasped.

His eyes shone with sadness, and he shook his head. "No, I don't. And I pray I never will." He cleared his throat. "But I do know what it was like to lose you." He waited a long moment as his words sank in, and he saw a dawning comprehension in her gaze. "Don't you have any idea what it did to me to have you turn away from me? To have you leave town with Silas, without even saying goodbye?" His eyes glowed with pain. "How could you, Deirdre? Leave without a word?"

She stared at him, her eyes shining with her misery, as tears flowed down her cheeks.

"Do you have any idea what it did to me to receive word of the crash? To believe ..." He closed his eyes for a moment, as though unable to utter his worst fear. He opened his eyes and spoke in a low, earnest tone, laced with terror. "To believe for the entirety of that harrowing trip to the crash site, that you might have been hurt? That I might have lost you?"

"Ardan," she breathed.

"How can you not comprehend what that did to me?" he asked with a shake of his head. He closed his eyes, as a tear streaked down his cheek before meeting her gaze again. "I love you, Deirdre. I love you with all that I am and all that I hope to become. But I can't continue thus." He released her. "I refuse to wait in vain for a woman who has no hope in the future. Who is not brave enough to dare to dream again."

"Ardan," she whispered, her voice cracking. She stared at him a long moment, but the only sound in the room was that of their harsh breathing.

"Goodbye, Deirdre." He picked up her hand, kissing her palm, his eyes closing for a moment at the touch of her skin against his lips. "I will always cherish what we had." He released her hand and slipped from the room without a backward glance.

Deirdre fell to her knees, watching Ardan leave. A deep keening sob tore from her as his words reverberated through her mind. *No hope in the future. Not brave enough to dream again.*

"No, no, no!" she cried out, as she reached toward the door, willing him to turn around. To comfort her and to listen to her avowals of love. Of *love?* Oh, did she dare? Could she be as brave as he believed her to be?

However, he failed to return, and she remained alone in her misery on the floor.

After long minutes, she pushed herself to standing, groaning at the stiffness in her joints. She shuffled to her room, moving through her nightly ablutions with little thought, as an overwhelming grief settled over her. Like the shroud of grief that had enveloped her with the death of Lydia. At the news of Alonzo's death.

She curled under the covers of her bed, staring at the wall, as tears leaked from her eyes. "This time, I did it to myself," she whispered. She fought the urge to scoot backward, her body eager to feel Ardan curling around her as she slept, bereft at the realization he wasn't here. That he'd never be here again.

Early the next morning, Ardan stood staring in the direction of the Missouri River. Rather than the current carrying driftwood downstream, he saw his memories of Deirdre. Her eyes lit with joy as she told him a story in the kitchen. Her head tilted back as she laughed. The dawning passion in her gaze the moment before he first kissed her. The contented smile on her face as she leaned into him for comfort after she hurt her ankle.

He closed his eyes to stop the onslaught of memories, but they continued until he had relived the previous night's argument. He bowed his head, rubbing at his temple as he sighed.

Kevin joined him, sipping at a cup of tea. After many minutes, he murmured, "What happened?"

Ardan took the cup from him and swigged down a large sip. "Ah, heaven." He sighed and shared a sardonic look with his brother. "I lost my patience with her fear." His shoulders slumped. "I thought I could wait forever. That I would be satisfied with whatever she was willin' to give me. I was a fool."

"What changed?" Kevin asked, as he took another sip of the tea and then handed the mug to Ardan to finish the beverage. "You've always been the most patient of us all, Ard."

"Perhaps," he murmured, as he stared at the golden hills across the river. "But I found I had little tolerance for her using her grief as a shield against loving me." He ducked his head.

Kevin sighed. "We all know what fear can do."

Turning to face his brother, Ardan stared at him intently. "You didn't allow your fears to prevent you from loving Aileen. You believed. You had faith in the future, rather than clinging to the disappointments of the past."

Smiling, his brother shrugged. "I had no choice. 'Twas as though I'd been struck dumb at the sight of her, an' I knew life would never be the same again." He gripped Ardan's arm. "I suspect it was much the same for you, although you were slower to admit it."

Ardan chuckled. "Aye. But now that I have accepted how much I care for her, I can't accept the little she's willing to give me. I deserve more."

"You both do, Ardan." He sighed. "I believe she'll discover fear is a cold bedfellow, and she'll soon seek you out. Be patient, Ardan."

He let out a deep sigh. "For the first time in my life, I don't want to be. I want to grab at life and dare it to spite me." He closed his eyes. "And that makes me a fool. For it already has."

"No," Kevin said with a wry smile, his hazel eyes shining with love for his eldest brother and best friend. "It means you're no longer hindered by the past."

They stood side by side as the river gurgled and a group of white pelicans swooped by. "What should I do?" Ardan whispered.

Clapping his brother on the shoulder and squeezing it, Kevin said, "Nothin'. There's nothin' more for you to do. If she doesn't see her way free of her fear, feeling pushed into a corner by you won't help her."

~

Deirdre worked in the kitchen, fidgeting at being surrounded by O'Rourkes. Mary and Maggie helped her in the kitchen, with Seamus charming the men in the dining room. As though by tacit agreement, Mary and Maggie sang songs throughout the morning, sensing that Deirdre had no patience for conversation.

The few times the back door opened, only to find Eamon or Finn had entered, Deirdre had to fight disappointment that Ardan had not come to see her. To ensure she was well after the previous night's argument. She silently chastised herself, as he had told her that he would not seek her out. However, the thought that he would never walk up the back steps again made her want to sob.

"Where is Mr. Hunt?" Deirdre finally asked, as they prepared for the midday rush.

Mary stared at her, as though she were confused by the question. "Don't you know?" Mary asked, as she wiped down the butcher block countertops.

Deirdre shook her head. "All I heard was that you had bought the café. I don't know where he went."

Mary smiled. "He knew his talents did not lie in the café business. He departed yesterday for Helena." Mary sighed. "I fear he'll have as little sense as he did here and will attempt to run another café. Seamus urged him to try running a saloon instead."

"He could become a miner," Maggie said with an impish smile.

Mary laughed. "Oh, could you see him dirtyin' his fine clothes as he toiled in the muck, searchin' for gold?" Her eyes were lit with merriment at the thought, before she shook her head. "No, he'll hire someone to do the work for him, just as he hired Deirdre here." Seamus called for Mary in the main café area, and she walked out to speak with her husband.

Deirdre stood staring in space, wrist deep in bread dough to knead.

"Are you all right, Deirdre?" Maggie asked, as she dried dishes and put them away. "You seem out of sorts."

Deirdre cut off her instinctual protestation that she was fine and shook her head. "No, I'm wretched," she whispered.

"Oh, no." Maggie set down her cloth and pulled Deirdre into her arms, uncaring of the mess that would mar her dress. "Nothing can be so bad as to make you miserable like this."

"I pushed him away," Deirdre gasped out between her halting breaths. "I … I … wasn't the woman he needed."

Maggie laughed and shook her head. "I don't know Ardan well, as I've only been reunited with him for a short time." She bit her lip. "But, from what I do know, you are exactly the woman he needs." She swiped a hand over Deirdre's head.

Deirdre leaned forward, taking comfort in Maggie's soothing words and sisterly hug. "I never had a family like yours. A family who truly cared for everyone and wished for the best for each other." She let out a stuttering breath. "I thought for the longest time I had to live away from any familial entanglements because the loyalty they would exact from my husband would always run contrary to what I needed as a wife."

Maggie made a soothing noise. "That's what you knew with your first husband's family. We're not that way. You know that, Deirdre."

"It's hard to have faith that all this isn't simply to entice me to be with Ardan," Deirdre said, ignoring Maggie's shocked gasp.

Maggie stepped back a pace and stared at her in confusion. "You believe Da bought the café to control you?" She furrowed her brows. She bit off what else she would have said as Mary reentered the kitchen with orders and a story to tell about a recent Indian altercation at Cow Island.

"Seems you were lucky to have no interaction with them when you spent your night in the wilds," Mary said. "I'm glad my prayers were answered, and you all came home safely to me." She ran a hand down Deirdre's arm as she moved to the stew pot to ladle out the meals.

Deirdre nodded and fought tears—confusion, hope, and longing warring within her.

Ardan sat at the family dinner table that night, his plate of food largely ignored as he stared into space. He had hoped all day that Deirdre would come to him. Instead he had found ways to keep himself busy, and now he was filled with a restless energy. Conversations flowed around him, as they always did when all his siblings were together, and he focused on their chatter.

"Maggie, you seem quiet tonight," Ardan murmured to his sister, sitting a few seats away and across the table from him.

"The same could be said of you," she said with a wry smile. However, no joy lit her gaze, and she bit her lip, as though battling a worry.

"What is it, lass?" he asked. "You've not acted like this since ..." He shook his head, refusing to say Jacques Bergeron's name. "Have you heard something?" At the flare of terror in her gaze, he silently swore.

"No!" she gasped. "No," she repeated in a calmer manner. By now the other conversations had abated, and everyone focused on him and Maggie. She flushed as she slid a furtive glance in their da's direction. "I spoke with Deirdre today." She smiled apologetically in Ardan's direction, when he stiffened at her words. "I fear there is confusion, Da."

Seamus set down his fork and knife, ignoring the meat loaf, potatoes, and beans in front of him, as he focused on his youngest daughter. "Confusion?"

Maggie took a deep breath and said, "Deirdre believes we have bought the café to coerce her into being with Ardan. That we wish to control her in some way." She shrugged as Seamus gaped at her, and her brothers burst into outraged protestations.

Ardan pushed back his chair and rose from the table. "She's uncertain about her role, Maggie, and she wants someone to blame for her fear. If she had paid attention to how we are rather than let her fears rule her, she would know we would never have meant to control her. To coerce her." His gaze was filled with pain, as though he had just suffered a bodily injury.

He spun and fled the room, his boot heels clattering down the back steps as he strode away from the family home. He avoided the gopher hole that had tripped up Deirdre and walked farther away from the house until the light in the kitchen window acted like a beacon. Turning his back on the house, he took a deep breath and stared into the darkness. After a moment, he tumbled to the ground and laid flat on his back to stare at the stars.

The Milky Way shimmered in the moonless night, as though beckoning all who beheld it to become lost in its depths. A shooting star raced across the sky, and Ardan closed his eyes to make a wish. He allowed the cool night air, the soft breeze, the call of a distant owl to soothe his restlessness. However, nothing eased the ache in his heart.

After nearly an hour, Ardan reentered the family kitchen to find his family sipping tea and furtively watching the door for his reappearance. He accepted a cup of tea, adding milk and sugar, and sipped at it with a sigh of appreciation.

"What did you decide, Ardan?" Seamus asked. He sat at the head of the table, with a sleeping Maura in his arms.

Ardan gripped his thighs and looked at all his siblings before finally meeting his father's patient gaze. "I know we're nearly out of capital. With the money we spent sending Jacques away and the need for Declan to go south soon to purchase supplies for next year." He paused. "And then you bought the café."

"Aye," Seamus said, "it's been an expensive year. But we've had our fair share of profits." He waited for Ardan to continue.

Ardan lowered his head a moment, as though marshaling his thoughts, before raising his head to meet his father's implacable gaze. "I want Deirdre. I love her. But I don't know how to fight her fears."

"She must overcome them herself, Ardan," Mary said. "You can help her, but those sorts of fears she must battle on her own."

"Aye, love," Seamus said, as he gripped Mary's hand. "But it always helps to know the one you love is there beside you. Supporting you the entire time."

Mary flushed and nodded her head.

Ardan watched the exchange between his parents, battling envy and a desire for the same with Deirdre. "She fears we will see her as little more than a cook. That she will be seen as a role, not a person." He closed his eyes. "She doesn't understand she could never cook again, and I'd be a happy man. As long as she was mine to cherish."

Seamus let out a deep breath and sighed. "You want me to give her the café. For the O'Rourkes to have no claim on it."

His siblings gaped at him, as Ardan nodded. "Aye."

"Feck," Eamon hissed, as he rose to pace the kitchen, muttering his apologies to his mother and sisters for swearing. "Are we to work for her for free too? Are Mum an' Maggie an' Niamh to become *her* indentured servants?"

Ardan flushed with anger and rose to face his brother. "No, Eamon." Soon he was nose to nose with his younger brother, Finn standing behind Eamon, with Kevin behind him. "That's not how it would be."

Declan, who stood to one side, watching his brothers with mild interest, as though waiting to see which group to join, asked, "Then how is it, Ard?"

"If she doesn't have the pressure of our ownership of the café, if she believes she is free to choose and to do what she wants, I believe she will come to understand that we value her for who she is." He stared at his siblings. "We lost Mum and Maggie. Aye. But we were never alone. We had Da. We had each other." He saw the flash of understanding in their gazes. "Deirdre lost everything on her journey from Ireland. She doesn't understand *family*, like we know it. *Love*, like we know it."

Mary rose, pulling him into her arms, effectively ending any chance for a fight, as no son of hers would ever risk harming her. "Oh, I'm so proud of you, my sweet, sweet boy," she whispered. She cupped his face in her hands and nodded. "Of course Deirdre will have the café. For soon it will be yours with her. For she loves you, and she will find her courage. Have faith in her, as your da had faith in me."

"Mum," Ardan breathed, pulling her close.

Kevin slapped him on the back and sat, tugging Aileen to his side.

Although there were a few grumbles, no further discussion occurred, as they all knew the decision had been made once their mum had spoken.

CHAPTER 10

The next day, Deirdre stood at the stove, pulling out a loaf of bread, when she heard footsteps behind her. She turned, stilling at the sight of her brother-in-law, Silas. "You are not welcome here."

He chuckled, limping his way into the kitchen. After he sat on one of the stools around the large butcher block table, he ran a hand through his freshly washed blond hair. Hair that reminded her of Alonzo's honey-gold hair that felt like silk when she ran her hands through it. However, the calculating gleam in Silas's cold brown eyes proved he was her brother-in-law, rather than her beloved husband. Alonzo's pale-blue eyes had always reminded her of the sky at dawn. "And you have no right to throw me out. You don't own this place."

"You're incorrect, as you always seem to be," Ardan said, as he stepped into the kitchen from the back door. "And if Deirdre doesn't want you here, you aren't to be here."

Deirdre gazed at Ardan in confusion, at his sudden presence and at his words, then focused again on Silas. "I know you lie, Silas. You haven't changed since we were children."

Silas scowled at her, the expression only making him appear less attractive. "I was always the responsible one. While you and Alonzo raced about, as though you were free to do whatever you pleased."

She gaped at him for a long moment before letting out a huff of incredulous laughter. "Have you forgotten that I worked as a servant in your house? I was never free to run around and *do what I pleased*." She took a deep breath. "You never liked that Alonzo and I were close. And rather than rejoicing in our friendship, you tried to sabotage it."

His brown eyes glinted with disgust. "You were never good enough for him. He should have married a woman with prospects. Someone who would have brought fortune or connections to the family. Not a penniless orphan who has to peddle her second-rate pies to customers." He cast a mocking glance at Ardan. "No wonder you find him attractive. You both have to sell your wares for a living."

"Your insolence will only garner you trouble," Ardan murmured.

"You've played at opening another café long enough, Deirdre. You're coming back with me. Alonzo's waited too long as it is to hold you in his arms again." Silas frowned as his words appeared to have little effect on her.

"First you came here, claiming I'd stolen money from your family and that you wanted it back. Then, when you realized that tactic wasn't working, you claimed Alonzo was alive." She shook her head, as she picked up a cast iron skillet, which she planned to use for a skillet corn bread. "You'll say whatever you have to, so as to induce me to leave with you again."

"You're being swayed by this man's charm," Silas said as he stood, hobbling until he found balance on his good leg.

Deirdre glared at Silas as she set the skillet on the countertop. "This has nothing to do with Ardan." She paused as Silas flushed red with indignation. "And I know you lie about Alonzo." Taking a deep breath and standing tall, she faced Silas with her head held high. "Unlike you, Alonzo would never have let two years pass without informing me that he was alive. Even if he were injured, he'd know I'd want him back. No matter what." She blinked away tears. "If he were alive, you'd have a letter for me."

She smiled with smug satisfaction at the panic in Silas's eyes. "You always were the worst tactician, Silas. Blustering your way through your lies, hoping if you were a big-enough bully, we'd go along with whatever you said. Slamming and pounding on doors to provoke fear and to coerce me into doing what you wanted." She shook her head. "Not this time. Not when it's this important."

"You are to return with me. I am your family," he snapped. He raised and lowered his arm, pointing to the spot next to him, as though she were a recalcitrant hound to heel at his side. When she failed to follow his command, he took a menacing hobble in her direction.

"No, you were never my family. You doubted the existence of my daughter. Your niece," she said in a tear-laced voice. "Ardan and the O'Rourkes, they never doubted. They exulted in her, even though they never met her, and accepted my grief." Tears leaked down her cheeks. "Other than Alonzo, they are the only ones to ever see me as more than a servant."

When he reached for her, she shrieked and raised the skillet, clobbering him on the head with it. She watched, wide-eyed, as he groaned and then collapsed at her feet. "Oh, dear God. What did I just do?" she whispered, as she stared at Silas, crumpled on the floor. "Did I kill him?"

Ardan chuckled. "No, you gave him a lesson he won't forget." He paused as he was about to kiss her forehead, backing away a step instead and clearing his throat, as though embarrassed by his action. He focused again on Silas. "And a headache he'll regret." He poked his head out the back door and bellowed a list of his brothers' names.

"Why did you call for so many of them?" she asked.

"I don't know who'll hear. Those who do will come," he said, as he stared at Silas on the floor, refusing to look at her. "Are you well, Deirdre?"

She nodded, canting toward him, resenting he was not reaching for her or holding her in his arms. Just as she mustered the courage to push herself into his embrace, clattering footsteps sounded on the back steps, and Niall, Oran, and Bryan O'Rourke burst into the kitchen.

"Oh, a body," Bryan said with glee in his gaze. "Do we get to dig a grave?"

"No, you wee imp," Ardan said, as he ruffled his youngest brother's hair. "He's alive, but he's badgerin' Mrs. Finnegan. Help me carry him out of here, aye?"

Niall and Oran puffed out their chests, elated that their eldest brother, who was their hero, had asked them for help. They shared carrying one side of Silas while Ardan hefted the other side. Bryan opened the door and raced ahead, calling out for all to hear about the incident in the café's kitchen.

Deirdre watched them leave, dragging Silas's good foot in the dirt. Soon Declan and Kevin had emerged from the warehouse, and they lifted Silas's legs, carrying him with ease. She waited until they were out of sight, wishing Ardan had turned to smile or to wink at her. However, he never looked back.

Three days later, a cool breeze blew, and Deirdre sat on the rear porch steps, enjoying the quiet evening air after finishing her chores in the café. Mary's sons, from her marriage to the Canadian Frenchman Francois, had come by in the afternoon to help with dishes. Lucien and Henri had jabbered in a foreign language she presumed was French, while casting curious glances in her direction. *Probably because I had knocked Silas unconscious with a fry pan*, she thought to herself. She had been informed he lived, which she was mostly grateful for. She had smiled at Lucien and Henri as they worked but had resented feeling out of place in her own kitchen. When they were done with their tasks, they had nodded in her direction and departed.

Niamh had remained at home, caring for a fussy Maura, and Deirdre had worked the café alone for the first time in weeks. For the past few days, neither Mary nor Maggie had come to work at the café. Deirdre had forgotten how lonesome she could be without the companionship of the O'Rourkes. Without them continually wandering in and out of the kitchen, snatching at a cookie or a roll, and winking at her as she laughed at their outlandish tales.

Was this how her life would be in the future? Devoid of any true friendship now that she had spurned Ardan? She shivered as she wrapped her arms around her middle. Did she truly want to spurn him?

At the sound of footsteps, she fought hope and glanced up. Her weak smile and defeated posture heralded her disappointment as Seamus approached. "Hello."

"Mrs. Finnegan," he said with a deferential nod. "I suppose I should call you Mrs. Fiske, but I'm too used to calling you Mrs. Finnegan. Besides, 'tis a proper Irish name." He winked at her, frowning when he saw his teasing provoked tears rather than a smile. "Are you all right, lass?"

"I'm fine," she gasped out. "Merely a little tired."

He rocked back on his feet. "I'm sure you are confused as to why my Mary and Maggie didn't come to work lately." He paused. "I also know you had trouble with Silas before Ardan could inform you of the reason he had come to call."

She shook her head in confusion. "I don't understand."

"We decided, as a family at that night's supper some evenings ago, that you are to own the café. Not the O'Rourkes. You do all the hard work. Thus it should be yours. And you should hire as you deem fit."

She stood from the stoop, nearly tumbling down the steps in her haste to rise. "What? You can't just gift me something of such value. It's … It's …" She shook her head as she attempted to catch her breath.

"'Tis yours, Deirdre, as it always should have been." He caressed her arm. "If you'd like Maggie an' Mary to continue to work for you, please send word. I think they've missed havin' a purpose these past few days." He winked at her, as she continued to gape at him. "Good night, lass."

She stared in dumbfounded confusion, as he strolled away from her. How had they managed to turn her world upside down again?

T he following morning, Niamh arrived to work at the café with faltering, halting steps. Deirdre watched her with concern but was hesitant to pry into her personal life. She ducked her head. She knew she had no right to inquire into another's life when she was reluctant to examine her own. However, when Niamh whimpered as she attempted to lift a pot to carry to the sink, Deirdre stilled her baking.

"Niamh?" she asked. "Are you all right?"

"Aye," she said. "I fear I'm comin' down with what ailed wee Maura."

Deirdre approached her, holding the back of her hand out, as though to touch it to Niamh's forehead to check for fever. Niamh flinched away, backing into the countertops and then yelped in pain when her hips hit the hard wood. "Niamh," Deirdre whispered, her eyes widened in shock. "Who are you afraid of?"

Shivering, Niamh stood staring into space, a wild, terrified look in her eyes. "I'm afraid of no one."

Deirdre made a soothing sound as she approached Niamh, softly stroking a hand over Niamh's arm. "Of course not. You're a strong woman." She broke off what else she would have said when Niamh gripped her arm in a fierce clasp.

"Promise me you won't say a word to anyone in my family." Her hazel eyes bore into Deirdre's, her jaw firming at the evident hesitation in Deirdre's gaze. "Promise me."

Deirdre nodded. "I promise. But the man who hurt you should suffer consequences for what he did."

Niamh's eyes filled, and she shook her head. "Connor—Cormac," she broke off what more she would have said when the back door opened. She spun to the sink to wash dishes.

Her mind spinning with uncertainty, Deirdre turned to smile impersonally at Declan. "Hello. How might I help you?"

"I'm leavin' soon for Cow Island and then on to Saint Louis. I wanted to ensure I had the list of supplies you'll need for next year. Have you thought of anything else you'll need?"

Deirdre held a hand to her forehead and stared at the butcher block top for a long moment. "I'm uncertain."

"'Tis all right. You have a few days." He looked at Niamh, who had yet to turn around to acknowledge him, and then to her. "Good day, missus."

Deirdre sat on her stool, her work forgotten, while Niamh sniffled at the sink, and Deirdre's head spun with all that had been revealed that morning.

A rdan poked his head into his father's office, letting out a sigh of relief to find his father seated behind his desk. However, rather than working on last-minute details for his sons' impending trip to Saint Louis, Seamus sat staring in space, with a mutinous expression. "Da?"

"Ardan," Seamus murmured, failing in his attempt to smile in a soothing manner.

"What troubles you?" He sat, although he did not relax. A tension coiled through him, as though preparing him for battle at any moment.

"I've deluded myself into believin' I took good care of my children." At Ardan's instinctual attempt to contradict him, Seamus waved away his protestations. "I failed Niamh, Ardan."

"Da," Ardan whispered. "None of us could stop her once she met Connor. 'Twas like he cast a magic spell over her, and she couldn't do anything but his bidding."

Seamus rose and paced to the window behind his desk. He slammed his hand against the windowsill. "'Tisn't love, Ardan." He turned and saw his son nod. He sat on the window ledge and held his head in his hands. "Wee Maura's been ill. You know how much I adore her." His contented smile was short-lived. "I went to Niamh's house two nights ago. To bring her stew Mary made."

Ardan frowned, as his father paused. "I know this, Da. You came back upset because you feared Niamh was catchin' what Maura had."

Seamus shook his head. "No. 'Tis what I told your mother. May God forgive me, but I lied to my Mary."

"Why?" Ardan asked, canting so far forward in his chair he risked falling out of it.

His da stared at him with a bleak look in his eyes. "I stared in through the window, as I watched my Niamh sob on the floor. Begging that worthless beggar Connor to love her. To care for her, as he had promised on the steamboat." Seamus closed his eyes. "An' I realized I had failed her. She saw Colleen, beggin' me, an' thought that was how it should be between husband and wife."

"Da," Ardan breathed.

"I'd hoped, now that Mary's back, Niamh would remember." His voice caught. "Remember the time before we lost your mum."

Ardan rose, taking his father by the shoulders. He squeezed them to reassure him. "She does, Da. She was ten. She remembers Mum. She remembers how it was between you." He shook his head and then shrugged. "For some reason, she doesn't believe she has the right to such joy."

"Ah, lad, I don't know what to do to help her."

Ardan sighed. "Support her so she knows, no matter what, that she always has your love."

Seamus focused on his eldest and smiled his thanks. "Ah, my brave, strong lad, how are you?"

Ardan attempted a smile, before he suddenly fought a sob. "I don't know what to do, Da. I can't remain in this town. Waitin' for a day that will never come." He turned away and sniffed, as he swiped at his eyes. His head was bowed as he faced the rear of the office. With shaking shoulders he attempted to corral his strong emotions. After a moment, he blurted out, "I think I should travel with Declan. I must leave."

Seamus's breath hitched. "Four of you to leave?"

Ardan turned to stare at his father, his gaze filled with desolation. "If I go, there's no need for Eamon and Finn to travel too."

Rolling his eyes, Seamus let out a snort. "Try tellin' that to the lads. 'Tis all they can talk about. The adventures they'll have. Declan's on the verge of tellin' me that he has no desire to go, as he doesn't want to be stuck with the twins for months on end."

Ardan collapsed into the chair again, his gaze distant and lost. "I don't know what to do, Da." He stared at his father with admiration and respect. "I always thought my greatest fear was being left alone, like you were. Like we all were." He paused as he saw the flash of pain in his father's gaze at his words. "But I've come to understand, 'tisn't my true fear."

When he paused for a long time, Seamus murmured, "What is?"

"Loving and not being loved in equal measure." He closed his eyes. "'Tis a special form of hell."

"Oh, lad," Seamus whispered. Crouching in front of his eldest son, Seamus was reminded of all the times he had soothed his children. And he gave thanks they still sought him out for his counsel and love. "Don't run away from your heart's desire, my lad. You'll only regret it if you do."

Ardan fell forward, into his father's arms, the strength of his emotions far more powerful than any control he attempted to exert. He clung to his father as though a boy, thankful for his father's constancy.

After a quieter-than-usual evening at the café, Deirdre stood in her kitchen, staring at her back door, as though willing Ardan to walk through it. However, the door remained closed, and no O'Rourke walked through. Bowing her head, she thought about her current predicament. Although she had always wanted to believe herself a brave woman, she knew many of her decisions had been borne out of desperation. Due to the generosity of the O'Rourkes, she had the chance to never have to live that way again.

With the soothing scents of baked bread and coffee, she closed her eyes, as a vision of her dream future appeared. She stood, smiling and laughing in the kitchen, as Ardan served customers in the café, while his mother and sisters helped her in the kitchen. Children's joyful voices could be heard playing outside, and her heart skipped a beat, as the ferocious desire overwhelmed her for another child. For another chance.

She gripped the butcher block, her eyes squeezed shut, reluctant to disturb her dream. For, if she didn't take a chance, would it ever be her reality?

The slamming of the back door jerked her out of her reverie, and she stared with a bleary gaze at the woman watching her with amused understanding. "Why are you here?" she whispered.

"I worry you have less sense than before you left for the stagecoach accident." After a pause, she held out her hand. "I'm Madam Nora, and business owners should introduce themselves and get to know each other. I failed to introduce myself properly to you before you left on Bailey's stagecoach." Tonight, Nora wore a brilliant green dress in a shiny satin that appeared to sparkle in the kitchen light. Her brown hair softly framed her face, held back by tortoiseshell combs, while her brown eyes held a stark inquisitiveness.

Deirdre shook her hand, nodding in confusion. "I agree, although I'm uncertain I should associate with you."

Nora shrugged. "I wouldn't worry about the O'Rourkes. They are generous with their friendship and affection. Besides, Aileen has become a close friend, as she aids my girls."

Deirdre nodded dumbly, staring at Nora again with abject uncertainty. "Would you like supper? A cup of something?"

Waving her hand at the offer, Nora smiled. "You are too kind. I have a decent cook, although I wouldn't mind convincing your helper, Niamh, to work for me. I had thought her talents lay in another area, but I can see I was wrong." When Deirdre continued to gape at her, Nora laughed. "She's a fine seamstress herself."

"Oh," Deirdre said, her shoulders relaxing. "I ... was uncertain what you meant."

Nora raised her eyebrows in a sardonic manner, indicating she knew exactly what Deirdre had suspected. "Tell me, Deirdre. Do you care for the man, or was it mere friendship for you?" At the deafening silence, she continued. "Or was it all a game?"

"I don't know why you would presume to speak to me in such a manner." She stood tall, and any curiosity or burgeoning friendliness was hidden behind an aloof wall of propriety.

"I presume so because I count the O'Rourkes as friends. I know you've broken a good man's heart. His spirit." Nora frowned, as though perplexed. "Which makes no sense. I thought you were a woman able to distinguish between a charlatan and a gem. I never like admitting I was wrong." She stared at Deirdre, who seemed to deflate in front of her, before collapsing onto a stool.

"Why should you care what happens in my life?"

Nora smiled. "I was like you once. Scared and alone, with too many around me attempting to take advantage of me or giving me wrong advice." She paused as the shadow of regret crossed her features. "I had the opportunity to choose differently, and I didn't. I'd hate for you to make a similar mistake."

Deirdre raised an eyebrow, as though mocking the Madam in a subtle manner. "I have a café, Madam Nora, not a brothel."

Nora stiffened. "How sad that you cannot see past the occupation to the person, as the O'Rourkes have." She turned toward the back door, pausing with her hand on the door handle. "I hope you do not live a life filled with regret. Especially as Ardan O'Rourke has made plans to leave Fort Benton for Saint Louis." She looked over her shoulder to meet Deirdre's devastated gaze. "And there is uncertainty if he'll ever return."

Deirdre sat rooted in place as she watched the Madam leave. How was she to live here without Ardan?

Ardan sat in the warehouse, eschewing joining his family for dinner. He had no desire to sit around the table and to force a gaiety he didn't feel. He lowered his head, considering his conversation with Da. Although Ardan understood his father's point of view—to stay and to continue to fight for the woman he loved—Ardan did not know how he could remain in Fort Benton, when she wanted little to do with him.

For the past few days, the running of the café had been her endeavor. From what he had gleaned from listening to his family's dinner conversations, she appeared to relish the challenge. "*Eejit,*" he muttered to himself. He rubbed at his temples, cursing himself for being a fool. Now that she had everything she wanted, why would she desire him?

He rose to answer the knock at the rear door. Few men in town needed supplies, but his father had raised him to always be a good businessman. He pasted on a friendly expression as he opened the door. "Deirdre?" he asked, as he saw her gasping for breath, a wild gaze in her eyes. "Who hurt you, lass?"

"You did!" she cried out. "How could you, Ardan?"

He shook his head in confusion, pulling her inside. "You're not making any sense." He grunted when she pelted him in his chest as he said that. He grabbed her hands, holding them gently in his, as he studied her tormented expression. "Deir, what is it?"

"You're leaving me. Just like I knew you would." Her shoulders stooped forward, and she curled into herself as a sob burst forth.

Murmuring soft words of nothing into her ear, he pulled her close. He breathed in her light lilac scent, both a temptation and a tease at the same time. "All will be well," he whispered.

"How?" she stammered out. She wiggled until she had freed herself of his embrace and swiped at her wet cheeks. "How am I to live in this town without you?" When he stared at her in wonder, she took in a stuttering breath. "The past few days have been wretched enough. I can't imagine weeks and months."

"*Wretched?*" he whispered, his brilliant blue eyes lighting with hope.

"Horrible," she said, as she hiccupped. Her cheek moved into his hand as he caressed her skin. "Every night I've waited for you. Needed you to hold me in your arms."

"I thought you didn't want me anymore," he whispered.

"I was a fool." She took a step closer, her eyes shining with sincerity. "I thought what I feared most was what I had already lost." She shook her head at her daft notion. "I hadn't realized what my life would be like devoid of your company." She closed her eyes. "I'm so ashamed."

"Why, Deirdre?" he whispered.

"I made you believe I didn't want you. That I wanted a business more than I wanted you." She took a deep breath. "I don't want it," she proclaimed. "I'll speak to your father tomorrow, but I don't want the café."

His eyes bulged at her declaration. "Deirdre, no," he rasped. "I wanted you to have it. Please, don't turn your back on your dream."

Tears streamed down her cheek, as she took another step toward him, bridging the final step that separated them. "Don't you understand? That dream means nothing if you aren't there with me?" She stared for a long moment into his eyes. "May I share my genuine dream with you now?"

He nodded, too overcome by strong emotions to speak.

She closed her eyes, as though bringing her vision into focus. A contented smile spread, and she sighed. "I work in the kitchen, baking with your mother and sisters when we are busy. Running the kitchen alone during the slow season. Through it all, you are there. Talking and cajoling our customers. Slipping your arms around my waist in an encouraging embrace, when you come to tell me of an order or for a break. At night, we have dinner with your family and then return to our home above the café. There's laughter and joy and an abundance of love." She opened her eyes, unable to hide the yearning within. "That's what I desire."

"Is that what you had with Alonzo?" he asked.

She shrugged. "Partially. He was a good man. But he never would have carried me to the privy every day for a week, as you did. He never would have done the dishes. That would have been beneath him." She flushed, as though she had been disloyal to her first husband.

"Why, Deirdre?" he asked in a passionate voice. "Why do you want such a life with me?" He bent forward until their foreheads were almost touching, and his hand cupped the side of her neck.

"I love you, Ardan. I can't imagine a life without you in it. Please, don't leave me alone."

He yanked her into his arms at her declaration, his strong hands caressing her back. He shuddered, as though overwhelmed by her words. "Oh, my darling, how I love you. I'll never leave you alone. I promise."

He pulled back, lowering his head. His warm breath provoked a shudder as he kissed the side of her neck. Soon he had kissed his way from her neck to her forehead and then to her cheeks. His fingers traced patterns over the soft skin exposed above her collarbone, and he smiled as she gasped at the gentle touch.

"Kiss me, Ardan," she begged as she arched back.

"I am," he teased. Before she could protest, he kissed her softly on her lips. Soon the kiss deepened, and he pulled her tighter into his embrace. His hands tangled in her hair, freeing it of its pins, while her hands raced over him, eliciting shivers of her own.

After many minutes, he raised his head and pulled her with him to sit on his lap as he collapsed on a crate. "Let me hold you, *a stoirín*," he murmured. "For you are my treasure."

After their breaths had calmed, he murmured, "Will you marry me, Deirdre? Will you allow me to make your vision a reality?"

She raised her gaze, her cognac-colored eyes watery as she met his gaze. "Yes." She sighed, as he kissed her again. "Yes, my love. I will marry you."

"Oh, love, we will have the most wondrous life." He tensed, although his hands continued to caress her in a reassuring manner.

"What is it, Ardan?" she whispered.

"Will you be upset if we have children?" he asked. When she stared in wonder at him, he ran a finger over her cheek. "My dream of our future would have children in the kitchen with you, as you teach them how to cook." He fought to hide disappointment in his gaze as she gaped at him. "Forget I said anything."

"No!" she said, as she held his head in her hands, her fingers caressing his soft beard. "No, my Ardan. Of course I want children with you." She closed her eyes. "It's a dream I never allowed myself to dare to have. I've always feared I was tempting fate by wanting too much. For, if I had you, why should I want more?"

"Oh, my love," he whispered as he kissed her soundly. "I want to be by your side, as I help make every one of your dreams come true."

She beamed at him. "You will, Ardan. As I will yours. We will have a marvelous life."

CHAPTER 11

The following morning, Mary arrived at the café without Maggie. Niamh had yet to arrive; thus they worked alone as they prepared food for the midday meal. During the customary midmorning lull, Deirdre sat, staring in space, as she held a cup of tea in her hands. However, she did not sip from it, nor did she sing or chat with Mary. A half-finished cake batter and bread to be kneaded stood nearby, but she remained lost to her daydream.

"Whatever has you mesmerized, I hope it brings you joy," Mary murmured, as she watched Deirdre with concern.

Deirdre jumped at Mary's words, spilling a few drops of tea and focusing on her friend. "Oh, I'd forgotten you were here." She blushed as she belatedly heard what Mary had said. "And it does."

"Good." Mary smiled with pleasure, as she returned to the stew, which she had prepared for the midday meal. "I saw Ardan this morning, and the black cloud hangin' over him seems to have disappeared."

Deirdre's flush brightened. "We reconciled last night." She beamed at Mary, as the older woman stepped away from the stove to fully focus on her. Mary pulled out a stool and sat, waiting with patient acceptance as Deirdre collected her thoughts. "I spoke with the Madam."

Mary sobered. "Again?" Her fingers rubbed at the countertop. "Why did she interfere again?"

Deirdre shrugged. "I think she genuinely likes our family. And I could never blame her for yearning for what we have." She flushed at including herself as part of the O'Rourke family. When Mary merely nodded, as though her comment made perfect sense and took no objection to Deirdre's statement, Deirdre relaxed. "I'll always be thankful to her. Even if we aren't destined to be friends."

Mary sighed. "I've been hesitant to call on her. First, she's a Madam, and 'tisn't proper to associate with women like that." She paused and shook her head. "But Seamus liked her. Found her to be a wise woman and sought out her counsel before I returned." She paused, sharing a chagrined look with Deirdre.

Deirdre smiled reassuringly. "You never have to worry that Mr. O'Rourke will look to anyone but you for wisdom or support." She watched with wonder as Mary relaxed, her faith in her husband complete.

"Nay," Mary murmured, a small smile playing around her lips. "And Seamus assures me that she treats her girls well." She shuddered. "I couldn't imagine such a life."

"Nor I," Deirdre whispered. "The Madam informed me that Ardan was to travel with Declan. And challenged me to be brave." She smiled. "I realized what my fear was costing me. My dream of a future with a man I love."

She laughed as Mary launched herself from her stool and pulled her into a tight hug. "Oh, please tell me that you told Ardan that." Mary backed away, her hazel eyes sparkling with hope. At Deirdre's nod, Mary gave a girly squeal of glee and pulled Deirdre close again. "Oh, you'll be a daughter in truth, rather than merely a daughter of my heart," Mary breathed.

A sob burst forth, and Deirdre clung to Mary. Unable to speak, her hands dug into Mary's back.

"Oh, sweet girl," Mary crooned. "You've a family now. You've had one for some time, but I know it takes a while for the reality of such a drastic change to seem real." She continued to murmur reassuring words to Deirdre, easing away as Deirdre's sobs abated. Smiling at her, she swiped at her cheek. "Feel better?"

Deirdre nodded but ducked her head in embarrassment. "I don't know what happened."

*Tsk*ing, Mary handed her a clean handkerchief and sat again on a nearby stool. "If anyone understands how overwhelming it can be to find a family, 'tis I." She shrugged. "Or any of us O'Rourkes." She made a waving motion with her hands. "In one day, my children went from seven to one. Then, in another single day, from three children to twelve!" She gave a wondrous laugh. "An' now I have two more daughters to love. Never doubt. I understand a great deal of what you're feeling, darling Deirdre."

A wondrous smile spread as Deirdre sat in awestruck silence. "He wants to marry me. And hopes to have children with me." She swiped at a lone tear that tracked down her cheek. "We'll have family to love and to cherish us." She shook her head, as though it were almost too much to comprehend.

Mary rose, cupping her cheek. "Seamus prays nightly for our lads to marry good Irish lasses who bring them joy. While I pray for that too, I also have another prayer." She paused a moment. "I pray that whoever marries my children also loves our family. For I could never bear to be parted from any of them. Thank you for understanding our closeness, Deirdre."

Deirdre leaned into Mary for another hug, saying a silent thanks for her second chance at love and a family.

Deirdre leaned on an elbow, her head cocked toward the door, as she heard a soft tapping at the entrance to her upstairs rooms. She had locked the door again, as Ardan hadn't visited her in the evening since the arrival of Silas. When the tapping occurred again but louder, she pulled on a robe and tiptoed to the door.

"Deirdre?" Ardan called out. "Will you let me in?"

Gasping with surprise as an exhilarant joy filled her, she pushed over the bolt and yanked the door open. "Ardan," she breathed. He stood in shadows, but his eyes acted as a beacon. Flinging herself in his arms, she pressed herself against him, wrapping her arms around him like a vine. "Hold me and never let me go," she whispered.

He chuckled and kissed her head. "I'll have to if I'm to sleep beside you, love," he teased. "Come. 'Tis late, and you need your rest." He shuddered as she kissed the underside of his jaw. "Deirdre, no, we should—" He gasped as her hands roved over him.

"We should rejoice that we are together. That we will be together forever." She cradled his face in her hands, her fingers playing in his trimmed beard. "Celebrate with me."

"Oh, love," he breathed. "I thought you'd want to wait for the wedding." He shucked his jacket, grinning down at her as she slipped his shirt buttons lose. He shuddered again as her hands ran over his muscled chest, her fingers playing through the black hair there. "I feel like I've dreamed of you forever."

She kissed his shoulder. "What do you mean?"

"I never allowed myself to believe I could have a marriage like my parents'. A woman to love, who loved me." He sighed with pleasure as she again kissed the underside of his jaw. "From the moment I started helping you here in the café, I couldn't fight the vision of us here. Building our life together."

She paused to stare at him in wonder. "Just like mine?"

He nodded, his smile widening. "Yes." Unable to prevent himself from touching her, he yanked her against his chest, cradling her for a long moment before his nimble fingers worked on the buttons of her robe. "I've wanted you from the moment I kissed you." He shook his head. "From long before then. From the moment I saw you in the café window the day we met."

When her robe pooled around her feet, his breath caught. "I need to see you in the light." They shuffled backward as they peppered each other with kisses. She giggled as he tripped over a side table before grunting as he backed her into the doorjamb.

"A walk that should take seconds is taking minutes," he rasped, as he continued to scatter kisses over her collarbone.

"I'm not complaining." She giggled again as he stumbled upon entering her room. With hope, uncertainty, and vulnerability shining in her eyes, she spread her arms wide, standing in her nightgown.

He approached her with a reverent solemnity, his gaze ablaze with longing, love, and devotion. "If you want to lie on the bed with me holding you in my arms, I will not complain. 'Tis more than I hoped would ever occur again." He paused as he saw the momentary flash of shame in her gaze. "What did I say?"

Deirdre ducked her head, her arms falling as she held them over her chest and belly, then curled inward. "I'm sorry you don't find me pleasing."

"For the love of …" Ardan crossed the short space separating them and clasped her face between his palms, tilting her face up to meet his ardent gaze. "You are the most beautiful woman I have ever seen. The sight of you in your nightgown, smiling at me?" He shook his head as his eyes glowed. He leaned forward until their foreheads touched. "I want to honor you. To cherish you. And, if you want to wait until we are wed, I want to give you that chance."

"No," she whispered. "I want you, Ardan. Now and forever." She kissed him. "Make me believe what you say." She paused. "Touch me. Bring me alive."

He picked her up, settling her on her bed. "With pleasure, *a stoirín.*"

Deirdre rested with her head on Ardan's shoulder. His hands continued to wander over her back, caressing and tracing lines over her soft skin. She relaxed into his touch, unable to prevent a soft moan of pleasure. "I beg your pardon," she whispered, becoming as rigid as a board before attempting to push herself free of his embrace.

"What's the matter, love?" Ardan murmured, kissing her softly and never ceasing his soft touch. "Hearing that you enjoy being in my arms brings me joy."

"It's unseemly," she gasped.

He laughed, the sound reverberating in her ear as it was settled on his chest. "No more than what we just did." He eased away so he could brush at her loose hair and stare into her chagrined gaze. "Never feel embarrassed to show me what you enjoy. Or the pleasure you feel." He kissed her. "I'd hate if it were all one-sided."

She smiled, cupping his face. "You know it wasn't that."

Kissing her nose, he whispered, "I hoped it wasn't, but a man likes reassurances too." He sighed as her fingers played through his hair. "I love holding you like this. Knowing that I can and that, in a few days, I won't have to sneak in after the townsfolk have left."

"A few days?" She watched him with wide-eyed shock.

"Aye, the priest will soon leave to winter in Virginia City or Helena, and I don't want to wait until he returns. I want his blessing." He paused as she continued to stare at him. "Or would you prefer to wait?"

Her hands tightened on his shoulder. "No! Not at all. It's all happening so fast. Yesterday I feared I would never be held in your arms again, and now we plan to marry in a few days." She gave him a smile meant to mollify him.

"Aye, 'tis fast. But I know we'll never regret it, love."

"No, we won't." She said. "However, until we are married, I believe you should continue to spend your nights at your parents' house." Her smile broadened at the disappointment in his gaze. "Starting tomorrow," she whispered, as she leaned forward to kiss him, losing herself to their passion again.

The following evening, Ardan watched the back door of his family's home, as he waited for Deirdre to arrive to share a meal with all the O'Rourkes, before three of his brothers headed south. With no more steamboats expected to arrive in the Territory this season, there would be no further influx of men clamoring for her delicious food. However, enough townsfolk were in need of a decent meal for the café to remain open during the off-season, although

Ardan wondered if she shouldn't focus on one meal a day during the slow period.

He watched as Declan stood beside Eamon and Finn, attempting to join their laughing and cajoling. In that moment, Ardan realized how challenging the next months would be for Declan: always with family but never feeling as though truly part of the group.

While Kevin stood in a corner of the room, flirting with Aileen, Ardan approached Declan and slapped him on his arm. "Are you ready, lad?" he asked, unable to hide the worry in his gaze. This would be the longest stretch of time his younger brothers would be separated from the family.

"Of course I am. I'll be as successful as you and Kevin." Declan lifted his chin in defiance, as he stared at both his older brothers, daring Ardan to contradict him.

"'Tisn't what I meant," Ardan muttered. "You'll be with the young *eejits,* and I fear they'll get into mischief. You'll have no one guarding your back, as I had Kevin." He sighed but couldn't hide a relieved smile. "If things hadn't worked out between Deirdre and me, I would have traveled with you."

Declan laughed and slung an arm over his shoulder. "You know I would never have wanted you to leave your ladylove." He nodded toward the back door. "Besides, she's mad for you."

Ardan looked toward the door, unable to hide the broad smile, nor the joy lighting his gaze at her entrance. "Aye, she is. As I am for her."

"You're a lucky man, Ard." Declan squeezed his shoulder.

Watching his younger brother with an amused smile, he asked, "Have you no desire for a mail order bride?"

Declan shrugged. "Perhaps. It seems unlikely to me that I'll ever find what you and Kevin have." He looked at Kevin canoodling with Aileen and bit back a sigh. "Seems more like a dream to me."

Ardan focused on his brother, his eyes shining bright with sincerity. "I will continue to pray you find someone who makes your heart leap, as Deirdre does mine. That you discover it doesn't have to be a dream." He paused. "And that you're brave enough to leap at the chance to love."

"I'm sorry I'll miss your wedding," Declan said.

Ardan nodded. "Aye, it can't be helped. We were fools an' took too long to reconcile." He smiled at his brother. "I expect you home in time for the first christening."

Declan laughed and slapped his brother on his back. "Never fear. I'll have no desire to remain in a large city. I've had enough of those."

Squeezing Declan's shoulder, Ardan said, "Stay safe. I couldn't imagine this world without you."

Ardan and Declan embraced for a moment, before others crowded around the soon-to-depart brother. Ardan left Declan to deflect the curious questions from *the pack*, the new nickname given to the expanded group of younger brothers. Unable and unwilling to hide his delighted smile, he approached Deirdre, lifting her hand to kiss it. "Hello, love."

Her eyes glowed with adoration, and she leaned into him, wrapping her arms around him. "It's only been a few hours since I saw you, but I missed you."

He chuckled and kissed her head. "The day finished well?"

"Yes," she murmured. "Not nearly as busy as last month." She breathed in deeply of his cologne and the subtle scent that was all Ardan.

He eased away, bracketing her face with his palms. "I spoke with the priest. In three days, he'll marry us. He wants to have all his business here finished by the time Dunmore returns from Cow Island and does another run to Virginia City."

"Good," she whispered. "I dread the nights without you by my side."

Two mornings later, on the day before her wedding, Deirdre slipped out of the café early, approaching the men boarding one of the last stagecoaches to make the trip to Cow Island this season. Dunmore had left the day before with Declan, Eamon, and Finn. Today Bailey would leave with a borrowed stage. She approached her brother-in-law and paused as she saw Silas stiffen as she neared. "Silas."

"I can only imagine you came here today to crow at your ability to deceive an honest man into becoming a bigamist," he snapped. He wore a perfectly tailored suit, and he watched to ensure his trunk was loaded onto the back of the stagecoach. When he was assured his belongings had been strapped on, he faced her again. "Why are you here?"

A sense of calm enveloped her, and she smiled at Silas. "I'm here because I know, deep inside, you lie. Why won't you tell me the truth about Alonzo?"

He smirked at her. "If you know the truth, why is it important to hear it from me?" He gripped her arm, frowning when she did not flinch at his tight hold of her arm. "Why?"

"Have you ever loved anyone, other than yourself, Silas?" she asked. "Do you have any idea what your announcement did to me? Did to Ardan?" She took a calming breath, as she feared she would express more emotion than she desired to share with her soulless brother-in-law.

"You only wanted money," Silas jeered. "Just like now. You arrived in this town, and miraculously the eldest son of the most successful businessman fell in love with you. It's not a coincidence, Deirdre."

She leaned forward and whispered, "You remain bitter that I never loved you."

He flushed with agitation.

"Tell me the truth about my husband, Silas." She stared at him with impassioned determination.

"Of course he's dead. He was dead long before you ever received the notice!" He snapped and then swore under his breath at the startling veracity to his words.

Deirdre backed away from him, her gaze filled with relief and sadness. "I knew." She placed a hand over her chest. "Deep inside, I knew I'd lost him." She blinked away tears. "Safe travels, Silas. I know we shall never meet again."

She backed away until she stood beside the boardwalk near the hotel, relieved when Bailey signaled it was time for passengers to board or to miss their chance for a ride. A movement to her right caused her to glance in that direction, and she relaxed. "How long have you been here?" she asked Ardan, who moved to enfold her in his arms.

"Almost from the moment you arrived to speak with him." He kissed her head and held her close. "Why not have one of us come with you? If you didn't want me here, my da or one of my brothers would have come with you."

She pressed farther into his embrace. "I know," she whispered. "It was something I needed to do on my own. To prove I can continue to be brave." Turning her head, she watched as the stagecoach rolled into motion. They stood in silence as it disappeared down the street, before turning to head out of town and up the winding road, carved into the side of the bluff, that led to the primitive road to Cow Island.

"What did you learn, love?" he whispered into her ear.

"As I knew, deep in my heart, Alonzo is dead. Silas wanted me." She clung to Ardan a little tighter. "I don't know why. Perhaps because I was Alonzo's, and he always resented anything Alonzo had that he didn't. In the end, it doesn't matter."

He kissed her head again, the tension leaving him. "No, all that matters is he told you the truth. And he left."

"Yes," she whispered, leaning back so she could meet Ardan's adoring gaze. "And that tomorrow we marry." She met his answering smile with one filled with the promise of an abundance of joyful tomorrows, sighing with pleasure as he kissed her softly as dawn's early rays lit the town.

CHAPTER 12

Deirdre stood upstairs in the room that she would soon permanently share with Ardan and ran a hand down the cream-colored dress Aileen had sewn for her. There was little adornment except for the row of buttons down the back of the dress. Although simple, it fit her perfectly, and she felt like one of the fairy princesses she had learned about from Finn, when they sat around telling stories one evening.

"Oh, look at you," Mary breathed, as she bustled into the room. "If you aren't the most beautiful woman to meet her groom."

Maggie rolled her eyes and laughed. "You say that every time you see a bride."

Mary nodded, unapologetic in her praise. "An' 'tis true. Every bride is beautiful." She gave Aileen a squeeze. "Look at your beautiful work."

Smiling with pride at the dress, she nodded. "Yes, it's lovely, but nothing compared to what Niamh can create." She looked at Deirdre. "You should have seen the intricate embroidery Niamh placed on my dress." She sighed with pleasure.

"Where is Niamh?" Deirdre asked.

Mary shuffled her feet, appearing momentarily uncomfortable. "I'm uncertain. I fear Maura's fussy again."

Deirdre froze, afraid for a moment what that meant but then forced herself to focus on her wedding day. "As long as she is at the wedding." At Mary's brisk nod, Deirdre relaxed. "Are all the townsfolk invited?"

"All except my aunt," Aileen said. "She's never welcome."

Turning to face the women who would soon be her family in fact rather than only in her heart, Deirdre smiled. "Even if she were to appear today, nothing could diminish my joy." After a few more moments where the O'Rourke women fussed with her lace veil, Deirdre followed Mary down the stairs.

In the distant field, she saw a small crowd, and her heart skipped a beat. Today she would marry Ardan. The man she loved. How was she this fortunate? She gave a small giggle of glee and picked up her skirts as though she were to race to him.

"No, Deirdre," Maggie said, holding on to her arm. "Remember what happened the last time you raced through the field? Don't ruin your wedding night." Maggie flushed at her mother's admonishment but winked at Deirdre.

"You're right, Maggie," Deirdre said with a chuckle, slowing her pace and walking with the outward appearance of far more patience than she truly had. Her breath caught at the sight of Ardan, in a formal black suit with a starched white shirt. His beard had been trimmed, but she was thankful he had not shaved it off.

Seamus approached, winging out his arm to lead her forward. "Ready, lass?" At her nod, they started the slow march up the aisle.

Standing beside Ardan, her fingertips played with his, and she fought a shiver at the emotions his soft touch evoked. Although she tried to focus on the priest's solemn words, all she could hear was Ardan. Ardan proclaiming his love of her. His devotion. She took a deep breath, and her senses were filled with the soft scent of his cologne mingled with trampled prairie grass. Standing beside him, but not touching him, was a torment. All she wanted to do was lean into him, be in his arms.

When Ardan squeezed her hand, she jumped. "What?" she whispered.

Chuckling, Ardan nodded toward the priest. "Repeat after Father Mac," he murmured.

Flushing, Deirdre realized she had missed her first cue for her vows. She concentrated on what the priest said, repeating in a loud, precise voice every word he said. She flushed as she realized she'd missed Ardan repeating his vows. When he slipped on his ring for her, she met his amused gaze.

"I love you," she whispered, smiling as her words provoked a flash of deep pleasure in his beautiful eyes.

After he motioned for her to pay attention to the priest for the final blessing, she sighed with relief that he would finally kiss her. However, it was a short kiss, and he soon led her down the aisle.

"Why the sad face?" he asked, when they reached the small area near his parents' house, set up for the festivities.

"I hoped for a longer kiss."

"Those are for us, Deirdre," he said, as he traced a finger down her cheek. With a sigh, he turned to face the many guests walking the short distance to congratulate them. "Soon, love. Soon."

"I'll keep you to your promise." At his chuckle, she laughed and leaned into his side. A place she knew she always wanted to be.

Ardan stood beside Deirdre, beaming and laughing as friends and family congratulated them. Although he continued to smile, he stiffened as Niamh approached. Rather than pulling her into a hug, as he would have customarily done, he stood beside Deirdre, waiting to see what Niamh would do.

"Ardan," Niamh whispered, beseeching forgiveness in her gaze. "Deirdre," she said around a throat-clogged tear when Ardan remained quiet. "I wish you both so very happy." She nodded and then walked away.

Ardan took a step in her direction before forcing himself to remain beside Deirdre.

"Speak with her, Ardan," Deirdre urged. "I understand."

"No," Ardan said with a reassuring smile. "Today is not a day for discord. I'll speak with Niamh when the time is right." His gaze tracked his sister, frowning to see her avoid Cormac, a man she had always liked. "I don't understand what is occurrin' in her life."

"Nor do I, but I fear she is dreadfully unhappy," Deirdre murmured. "One day, soon, we will learn more."

As another man approached to congratulate them, Ardan stiffened, his arm beneath Deirdre's hold taut. He was nearly Ardan's height, with broad shoulders, blond hair, and bloodshot brown eyes. "Connor," he said. "I just had the pleasure of speaking with Niamh." At Connor's blank stare, he snapped, "Your wife."

"I'm glad you found something pleasurable with Niamh." Connor spoke with slightly slurred words and nearly toppled headfirst to the ground in front of them when he tried to bow deferentially. "I should think the true pleasure would be found in your father's fine whiskey."

Ardan clamped his jaw closed so tightly that the muscles ticked. "Leave, Connor. No one wishes you here."

Connor shrugged and then clapped Ardan on the shoulder before leering at Deirdre. "I hope you made a wiser choice than I did." He stumbled away, making a wide berth to avoid both his wife and his brother.

Ardan relaxed as Connor melted into the crowd, quickly escorted away by Kevin and Niall. "Come, love. Dance with me. We've spoken to enough people. I want to hold you in my arms, before we speak with anyone else."

Seamus coaxed Mary onto the dance floor of crushed grass, easing her into his arms as the sweet sounds of one of their favorite songs floated on the breeze. Niall had learned the fiddle from Eamon and had learned all the songs from Ireland. The celebration today had helped to diminish a small amount of the loneliness he and his wife felt, already missing their three sons on the way to Saint Louis. "Do you remember, love?" Seamus asked, as Mary swayed in his arms.

"How could I forget?" she murmured, her arms holding him close. "This is the first song we ever danced to together at the Harvest Dance, all those years ago." She sighed with pleasure, pushing closer to him.

"Ah, love, I'd never forget." His eyes sparkled with love and pride. "An' 'tis grand to see our sons are as romantic as we are." His smile dimmed as he saw Niamh scowling at them. "Niamh's never liked this song."

Mary ran her hands over his back. "'Tis because it reminds her of me. Of the time I was away from all of you." She followed his gaze and gave a soft sound of distress. "She's miserable, but I don't know how to ease her despair."

"Ah, love, all we can do is help her when she desires our aid. Unfortunately she doesn't believe she deserves our help. There isn't much we can do for her until she does."

"Was her husband even at the ceremony?" Mary met her husband's irate gaze.

"Aye, to hear the blessing and then to drink of the fine whiskey. He always manages to appear when there's something better than fire-water to drink." He gave a grunt of disgust. "By now, he'll be in the Sunrise, playing cards."

Mary rested her head on Seamus's shoulder. "Today, let's celebrate Ardan and Deirdre. At least two of our three married children are happy."

"Aye, *a ghrá*, they are," he murmured, as he kissed her temple. "And you are in my arms, dancin' with me again. 'Tis always somethin' to celebrate." He smiled as she giggled and continued to twirl her around the dance floor.

After the townsfolk had returned home, the last public cask of Seamus's whiskey had been imbibed, and the musicians had ceased playing, Ardan led Deirdre to their home over the café. After locking the back door to the kitchen, he led her upstairs. In the cramped hallway in front of the door to what would now be their home, he stared at her and shook his head. "I don't see how I can do this without killin' one or both of us."

She laughed. "Do what, Ardan?" Her smiled widened as she elicited a shiver as she stroked a hand down his back.

"Carry you over the threshold. I fear I'd tumble backward as I hefted you into my arms. An' then we'd both end up on the bottom of the stairs, injured an' unable to enjoy our weddin' night." His eyes gleamed with passionate intensity as he stared at her. "I have many dreams I hope to fulfill with you tonight."

She giggled and pushed open the door. "I love traditions, Ardan, but let's make our own." She clasped his hand and squeezed it. She hopped over the threshold and winked at him. When he did the same, she burst out laughing. "Oh, how I love you," she gasped, as she threw herself into his arms.

He held her close, burying his face in her hair. "An' I you, my darling. You fill my life with laughter and joy, and I wake every mornin', excited to see what the day will bring." He cradled her face with his hands, his thumbs stroking over her cheeks. "Thank you for being brave."

Her eyes filled, and she nodded. "As long as you are by my side, I will have all the courage I need."

He stilled her movement to the bedroom. "I know we said our vows today in front of the priest and our families." He paused as he looked at her. "But I have a few more I must say." He took a deep breath. "I promise to cherish your dreams and to make them my own. I promise to stand by you every day and to never leave you alone, as long as there is breath in my body. I promise to love you forever."

With shimmering eyes, Deirdre's breath caught. "Oh, Ardan. I promise to cherish the family we already have and any family we may be blessed with in the future. I promise to have faith in the future because you are by my side. I promise to love you eternally." She arched onto her toes to kiss him.

Taking one of his hands, she winked at him and led him to their bedroom. "Come, husband. Let's enjoy our wedding night. The townsfolk know the café will be closed tomorrow. We have a little time, just for us."

"I'll follow you anywhere, love."

Do you want to know what is occurring with Niamh? Click here to order her book, Pioneer Yearning, now!

SNEAK PEEK AT PIONEER YEARNING!

Chapter One

Fort Benton, Montana Territory; October 1865

The pouring rain prevented many of the townsfolk from attending the funeral. Anyone related to the deceased man, dedicated to those mourning or foolish enough to otherwise attend stood next to the gaping hole, dripping from the incessant fall deluge. The priest's voice, nearly drowned out by the sound of the downpour pelting hats and the ground, rose as he said his final prayer.

Those gathered looked to the widow, eager for her to get on with it, so they could return to their homes or the saloons.

"Does she want the priest to have more business?" one man muttered, as he stared at the woman standing stock-still as she peered into the yawning hole in front of her.

"Still can't believe Dunmore found a priest so near winter," another murmured.

"No one can deny an O'Rourke," a third grumbled.

Unaware of the murmuring and the speculation around her, Niamh O'Rourke Ahern stared into her husband's grave. She bent, scooping up a handful of mud to sprinkle over his casket. Rather than the priest's final blessing ringing in her ears, she heard the final words her husband had spoken to her, before he had stormed out of their house that fateful night.

Her hand shook as she opened her palm, the mud landing on the casket in a *splat*. Thankful for the rain, it concealed the fact she did not cry for Connor. How could she mourn such a man?

At her father's urging, she turned away from the grave to return to her family home and to her daughter, Maura, ignoring the echo of her husband's words, as though carried on the vicious wind.

I never loved you, you faithless harpy.

~

Cormac Ahern stood beside his brother's grave, long after all the other mourners had departed. Against his will, he had watched Niamh leave, leaning against her father for support, as her brothers hovered around her. He fought anger and rage at all that had transpired.

"Damn you, Connor," he rasped, as he swiped at his face, smearing tears, snot, dirt, and raindrops across his bearded cheeks. "How could you do this to her?" He closed his eyes, as he knew he would have one-sided conversations with his brother for the rest of his life. How was it that his beloved elder brother was dead?

Swaying, he fell to his knees and bowed his head, taking off his hat in deference to his deceased brother. "I shouldn't swear at you. Not on the day of your burial." He slammed his hand onto the packed-down earth. "But how could you?" he asked again, his shoulders shaking with sobs. "We were supposed to go through life together. Fight all our battles together."

He put his hat back on, ignoring the horrible weather. Today he refused to remember the distance that had sprouted up between him and his brother since they had arrived in Fort Benton. The disappointment and the frustration which Cormac had felt in equal measure. Instead he mourned what should have been. What *could* have been.

A hand squeezed his shoulder, and he looked up into the eyes of Ardan O'Rourke, the eldest son of Seamus O'Rourke. "Come, Cormac. You'll give yourself pneumonia, sittin' out here in the rain, an' you know Connor would never want that for you." He took a step back, granting Cormac a few more moments alone beside his older brother's grave.

Finally Cormac stood and faced Ardan. "I can't go to your family's home tonight."

Ardan stood in front of him, as tall as Cormac, although not nearly as brawny. Cormac had earned his strong lean muscles from the hours steering a team of oxen hitched to supply wagons to various destinations throughout the Montana Territory. Ardan knew he could never force Cormac into doing something he didn't want to do. However, Cormac was as loyal to the family as any O'Rourke. "Niamh needs her family around her, Cormac. *All* of her family."

Swearing under his breath, Cormac ducked his head and kicked at a rock, inadvertently pushing it into a puddle. "Fine. I'll come for a few minutes. But then I'm leaving."

Ardan slapped him on his back, letting it rest there to give further solace to Cormac. "You won't want to leave. Not after you taste the fine whiskey Da unearthed."

"I thought we drank all the whiskey last night."

Ardan rubbed at his head with his free hand and shook his head with chagrin. "So did I, Cormac. So did I." He gave a slight tug on Cormac's shoulder, urging him into motion and away from the grave. Murmuring in a soft voice, he said, "You know we'll help with a grave-stone. We'll ensure he's remembered."

Cormac jerked his head in acknowledgment, walking beside Ardan in silence to the large O'Rourke house. Although the two eldest O'Rourke sons, Ardan and Kevin, had married and no longer lived there, and the next three sons—Declan, Eamon, and Finn—were in Saint Louis for the winter, procuring supplies for their business, still the house was always full. Rarely did Ardan, Kevin, and their brides miss a family dinner together. And, since Connor's death, Niamh had moved home too, with her fifteen-month-old daughter, Maura.

Cormac paused at the back entrance of the kitchen, attempting to scrape the mud and the muck off his boots before entering. Crossing the threshold of the kitchen, he saw a makeshift clothes rack near the stove. He shucked his hat and jacket, adding them to the pile of clothes steaming by the range. With a shy smile, he accepted a towel from Mary O'Rourke, the matriarch of the large family. Of middling height, she had a presence about her that commanded the respect of all her family, although a distance remained between her and her daughter, Niamh. Unlike most of her children, Mary had auburn hair, now shot with gray, and her hazel eyes were always filled with compassionate concern.

"Wipe yourself down, lad," she said, as she fussed over him with a worried smile. "Seamus has set out dry clothes for you, if you like." Although she had never taken to Niamh's husband, she had shown an instant affinity for Cormac.

Flushing, Cormac shook his head. "There's no need," he protested, as he ran the towel over his long brown hair. "I shouldn't stay long."

Mary tugged at his arm, urging him into the living room. "You'll stay as long as you like. An', if you want to spend the night, there's room. With too many of my boys away, there's always a bed for you." She squeezed his arm. "Don't allow your grief to turn you into a hermit." She stood on her toes to kiss his cheek and returned to the kitchen and a large pot of soup she was preparing with her youngest daughter, Maggie.

Cormac paused at the entrance of the living room to find the O'Rourke men, standing and chatting in low voices, while the women sat near Niamh in a far corner. Although Niamh's hair was damp, she appeared to have changed into dry clothes, although they were no longer black. The indigo-blue dress enhanced her natural beauty, making her auburn hair shine. He frowned as it also highlighted the circles under her eyes and the desolation in her expression. Kevin's and Ardan's wives, Aileen and Deirdre, sat on either side of the widow.

Cormac forced himself to stop staring at Niamh and to approach the O'Rourke men. He absently noted the priest, warming himself near the potbellied stove, talking with Dunmore, a successful stage-coach driver and friend of the O'Rourkes. Cormac accepted a glass of whiskey from Kevin, the second-eldest brother and husband to Aileen. Ardan stood beside Seamus, their father. Younger brothers, Niall and Lucien, stood tall, as though honored to be included in the group of older men. However, the three youngest boys loitered nearby, although they had begun to fidget. Cormac understood their restlessness. If possible, he'd be outside wandering, rather than cooped up inside, spouting niceties.

Seamus clapped Cormac's arm, and he focused on the men around him. "'Tis a tragedy," Seamus murmured.

Cormac nodded and lowered his head. "Yes. But Connor had lived a wild life for too long. It was only a matter of time ..." He broke off what more he would have said and took a sip of his whiskey.

"We've all had wild times in our lives," Seamus murmured. "'Tis a shock what occurred." Seamus shared a quick look with his two eldest sons, who nodded subtly.

"Thank you for finding a priest," Cormac murmured. "I don't know how you managed that this time of year."

Seamus looked with gratitude in the direction of the stagecoach driver. "Dunmore has his ways," Seamus said. "An' I'm glad of it, for we wanted to honor Connor too. It wouldn't have been right, burying him without a proper prayer."

Cormac made a sound of agreement, taking another sip of whiskey, as his throat had thickened and he was incapable of speaking. The image of the yawning hole with his brother's casket inside filled his vision.

"I know you must believe that no one understands how you feel," Ardan murmured, recalling Cormac to the present, "but we have an idea of what today is like." He paused. "We remember what it was like to lose our mum."

Cormac nodded to acknowledge their sympathy. He knew well the story of Mary O'Rourke's separation from her family, upon their

197

arrival from Ireland in 1847 in Montreal, Canada. She, and Seamus's youngest daughter, Maggie, had spent nearly eighteen years apart from them. Only in June of this year had they been reunited. However, Cormac fought a deep resentment because they had always had one another. They had never truly been alone, as Cormac now was. He paused as he took a deep breath to calm his anger and his grief. *Except for Mary*, he realized. She had been left alone with a newborn to care for. "Thank you," he finally rasped out, his voice roughened by his deep emotions.

Seamus cleared his throat and squeezed his shoulder, as though knowing instinctively what he thought. "You aren't alone, Cormac. You have all of us. We will always be your family."

A rising surge of emotions threatened to overwhelm him, and he thrust his whiskey glass at one of the youngest O'Rourke boys before fleeing the room. In the kitchen he snatched his hat and coat and raced outside into the rain. After a few steps, he shrugged into his jacket, jammed on his hat, and stormed away to his nearby one-room cabin. Grief and guilt threatened to swallow him whole. For, no matter what the O'Rourkes said, Cormac knew they would never be his family. How could they want him after what he did?

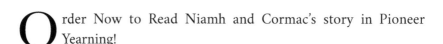

Order Now to Read Niamh and Cormac's story in Pioneer Yearning!

NEVER MISS A RAMONA FLIGHTNER UPDATE!

Thank you for reading *Pioneer Desire*! I hope you enjoyed it as much as I enjoyed writing it.

I love hearing from you, so please feel free to write me and let me know what you think!

You can reach me at: ramona@ramonaflightner.com

Join My Newsletter For Updates, and Sneak Peeks about the series you love!

Want new release alerts, access to bonus materials and exclusive give-aways, and all my announcements first? Subscribe to my weekly newsletter!

Want to be notified about freebies and sales? Try Bookbub!

Want to stay up to date on new releases, my life in beautiful Montana, and research trip adventures? Find Me On Facebook! Or Find Me On Instagram!

ALSO BY RAMONA FLIGHTNER

The O'Rourke Family Montana Saga

Follow the O'Rourke Family as they settle in Fort Benton, Montana Territory in 1865. Coming in 2020!

Sign up here to receive the prequel, *Pioneer Adventure* to the new Saga as a thank you for subscribing to my newsletter!

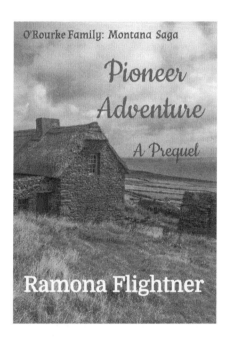

Pioneer Dream (OFMS, Book 1)- Kevin and Aileen

Pioneer Desire- (OFMS, Book 2)- Ardan and Deirdre

Pioneer Yearning- (OFMS, Book 3) Coming in May 2020- Niamh and Cormac

Pioneer Longing (OFMS, Book 4)- August 2020! Eamon's story!

Pioner Bliss (OFMS, Book 5) Coming Soon! Declan's story!

Bear Grass Springs Series

Never fear, I am busy at work on the next book in the series! If you want to make sure you never miss a release, a special, a cover reveal, or a short story just for my fans, sign up for my newsletter!

Immerse yourself in 1880's Montana as the MacKinnon siblings and their extended family find love!

Montana Untamed (BGS, Book 1)- Cailean and Annabelle

Montana Grit (BGS, Book 2)- Alistair and Leticia

Montana Maverick (BGS, Book 3) Ewan and Jessamine

Montana Renegade(BGS, Book 4) Warren and Helen

Jubilant Montana Christmas (BGS, Book 5) Leena and Karl

Montana Wrangler (BGS, Book 6) Sorcha and Frederick

Unbridled Montana Passion (BGS, Book 7) Fidelia and Bears

Montana Vagabond (BGS, Book 8) Ben and Jane

Exultant Montana Christmas (BGS, Book 9) Ewan and Jessamine

Lassoing a Montana Heart, (BGS, Book 10)- Slims and Davina—Coming July 2020!

The Banished Saga

Follow the McLeod, Sullivan and Russell families as they find love, their loyalties are tested, and they overcome the challenges of their time. A sweeping saga set between Boston and Montana in early 1900's America. Finally, the Saga is complete!

The Banished Saga: (In Order)

Love's First Flames (Prequel)

Banished Love

Reclaimed Love

Undaunted Love (Part One)

Undaunted Love (Part Two)

RAMONA'S READER NOTE

Hi!

Thank you so much for reading *Pioneer Desire* and for embracing another series!

As with all of my books, I greatly enjoyed the research for this book and the series. Fort Benton is **not** a fictitious town, unlike Bear Grass Springs in my other series. From Benton is as described in the novel, and it's one of my favorite places to visit in Montana. One day, I will float the Missouri River and have a little bit of that experience of what it felt like to be on a steamboat!

There was a powerful family in Fort Benton that ran a powerful trading empire, run by the patriarch Isaac G. Baker. I loosely based the O'Rourke family and their store on him and his business, although he did not have twelve children.

There was also a very powerful, popular Madam in Fort Benton. Again, I loosely based Madam Nora on her.

As for the Irish used in this short story, I did the best research I could and any mistakes are mine alone. Although *a chuisle* literally means my pulse, I also read it can mean my heartbeat, which I thought was more lyrical.

As always, my heartfelt thanks for being such a wonderful, loyal fan of my work! Never fear, there are many more novels to come!

Sláinte,

Ramona

ABOUT THE AUTHOR

Ramona is a historical romance author who loves to immerse herself in research as much as she loves writing. A native of Montana, every day she marvels that she gets to live in such a beautiful place. When she's not writing, her favorite pastimes are fly fishing the cool clear streams of a Montana river, hiking in the mountains, and spending time with family and friends.

Ramona's heroines are strong, resilient women, the type of women you'd love to have as your best friend. Her heroes are loyal and honorable, men you'd love to meet or bring home to introduce to your family for Sunday dinner. She hopes her stories bring the past alive and allow you to forget the outside world for a while.

BB bookbub.com/authors/ramona-flightner
🅟 pinterest.com/Ramonaauthor
🇫 facebook.com/authorramonaflightner
🅞 instagram.com/rflightner

Made in the USA
Monee, IL
13 January 2022

88903983R00125